Praise for the novels of

SHARON SALA

"Sala's characters are vivid and engaging."
—*Publishers Weekly* on *Cut Throat*

"Sharon Sala is not only a top romance novelist,
she is an inspiration for people everywhere
who wish to live their dreams."
—John St. Augustine, host, *Power!Talk Radio*
WDBC-AM, Michigan

"Veteran romance writer Sala lives up to her
reputation with this well-crafted thriller."
—*Publishers Weekly* on *Remember Me*

"A well-written, fast-paced ride."
—*Publishers Weekly* on *Nine Lives*

"Perfect entertainment for those looking for
a suspense novel with emotional intensity."
—*Publishers Weekly* on *Out of the Dark*

SHARON SALA

swept aside

MIRA®

Recycling programs for this product may not exist in your area.

ISBN-13: 978-0-7783-2802-5

SWEPT ASIDE

For questions and comments about the quality of this book please contact us at Customer_eCare@Harlequin.ca.

www.MIRABooks.com

Printed in U.S.A.

Family is everything to me.
I've grown into the woman I am because of the lessons I've learned from those who came before me.

I hope that, as I've gone through life, I have grown to become the person that my family wanted me to be. I pray that when I leave this earth, that I will have left behind enough of me to guide those who come after.

I want them to be able to speak my name with pride and love, and know that no matter how far away my soul will travel, my heart will always be with them.

So I'm dedicating this book to families. Good or bad. Large or small. They are our beginning, and ultimately, all that's left of us when we're gone.

One

Sunday afternoon—Bordelaise, Louisiana

A storm was brewing, and Nick Aroyo could tell, even from inside the Bordelaise Police Department, that it was going to be a strong one. The day had begun with sunshine and a breeze, but for the past couple of hours the wind had continued to rise, until now it had elevated to a high-pitched whine that he could hear through the three-foot-thick concrete block walls of his jail cell.

For Nick, jail was the last damn place he needed to be, but getting arrested on a Friday night in Bordelaise, Louisiana, meant you awaited the judge's pleasure when it came to a "prompt" arraignment, and for whatever reason, this time it wasn't happening until Monday.

In his other life, away from the undercover world of the DEA, Sunday meant sleeping in, hot wings and watching football on TV. But there would be none of that today. The jailer had yet to pick up their food trays from lunch, and the cockroach crawling on top of his leftover macaroni and cheese was so damn big he was afraid to turn his back on it. As for sleeping, at four inches over six feet tall, there was no way Nick could get comfortable on a jail bunk. So he paced, thinking about the three other men he'd been running with for the past eight months and who'd been arrested with him, and trying not to think of the luxurious extra-long mattress back in his Miami condo. Even though he knew his mother was keeping an eye on his place, he was anxious to put this case behind him and go home.

There had been a time when he'd thrived on undercover work, but the older he got, the more he realized that real life was passing him by. He had yet to have one serious relationship survive his unexplained absences, and at thirty-six, his own biological clock was ticking. He wanted someone to come home to and a kid who called him Daddy.

Suddenly he became aware that the wind outside had changed to a roar and a siren was going off somewhere, and when something hit the roof of the jail with such force that he felt the vibration beneath his feet, he ducked. To his horror, seconds later the corner of the roof began to lift. Knowing he only had moments to take cover, he grabbed his mattress, hit the floor, then slid beneath the frame of his bunk, pulling the mattress in on top of him.

The sounds that followed were like something out of a nightmare. The air became a living, breathing banshee—screaming nonstop and ripping the roof and rafters from above him before sucking them up into its vortex.

He clutched the mattress against him, then closed his eyes as he began to be pelted by rain and flying debris. Suddenly something hit the bottom of his boot with such force that his entire body slid a foot to the north.

Above the wind, he could hear a scream and thought it was Wayman French, one of the men with whom he'd been arrested. Then the winds ripped the mattress from his grasp, pulled him out from under the bunk and slammed him against the front of the jail cell. Before he could get a grip on the bars, his body went flying backward, slamming up against a wall; then he was turned around and slammed back against the bars. Realizing he'd just been handed a second chance, he locked his arms through the bars and ducked his head, trying to protect his face and eyes from the rain and wind-whipped debris. The last thing he was thinking was that his mother would have to identify his body; then something hit the back of his head and everything went black.

When Nick came to he was laying on his back, looking up at the sky, rain pelting his face. The roof was gone, as was the back wall of his cell.

His first thought was to make a run for it. He needed to contact his boss, Stewart Babcock, the deputy chief of the DEA, and tell him where he'd hidden eight months worth of intel. It would suck to have spent the last months of his life in the underbelly of society and then die before he could turn over the goods. The info was comprehensive—from the lowest of runners all the way to the top man in the drug ring—and it mattered too much for him to lose it.

Nick staggered to his feet, slipping once on the rain-slicked floor before he finally gained steady footing. A quick body check revealed he was bleeding in several places, although nothing that appeared deep or serious. There was a knot on the back of his head and it hurt to breathe, but he'd didn't think any ribs were broken. After a quick scan of the alley behind the jail, he crawled out over the rubble that had been the back wall and started moving, looking to see if the other three men were alive.

Lou Drake was the first to climb out to meet him—a stocky, bald-headed man of average height and less than average intelligence, and vicious without thought. He was wild-eyed and bleeding but obviously mobile, as he jumped over a hunk of drywall and clapped Nick on the back.

"Damn! Can you believe we lived through that? Let's make a run for it before someone comes looking to see what happened."

"What about Tug and Wayman?" Nick asked.

Lou shrugged as if the French brothers were no longer his concern, then frowned when Nick climbed back into the building.

"Fuck it," he said. "It's every man for himself."

Nick turned. "Then run, damn it. If they're still breathing, I'm not leaving them behind."

Lou cursed but knew enough to realize he would need more than his street smarts to get through the backwaters of Louisiana. He was originally from Detroit. His comfort zone was the streets, not alligator-infested swamps.

Wayman French was conscious, but pinned beneath debris. He could hear the others talking and was already calling for help. When he saw Nick climbing toward him over a pile of concrete blocks and rafters, he started waving his arms.

"My leg! I'm caught!" he said urgently, pointing to the piece of rafter that had fallen on top of the bunk where he'd been lying, pinning him to it.

Nick pointed at Lou. "Get in here and help me!" he said, and together, they began moving rubble, sliding around in the rain, until Way was free.

Way rolled out of the bunk onto his knees, then pushed himself up from the rain-soaked, debris-strewn floor.

"Thanks, man," he said, and then started looking for his brother, who'd been in the next cell. "Tug! Tug! Oh, damn, I don't see him!"

Lightning snaked across the sky, followed by a loud rumble of thunder, as Nick crawled over into the next cell and began digging through the rubble. Tug French was the undisputed leader of their gang, but he was nowhere in sight.

Way's panic increased as he started to sob. "The twister…the twister…it musta' took him."

Then they heard a moan and saw a hand slide out

from beneath a chunk of drywall. They scrambled forward, their movements frantic as they began removing rubble, knowing that with each passing second, their chances of escape were lessening.

When they heard the first siren, Nick's hopes fell. They were going to get arrested again before they even got off the block. He could, of course, confess his identity to the locals, but it would end his career as an undercover operative, plus, if word got out before his boss got the information, the possibility existed that the big dogs could make a getaway, and they were the ones Babcock wanted most.

The sirens set Lou off. He began to curse. "The longer we wait, the more certain we're gonna get caught!"

Wayman French was large in size and a little slow in the head, but the thought of leaving his big brother behind wasn't on the table. He grabbed Lou by the throat with one hand and started squeezing—just enough to remind the other man that he could still die today.

"You help get Tug free or I will break your fuckin' neck," Wayman said.

"Both of you! Shut up!" Nick said urgently. "Someone's gonna hear the noise. Lou! Grab the end of that rafter. Way, you grab Tug's shoulders. When I say so, you drag him out from under this, okay?"

Way gave Lou a last glaring look, then slid his hands beneath Tug's arms and waited. Nick and Lou grabbed opposite ends of the rafter.

"Okay, Lou. On three." Nick began the countdown. "One. Two. Three. Lift!"

They gripped and lifted in unison, putting every ounce of their strength into the effort—and the rafter moved—just enough.

Suddenly Tug was free.

Way swung him up into his arms, then threw him over his shoulder and started climbing out of the demolished jail. Nick and Lou followed.

The rain had become a downpour, and they could hear sirens as they ran—an indication that the rescue efforts had begun. Way was limping but showed no signs of stopping. Tug was bleeding profusely from the head, but the rain would wash away the blood along with their tracks. What they needed was a car and something to wear besides jail-bait orange if they were going to have any chance of making a getaway.

Just as they turned a corner, Nick saw that the department store across the street had taken a direct hit, and that most of the front of the building was missing.

"In there!" he shouted, and darted across the street and into the store with the others right behind him.

The once neat shelves had been emptied of goods and the racks of clothing strewn about in chaotic abandon by the force of the wind. They began combing through the jumble, looking for something in their sizes.

Nick was relieved to find jeans long enough to fit and quickly changed, ripping tags off the pants and a T-shirt before putting them on.

Tug had regained consciousness. He was groggy and in obvious pain, but he knew enough to get out of his prison garb. When Wayman found a pair of jeans and a shirt in Tug's size, Tug put them on. As Lou began to change, he tossed his prison uniform on the floor in plain sight.

"Hide it," Nick said, pointing to the neon orange jumpsuit Lou had just abandoned.

Lou shoved them in among the rest of the debris just as Tug staggered and slumped against a table. Wayman grabbed him, frantically trying to rouse his brother.

"Tug! Tug! Are you all right?"

"He needs a doctor," Nick said.

"Hell, no," Tug muttered. "No doctor."

Nick swore beneath his breath. "It's your funeral," he said, then grabbed a package of men's undershirts, tore them open, ripped one into strips and bandaged the open wound on Tug's head.

"That'll slow the bleeding down, but it won't fix what's wrong," he said.

Tug pushed away his hand. "Let's just get out of here."

Moments later they were back on the street, minus their prison garb but still afoot.

Nick's ribs were getting sorer by the minute, Wayman was definitely dragging his right leg, and Nick could tell by the way Tug was moving that he was about to pass out again. They needed a ride.

All of a sudden an ambulance shot across the intersection in front of them. Nick stopped, then held his breath, certain they would be seen, but the driver never even looked their way. As soon as it passed, Nick made a decision.

"Way, take Tug into that alley and stay out of sight. Lou and I will find wheels and come back for you."

"Hell, no!" Wayman said. "We don't split up."

"They'll be looking for four men, not two," Nick said. "And Tug's about to pass out. I won't leave you. I swear."

Wayman wavered. He glanced meaningfully at Lou and then back at Nick. "*He* would."

Nick put a hand on Wayman's arm. "He's free to go anywhere he wants. But I don't run with Drake. Tug's the boss. I'll be back."

Wayman took a deep breath, eyeing the expression on Nick Aroyo's face, then finally nodded.

"Yeah…okay, but hurry."

"As fast as I can," Nick said. "Just stay out of sight and stay put."

Wayman led his brother into the alley as Nick and Lou dashed across the street.

"Smooth move," Lou said as they continued to run, dodging downed power lines, broken glass and miscellaneous debris.

"It wasn't a move. I meant what I said," Nick said.

Lou glared "Then you're a fool, taking a chance on getting caught for them. They wouldn't do the same for you."

"I walk my own path," Nick said. "So…either you're part of the problem—in which case, beat it—or you're part of the solution, in which case keep an eye out for a pharmacy and wheels big enough for all four of us."

"Pharmacy? What the hell for?"

"Tug needs first aid."

Lou cursed beneath his breath, muttering something about ass-kissing and do-gooder.

Nick ignored him as they ran, making sure to stay out of sight of the growing number of rescue vehicles. When they finally found the drugstore, a tree from the town square had been driven through the plate glass windows and the door was standing ajar.

"Time for a little shopping," Nick said, and darted into the doorway, past the limbs and broken glass. He grabbed a large sack from behind the checkout stand and handed another one to Lou. "Get bottles of water and food...crackers, energy bars...candy bars...whatever you can find."

Lou headed toward the cooler on the west wall, while Nick started down the aisles, looking for first aid. The window between the pharmacy and the rest of the store had been shattered. He vaulted over the counter, scanning the shelves until he found antibiotics and painkillers, then headed back to the front, grabbing gauze, surgical tape and alcohol. After making sure no one was in sight, he and Lou slipped out of the store and bolted across the street.

They walked up on an older model Lincoln one block over. The doors of the big white car weren't locked, and when Nick slid in behind the steering wheel and pulled down the visor, a set of keys dropped into his lap.

Lou chortled as he jumped in beside him. "I love me some stupid, small-town hicks!"

Nick thrust the key in the ignition. The engine fired

up on the first turn. They pulled away from the curb, retracing their steps until they were back where they'd parted company. Seconds later Wayman came running out, dragging Tug along with him. The look on his face was nothing short of joyous.

"Way to score!" Wayman said, as he opened the back door and shoved Tug inside. "I didn't think you would come back," he added, and clapped Nick on the back. "I owe you, man...big-time."

"Just taking care of business," Nick said shortly. "All of you, get down. If anyone sees four men driving out of town in this car, someone might put two and two together later."

"Right!" Wayman said, and slid down in the back-seat, pulling Tug with him.

Nick accelerated carefully, not wanting to call attention to their exit from Bordelaise, but as he drove he realized he needn't have worried. The town was in chaos. People were running from one point to another, some covered in blood, others moving in zombielike fashion, all shocked by what they'd just lived through. No one noticed a big white Lincoln moving through the streets, and if they had, they wouldn't have thought a thing about it. Who wouldn't want out of this hellhole?

Still, Nick didn't relax until he could see the city limit sign in the rearview mirror.

"We're clear," he said.

Lou and Wayman sat up, but Tug didn't move. It was just as well. Short of a doctor and a hospital, rest was all they could offer him.

* * *

Amalie Pope was going home. Yesterday morning she'd left Jasper, Texas, for her grandmother's house in Louisiana—most likely for good. It was a safe bet that she wasn't going back to teaching—at least not there. The memories of Jasper's recent high school graduation still haunted her. She had yet to get through an entire night without reliving the sight of Pauly Jordan coming into the high school auditorium with a gun. Four students, two teachers and two parents had died that night, while six others were wounded before Pauly was taken down.

Amalie was one of the six.

Momentarily stunned by the outbreak of shooting, she had frozen in place, thinking that there had to be a rational explanation for what was happening. It wasn't until Pauly swung the gun toward a student who was standing right beside her that she'd jumped in front of the boy and taken the bullet meant for him. The miracle was that she lived to tell the tale.

But after her release from the hospital weeks later, staying in Jasper was no longer an option. All she could think about was going home.

Now she drove with one eye on the blacktop and the other on the sky. Hurricane-spawned storms were moving across the state but weren't predicted in this area until mid to late afternoon. She wanted to get to Nonna's house before any bad weather hit. It made her sad to know that her grandmother would never be there to greet her again, and she was still struggling with the guilt of how Nonna had died.

Upon learning Amalie had been shot, Laura Pope had suffered a heart attack and never regained consciousness. Being the only living relative, Amalie had inherited everything: the family home—a three-story antebellum house in need of a little TLC—and enough money to never have to work another day in her life. It hurt to think that Nonna had been buried without her knowledge or presence, but she knew it couldn't be helped. And after the month Amalie had just lived through, she was trying to turn loose of guilt, not add to it.

Her healing shoulder wound was beginning to ache from the long drive, and she glanced at the time, trying to gauge how much longer she had to go before reaching her destination, when something flew across her line of vision. Before she could react, it hit the passenger side of the windshield with a loud, shattering thump.

She ducked on instinct, and as she did, the car swerved toward the ditch. At the last moment Amalie thought to hit the brakes before she ran off the road, and as soon as she skidded to a stop she quickly slammed the car into Park.

Except for the heartbeat hammering in her ear, everything was quiet. Adrenaline was still rushing as she started to shake.

"Oh, my God…oh, my God," she whispered, then leaned her forehead against the steering wheel, fighting the urge to throw up. This was not the way to get over PTSD.

Frustrated by this weakness she couldn't seem to control, she looked up, combing shaky fingers through her short dark hair as she began to investigate.

There was a crack in the windshield, along with a good-size amount of blood and feathers. Upon closer examination, she could tell that the large bird now lying on her hood—it looked like a hawk—had just flown into the windshield. When her focus shifted to the blood and gore, the view began to morph. In a panic, she covered her eyes, but the memory was too strong. As she shuddered violently, the flashback overwhelmed her.

The auditorium was filling rapidly with graduating seniors, and their friends and families, anxious to mark this rite of passage into the beginning of adulthood. Normally Amalie Pope was the high school art teacher, but tonight she was handing out programs at the door as people filed through to get a seat.

The superintendent, Jacob Strand, was walking into the auditorium to take his place on the stage. The hall was full of people laughing and talking and snapping pictures, anxious to commemorate this night. There was nothing out of the ordinary to warn her of what was about to happen.

When she saw Pauly Jordan walk in alone, she frowned. He would have been graduating tonight along with his classmates, except for the fact that he'd been caught dealing drugs on the school grounds and expelled a month earlier. It occurred to her that he might try to make trouble, but that thought didn't prepare her for the handguns he pulled out of his pockets.

Before Amalie could think, he took aim at the superintendent and fired. Blood splattered on the wall behind Jacob as the bullet went through his chest. He was dead before he hit the floor.

The shot was still echoing when everyone began to scream.

After that, Amalie's memory became vague. She remembered seeing people falling and blood splattering, and vaguely remembered jumping in front of another student as Pauly screamed his name. After that, all she remembered was the impact of the shot and being knocked off her feet. Then she was falling…falling… as everything faded from sight.

She'd awakened the next day in a hospital. Four days later, when the doctors thought she could handle it, she was informed of her grandmother's death. After that, her world had come the rest of the way undone.

A distant rumble of thunder dragged her back to the present. She could hear her psychiatrist's voice telling her to focus—focus. She opened her eyes, then looked away from the window.

Still trembling, she put the car in Reverse and backed away from the edge of the ditch. Her stomach lurched again as she caught sight of the window.

"You are not a woman who faints at the sight of blood," she muttered, although it had been happening lately with some regularity. Even a paper cut made her stomach turn.

She got out of the car, pulled the dead bird from the hood and tossed it in the ditch.

"And you are also not going to throw up," she added, as she eyed the blue Chevrolet Impala, making sure nothing else had been damaged.

Satisfied, she got back inside the car, turned on the windshield washer and kept it running until the blood was gone, then put the car in gear and drove away.

Two

Even though the rest of the drive was uneventful, by the time Amalie reached her destination the pain in her shoulder was constant and she was fighting a headache.

She'd been coming to her grandmother's house her entire life and knew the road as well as she knew her own name, but as she began to slow down to take the turn, she realized the kudzu vines had become so thick that the house was no longer visible from the road. It gave her an eerie feeling, as if the old plantation house had disappeared along with Nonna.

She hadn't been here since Easter, and the overgrown property was an obvious reminder of Nonna's age and declining health. In years past her grandmother would never have let the grounds go in such a way. Guilt rose as she took the turn. She should have come back sooner, not settled for phone calls and letters.

But her guilt and her tension disappeared as she drove closer to the house. All she could think about was crawling into bed and sleeping for about a week. Even if the landscaping had been let go, in a way it wasn't such a bad thing—at least for the time being. She'd come here to recuperate, not to fill up her social calendar. If Nonna's neighbors knew she was here, they would all want to come pay their respects. A formal welcome-to-the-neighborhood and so-sorry-for-your-loss kind of thing. Something she wasn't ready to face. She wanted the first few days to herself.

Then she rounded the curve and the old three-story antebellum mansion came into view at last. Breath caught in the back of her throat as she hit the brakes. Still imposing, even though its splendor was slightly fading—and it was hers. The Vatican.

She rarely thought about the name, a presumptuous, if somewhat understandable, choice given to the place over a century ago. The house had always belonged to the Popes—from Joaquin Pope, who claimed the land in 1804, to herself, Amalie Pope, the latest heir. The name had seemed fitting.

Amalie's fingers curled around the steering wheel as she thought about the loneliness she was about to face. Then she stifled her self-pity and continued up the driveway, passing live oaks dripping with gray Spanish moss, unruly azalea bushes and wildly blooming crepe myrtles in various shades of pinks and reds, all of them sadly in need of a seasonal trim.

She drove around to the back, choosing, for the time being, to keep her car out of sight. As she got out, she glanced up at the sky. The clouds were building as the sky continued to darken, but that didn't matter to her now. The Vatican had weathered two-hundred-plus years of weather. Today would be no different.

She got her suitcase out of the trunk, unlocked the door and set the suitcase just inside the kitchen before going back to get the groceries. She'd brought enough food to last her for at least ten days, which should be long enough for her to settle in before she made the fifteen-mile trip into Bordelaise to set up a bank account and formally announce her arrival.

By the time she'd carried in the last of her things, her shoulder was in serious pain. As she shut the door behind her, she paused, admiring the stainless steel appliances, the white kitchen cabinets with china-blue knobs, and the salt-and-pepper colored granite on the countertops. But that was where renovation ended. The wide plank floors were still the original cypress, the hooks and nooks lining the walls still bore the marks of generations, and the kitchen table and chairs were antique cherrywood. To a designer, it would appear to be a successful blending of eras, but to Amalie, it was simply home.

Refusing to acknowledge the lump in her throat, she stowed the groceries—meat and dairy in the refrigerator, bread in the old breadbox, and the rest of the stuff in the pantry. Someone had obviously come in and cleaned out the refrigerator after Nonna died. Probably one of her grandmother's quilting friends. The only items still inside were the things that wouldn't spoil, like pickles and jam.

All the while Amalie was working, she caught herself listening for Nonna's footsteps, half expecting her to show up in the doorway with a big smile on her face and a welcoming hug. But that wasn't going to happen. Amalie slid the last can onto the pantry shelf while blinking back tears, then retrieved her suitcase and left the room.

As she paused in the hallway, she cocked her head to listen—something she'd seen Nonna do a hundred times, claiming that the creaks and groans, the pops and scratching, were just signs of the old mansion telling her things needed to be done, things ranging from something as simple as the grandfather clock needing winding to water leaking somewhere. But today the house felt different—even hollow.

Had it lost its voice when Laura Pope died?

Amalie felt as abandoned as the house appeared. Even when her parents had died in a wreck when she was eleven, she'd still had Nonna. Now the old matriarch was gone, and Amalie Pope was the last surviving member of a once prolific and thriving family.

She allowed herself another moment of regret, then proceeded up the hall to the grand foyer. She paused at the foot of the old staircase, remembering the countless times she'd come down the sweeping banister backward—to her parents dismay and Nonna's laughter—then considered her choice of beds.

There was a bedroom on the ground floor. It would be convenient but somewhat sterile. Nothing of her grandmother's personality would be there. The other bedrooms, including Nonna's, were upstairs on the second floor. The third floor, which had once been servants' quarters, was vacant of furnishings and no longer in use except for storage.

Amalie thought of all the times she'd awakened in the middle of the night and gone to her grandmother's bed for comfort. All the times she'd spent under the covers at Nonna's side, listening to her reading chapters of *The Wind in the Willows* and *Watership Down*. As the memories flooded in, Amalie realized her decision had been made. She chose the stairs, pulling the suitcase up behind her as she went.

When she reached the landing she paused again, gazing down the wide expanse of hallway toward the half-dozen bedrooms beyond. She had learned to roller skate down this hall, taking care not to bother the huge bouquets that always stood on the marble-topped tables standing sentinel midway down. Now the tables were as empty as the house.

For a moment she thought she smelled jasmine, Nonna's favorite scent, then chalked it up as a fantasy. A muscle jerked near the side of her mouth—a small but physical sign of her fragile hold on her emotional stability. Weighted down with a feeling of malaise, she moved to Nonna's room, opened the door and walked inside.

The room had not been redecorated in Amalie's lifetime, and the familiar sight of off-white walls and cypress floors polished by centuries of wear were more than comforting. Nonna's four-poster cherrywood bed seemed huge without her in it, but the mauve colored duvet with bolsters to match reminded her of Nonna. White lace curtains hung over a pair of long narrow windows, and across the room stood an ancient wardrobe, also made of cypress and now used to store linens. Part of the room had been remodeled during her grandfather's time to include a large walk-in closet and a private bath. A perfect room for the lady of the house.

It didn't take long to unpack her one suitcase. All the rest of her belongings, including her computer and art supplies, were still in Texas in storage. As soon as she had her things put away, she dug out her pain pills and headed for the bathroom. Her movements were mechanical as she downed the meds, used the facilities and then kicked off her shoes before climbing into bed. Once her head hit the pillow, she began to relax, comforted by the familiar in a world that kept letting her down. After a while, she slept.

Outside, the sky continued to darken as the storm front moved inland. Intermittent rain began to fall, dotting the dust in sparse polka dots that quickly turned to muddy rivulets. The sound was somewhat muffled by the third story of the house. But when the wind began to rise, causing tree branches to thump against the walls, Amalie woke abruptly, thinking she was hearing gunshots.

Heart pounding in a hard, erratic beat, she broke out in a cold sweat as she gave the room a panicked sweep. Although nothing seemed amiss, her stomach roiled.

Overcome by the sudden onset of nausea, she threw back the covers and bolted for the bathroom.

By the time the feeling had passed, her legs felt like rubber. It wasn't until she was washing her face that she began to realize there was more to the storm than a little rain.

Still shaking from the adrenaline rush of the flashback, she ran to the windows.

Wind was whipping the limbs on the trees as if they were nothing but tiny twigs and the rain was coming down in sheets. As she watched, a huge limb suddenly broke from one of the larger trees and went flying across the yard. Before she could react, more debris came flying past the window from another direction.

She'd lived in Texas long enough to know that winds coming from more than one direction at the same time meant a vortex. And that likely meant a tornado. Getting to the ground floor and an inside closet as fast as she could was paramount to survival.

Without taking time to get her shoes, she flew out of the room and down the stairs, unable to believe she was already facing another life-or-death situation. The moment she hit the ground floor, she took an immediate right, running for the closet under the stairs. The last time she'd hidden in there she'd been ten and hiding because she didn't want to go home. She grabbed the doorknob and gave it a twist, but the door wouldn't give.

"No, no, no, this isn't happening," she muttered, as

she continued to tug, but the wood was swollen from the ever-present humidity.

Suddenly something crashed against the house with a loud thud. Panicked that the next object might come through a window, she began to tug harder and harder until, suddenly, the door was open.

Amalie fell backward, landing hard on her elbows and jarring her healing shoulder and back. Ignoring the pain, she scrambled to her knees and crawled into the closet, pulling the door shut behind her.

She wouldn't let herself think about the possibility of spiders as she hunkered down inside. Outside, the wind had turned into a roar. She curled up into a ball and began to pray, although she'd already tempted fate by living through being shot. She couldn't help but wonder if her last free pass was already gone.

Amalie had no idea how long she stayed in the closet, but it was the absence of wind that gave her the courage to finally come out. When she did, all she heard was rain on the roof. Relieved that the storm had passed and she was still in one piece, she began going from room to room, then up through all three stories, checking windows and ceilings to make sure nothing was broken or leaking. To her relief, the house and windows seemed solid.

She was counting her blessings as she entered the kitchen, but when she glanced out a window and saw her car, her relief was dashed. A huge limb from one of the older live oaks was lying across the back half of it, crushing part of roof.

"Well, perfect," she muttered, then stopped and counted her blessings. If this was all that was damaged, she wouldn't complain.

She thought about going to inspect it more closely, then eyed the muddy yard and rain and changed her mind. So there was a tree on her car. It already had a crack in the windshield. That was all the information she could handle today.

With a slightly dejected sigh, she turned away. This wasn't how she'd pictured her first night at the Vatican. Thinking she should notify her insurance agent, she ran back upstairs to get her purse and his number, but when she tried to use the phone, there was no dial tone. No problem. She still had her cell. But that call wouldn't go through, either.

Tossing her cell on the bed, she glanced at the clock. It was almost 3:00 p.m., and she hadn't eaten since early morning, so she headed back downstairs. But when she opened the refrigerator and the light didn't come on, she realized the power was off, too. Hoping it wouldn't stay off so long that she lost her perishables, she got out stuff to make a sandwich, and then filled a glass with ice and Pepsi. As she sat down to eat, she took comfort in the fact that it was still daylight. If the power wasn't back on by nightfall, she would be digging out Nonna's hurricane lamps and candles.

As she ate, she ran through a mental list of things she would have to do besides calling her insurance company. She would need to call a tow service. Find a good body shop or—depending on whether or not the insurance company totaled it out—cope with buying a new car. All in all, it was a disappointing beginning to her relocation.

When she'd finished eating, she carried her dirty dishes to the sink, then began her search for flashlights and candles, as well as some oil for the lamps.

A short while later she moved through the house, setting a candle here and a lamp there until she was satisfied that, if necessary, she could navigate the house in the dark.

Tug French was in bad shape. He continued to moan as they drove through the back roads of the bayous. Nick was anxious to get as far away from Bordelaise as possible before someone noticed they were missing. He wanted to get back to New Orleans, take the intel he'd been gathering and make sure it got into the right hands.

Even though the rain had stopped, the unpaved side roads were slick and muddy, with water standing in the ruts. Some trees were down, while others were missing limbs, but it appeared the brunt of the storm had missed this area.

The odometer wasn't working, so Nick wasn't sure how far they'd driven. He was guessing about ten, maybe twelve, miles. But distance was almost immaterial compared to the fact that the gas gauge didn't work, either. He had no way of knowing how close they were to running out of fuel, although there was no going back.

As he took a sharp curve in the road, the back end of the old car began to hydroplane on the slick blacktop. Surprised by the sudden move, Lou grabbed for the dash. As he did, the bottle of Coke he'd been holding between his legs suddenly tipped backward into his lap.

"Son of a bitch!" he yelled, as he made an unsuccessful bid to grab it. "If you can't drive any better than that, get out and let me."

Wayman leaned forward from the backseat and slapped Lou on the side of his head.

"The roads are slick. It's not his fault."

"Keep your hands to your damn self!" Lou fired back.

Suddenly Tug rose up from the seat, pale and sweaty, but conscious enough to be pissed at what amounted to squabbling.

"Everyone shut the fuck up! All of you," Tug said. "My head is killing me."

The silence within the car was palpable.

At that point, Nick remembered the plastic sack on the backseat floorboard.

"Hey…Wayman, there are some pain pills and antibiotics in that sack. Lou, give Tug a bottle of water."

Tug groaned as he felt his head, then cursed at the sight of so much blood on his hand.

"Son of a bitch! I'm bleeding like a stuck pig."

Wayman shook out a couple of pills and handed them to Tug.

"Here you go. These will fix you right up."

Tug frowned and blinked, trying to focus on the pills in the middle of his palm, but they kept shifting in and out of focus.

"Where did you get the meds?" he asked.

"At a pharmacy, right before we got the car," Nick said.

"Way to go," Way said, as he began searching through the rest of the items in the sack.

"Don't give him more than two until we see how they affect him," Nick warned, then added, "Are you allergic to anything, Tug?"

"No."

Lou handed Tug a bottle of water, and the tension inside the car began to ebb. A few miles farther on, Nick realized Lou was going through the food sack as if it was his own private buffet.

"Go easy," Nick warned. "That's gotta last us until we get to New Orleans."

Lou glared. "Why? It's not like we're stranded on some desert island."

"The clothes we took from that department store didn't come with money in the pockets," Nick said.

Lou shrugged. "So we knock over a liquor store in the first town we come to."

"I did not just escape from jail just to get my ass thrown

back in for robbing a liquor store," Nick drawled, as if the thought of something so menial was beneath him.

Lou's voice rose in a challenging manner. "You're low enough to peddle drugs, but too good to heist a liquor store? Bullshit! Since when is one crime better than another, and by the way…why the hell are you suddenly the man in charge?"

"Since I'm not willing to go back to prison for stealing a few hundred dollars, that's why…and I'm not in charge," Nick said.

Lou muttered beneath his breath, but tossed the sack back onto the floor beside his feet.

Nick glanced in the rearview mirror, trying to gauge Wayman's mood. The last thing he wanted was to get on the wrong side of the French brothers, but he couldn't tell by the look on the other man's face what he was thinking.

"We all know Tug's the boss," Nick added. "I was only making a suggestion."

"Do what he said," Tug muttered.

Lou grabbed the sack and tossed it over the seat. "There! You are now the guardian of the damned peanut butter crackers. Is everybody happy?"

No sooner had he asked the question, than the car began to misfire.

"What now?" Lou demanded.

"I think we're running out of gas," Nick said.

Lou rounded on him viciously. "You didn't fuckin' think to check before you heisted the car?"

"I told you when we started, the gauge doesn't work," Nick said. "Remember?"

Sure enough, when the car jerked a few times and then began rolling to a stop, it became obvious they were out of gas.

"Now what?" Lou complained.

Nick glanced over his shoulder. "How's Tug? Think he can walk?"

"I'll carry him if I have to," Wayman said.

Nick nodded, then pointed to a bridge only a few yards ahead.

"I think we should roll the car off into the creek. If we're lucky, someone will just think it got dumped there by the storm. If not, at least it will confuse the authorities as to which direction we took."

Tug sat up and reached for the door. "I can walk. Them pills're already kicking in."

The four men got out, pushed the Lincoln closer to the bridge, then aimed it toward the creek below. It rolled past the entrance to the bridge, through a wire fence and some brush, before going nose down into the water. The runoff was swift from the passing storm. Water was almost to the windshield as the car shifted sideways just a little, then lodged between some submerged rocks, the back end sticking out of the water like the fin of a shark.

Nick picked up the sacks of food and medicine, tied them together, then slung them over his shoulder before pointing to the broken fence.

"Looks like a good place to cross. If we move into

the trees, we can still follow the road but stay out of sight."

"I am not walking in the fucking swamp," Lou said.

"Fine with me," Wayman said. "I'm tired listening to your bitchin' anyway. Do me a favor and take your ass on down the road alone."

Without looking back, Nick and the French brothers crossed the ditch and walked through the broken four-wire fence.

Wild-eyed and furious at the situation, Lou cursed at the top of his voice, then yelled, "Wait up!" and ran to catch up.

Bordelaise was in chaos. Police Chief Hershel Porter had been on his way into town when the tornado hit. He'd taken cover under an overpass and ridden out the storm, clinging to the underside of the bridge and praying that the tornado missed his home.

By the time he felt safe enough to crawl out, he was in a panic, wondering if the town had been hit and, if so, what kind of damage it had suffered.

He got back into the cruiser and grabbed the radio, only to find out it was dead. He dug through the console for his cell phone, then couldn't get a signal. Sure that was just the first sign of trouble to come, he headed into town with the siren running, only to find that entire streets had been leveled. Whole neighborhoods were missing. As he drove, he couldn't tell one street from another.

It wasn't until he passed a church that had been left standing that he got a mental picture of where he was. After that, he took a right and headed for the jail.

Friday night they had booked four men for possession of drugs and drug-related paraphernalia, and they'd been awaiting the arrival of a judge to arraign them. As usual when they housed prisoners overnight, he'd left retired deputy Edgar Shoe on duty. Ed was pushing seventy and a little hard of hearing, but he was reliable.

It took longer than expected to navigate the streets, and by the time he neared the office, he had a running list of places and people needing emergency services. But when he turned the corner and started down the block, his heart dropped.

"Lord, Lord," Hershel said as he parked, then jumped out on the run.

He sidestepped what was left of someone's sofa, and moved a large tree branch and a piece of rafter just so he could get in the front door. Within seconds he found Ed Shoe lying beneath an overturned chair.

He tossed the chair aside, then dropped to the floor and immediately felt for a pulse. It was there.

"Thank you, Jesus," Hershel muttered.

The old man groaned, then stirred.

Hershel put a hand on his shoulder.

"Ed? Ed? It's me, Hershel."

Ed blinked, then opened his eyes.

"Hey, Chief…what happened?" he mumbled.

"We were hit by a tornado. Are you okay? Can you sit up? Do you hurt anywhere?"

"My head hurts some, but I reckon I can walk all right. Help me up."

"No…no…just take it easy for a minute," Hershel said. "Let's just sit you up while I go check on the prisoners."

Hershel propped Ed up against an overturned desk, then began digging debris away from the doorway leading to his office and the jail. But when he opened the door, he couldn't believe what he was seeing.

The roof on the back of the building was gone. Water was standing everywhere, and it was still raining. He splashed through a hallway of puddles, and as he reached the cell block, he realized his problems had gone from bad to worse.

The back wall was gone, and the cells were empty. His first thought was that the men had escaped, and then he noticed the blood: on the bars of one cell, staining a mattress, darkening the wood on a piece of rafter and, in the last cell, enough blood that the puddle of water on the floor was a dirty pink.

Hershel's mind was racing as he hurried back to Ed. One of his deputies was just coming in the front door.

"Chief! Chief! Phones and electricity are out. The EMTs are dispatching ambulances by walkie-talkie and trying to evacuate the nursing home. I got our handhelds out of the trunk of my cruiser."

He handed one to Hershel.

"Good thinking, Lee," Hershel said. "But we got ourselves a big problem here, too."

Lee glanced at Ed. "Is he hurt bad?"

"It's not Ed. It's the prisoners. They're gone."

"Escaped?" Lee asked.

"I'm not sure. From the looks of the place, there's a real good chance the tornado took them. The roof is gone. The back wall is a pile of cinder blocks, and there's blood all over the place. Get radios to as many people as you can and tell them to be on the lookout for the men, just in case."

"Yes, sir," Lee said, then pointed to Ed. "What about him?"

"Help me get him in the cruiser. I'll drop him off at the E.R., then I'll be on the radio if you need me."

Once the rain ended and the sun began to emerge from behind the swiftly moving storm front, the air became a sauna. Wet heat radiated from the ground up as the four men slogged along the edge of a swamp. Kudzu vines that were hanging from trees and snaking along the ground were as rampant as the mosquitoes that buzzed around their heads. The sweat running from their hairlines burned the open wounds and abrasions they had incurred during the storm, and the bruises that they'd suffered were turning varying shades of purple.

Nick's belly was sore from being slammed against the bars of his cell. Tug was out of it, staggering without knowing where they were or where they were going. Wayman's limp was getting worse from having to bear his own weight and his brother's. Lou seemed to be the one with the fewest injuries, but he was complaining the loudest. The farther they walked, they more he bitched, until finally, Wayman stopped and grabbed Lou by the arm, yanking him to within inches of his face.

"If you don't shut the fuck up, I'm going to kill you."

It was the lack of emotion in Wayman's voice that drove the point home.

Nick waited, watching to see what happened next. It was of no consequence to him how this went down. If they all killed each other, then so much the better.

Lou opened his mouth as if to argue, then closed it and yanked himself free.

"Whatever."

"This appears to be a good time to take a rest," Nick said, and took the sacks off his shoulder and opened them. "Tug could probably use another pain pill about now, too."

He began passing around food and water. As soon as Tug had the water in his hand, Nick handed him two pills.

"Down the hatch."

Tug was swaying on his feet. He looked up at Nick, then down at the two pills in his hand.

"What?"

"You swallow them, Tug," Wayman said.

Tug blinked, then put the pills in his mouth.

"Did they go down?" Nick asked.

"Who the hell knows?" Wayman muttered, then eyed Nick anxiously. "Do you think Tug's gonna be all right?"

Nick shrugged. "I'm not a doctor. But if he was my brother, I'd get him to a hospital as fast as I could. Better he lives to go back to jail than dies in this damned swamp."

"Not goin' to a hospital," Tug mumbled.

"There's your answer," Nick said, then tossed the sacks back over his shoulder and proceeded to open a package of peanut butter crackers.

He ate without thought, easing the ache in his belly while his mind was racing. They needed to find food and shelter—and another vehicle to get them out of the area.

"While Tug is resting, I'm going to scout around."

"Hell, no," Lou said. "We stay together. Tug said so. You're not gonna leave us here while you make a run for it."

Nick took the sacks off his shoulder and handed them to Wayman, then looked him square in the face.

"Hold these, Way. I'll be back."

Wayman nodded as he took the sack. Nick had already proved that his word was good when he'd stolen a car in Bordelaise and come back for them. "Be careful. Watch out for snakes."

"You, too. I won't be long," Nick said, then headed into the swamp.

He could hear Lou and Wayman arguing as he walked away. If he was lucky, he would come back and find Lou with a broken neck. As soon as the thought crossed his mind, he realized how cold his emotions had become. He'd been undercover too long. However, his mental health was going to have to take a backseat to their immediate needs, which consisted of finding shelter or wheels, whichever came first.

Three

A cloud of mosquitoes buzzed around Nick's head as he pushed his way through the morass, knocking back kudzu, wading knee-deep through thick, murky sloughs with an eye on the water, making sure he wasn't about to be sideswiped by an alligator in wait. About fifteen minutes in, he walked up on an abandoned fishing shack, startling a small flock of ibis that had taken shelter from the storm. More than half the roof was missing, which ended the notion of using it for shelter. The heat was stifling as the sun continued to emerge from behind passing storm clouds. The cuts and scrapes he'd suffered during the tornado burned from the salt in his sweat, and more than once he'd felt something bump up against his leg as he waded through the muddy water.

Every time he heard something plop, he flinched, only to find out later it had been a frog, or a big, flat-shelled, snapping turtle. Well aware of the dangers in the bayous, he didn't linger.

He was still wading through runoff from the storm

and cursing bugs in general when he caught a glimpse of something in the distance. Although his heart was hammering from exertion, he decided to check it out.

Within minutes, his hopes rose. What he'd seen was the roofline of a house—a very large house. Hopeful this would be the answer to their needs, his steps lengthened as he hurried closer for a better look.

By the time he reached the clearing that surrounded the house, the muscles in his legs were shaking. He needed to rehydrate and rest, but that would have to come later. Instinct told him to check the perimeter—but time was not on his side. Although it was obvious the storm had passed through here, too, other than a few downed trees and a lot of broken limbs, he saw little physical damage.

His gaze moved to the house. Shades of Scarlett O'Hara! The three-story mansion had four massive columns and a veranda that ran the entire width of the front. The house itself was white with dark green shutters, and in need of a paint job. The structure appeared undamaged, but from where he was standing, he saw no signs of life—not even a dog. Either the owners were inside or gone. If it was empty, it would be a place to reconnoiter, maybe stock up on food. If someone was there, they could plead injuries from the storm, and beg food and the use of a phone. There were people Tug could call for a ride out of the area. But if the place was empty and they were lucky, there would be a vehicle to hot-wire. Excited by the discovery, he ran all the way back, anxious to get out of the swamp before nightfall.

When Wayman saw him coming, he stood up and waved.

"I knew you'd be back," he crowed.

Lou glared, then looked away.

Nick didn't have time for their petty squabbles, and from the looks of Tug, neither did he.

"I found a house…a big house," Nick said. "If someone's inside, we can ask to use the phone. Tug can call someone to come get us."

Wayman grinned. "Yeah, Whitey will come get us."

Nick nodded. "And if the place is empty, we can clean up, maybe rest and get some real food while we wait for our ride."

"What about just boosting another car?" Lou asked.

"Didn't see a car anywhere in the front, but we can look later. First things first," Nick said.

"Right. First things first," Wayman echoed, and dragged his brother to his feet. "Tug! Hey, Tug! Come on, bro…you can make it. Nick found us a place to lay low."

Tug's eyes were glazed as he staggered forward. Normally he was a very big man—almost as tall and wide as his younger brother—but right now, weighed down by his injuries and exhaustion, he didn't look much bigger than Lou. The makeshift bandage Nick had put around

Tug's head hours earlier was soaked with sweat and blood, and his skin was ashen.

"Follow me," Nick said, and led the way, with Wayman and Tug right behind him.

Lou brought up the rear, pissed about the situation but with no suggestions as to how to change it. Less than thirty minutes later, they had reached the property.

"Son of a bitch! Would you look at that!" Lou said, staring wide-eyed at the mansion. "I'll bet they're loaded."

He started toward the house, taking long, hurried strides without care that they might be seen.

Nick started to call him back, then realized there was no way to get there without being seen except to wait until dark—and that wasn't an option.

"You think it will be all right?" Wayman asked.

"We'll find out soon enough," Nick said, and then increased his stride to catch up to Lou, leaving Wayman and Tug to follow.

To Nick's relief, they crossed the grounds without being confronted, and when they reached the front steps, Lou ran up onto the porch and already had his hand on the door when Nick grabbed him by the arm.

"Wait, damn it!"

Lou yanked free but stepped back, impatiently watching the French brothers' progress. Wayman was bearing almost all of Tug's weight as they neared the house. When they started up the steps, Nick ran down and helped steady Tug.

* * *

As Amalie started down the main hall, double-checking that she was all set to get through a night without power, she heard voices, then the sounds of footsteps running across the front veranda. Curious, she moved to the living room and peered between the curtains. Expecting to see some of her neighbors, she was startled by the sight of four strange men.

A tall, dark-haired man with several days' worth of whiskers seemed to be arguing with a shorter, bald-headed man. Another man, a redhead, was leaning against one of the columns with a bloody bandage around his head. The man who was propping him up was also a redhead and massive, both in build and height. It was obvious from their soaked-through appearance that they'd been caught in the storm. Thinking they'd come looking for help, she opened the door.

"Hello?"

The men looked up in unison at the sound of a woman's voice.

Nick caught a brief glimpse of a young woman with short dark hair and almond-shaped, cat-green eyes. She looked pale and uncertain, but there was a smile on her face. Before he could blurt out an explanation for their arrival and appearance, Lou quickly spoiled the plan.

"Hot damn, would you look at that!" he cried, and leaped toward her.

"Lou, wait!" Nick yelled, but it was too late.

Amalie panicked as she slammed the door. Why had she opened the door like that? She knew better. Her heart was pounding, and her hands were trembling as she tried to shut the door, but it wouldn't close. When she realized the man had jammed his foot in the door, she screamed,

"Go away! Please…go away!"

"No way, bitch!" Lou's look was predatory.

Amalie cringed. She didn't have the strength to hold the door much longer, and it was four against one. Her only hope was to get out of the house. Maybe she could outrun them and hide in the swamp.

God help me.

She let go of the door and bolted toward the back of the house as fast as she could go.

Lou had been pushing hard against the door, and when she suddenly let go he fell inward, landing with a jarring thump on his hands and knees, biting his tongue.

"Son of a bitch!" he yelped, spitting blood as he scrambled to his feet. "She's gonna pay for that."

Nick rushed in, angrily grabbing Lou's arm.

"You idiot! Why did you have to scare her?"

Lou yanked free. "She's mine! I saw her first!" he cried and gave chase.

Nick knew his only chance to keep the situation from getting worse was to get to her before Lou did. At six-four, his stride was double that of the shorter man. He hurdled a sofa, outrunning Lou before they were out of the living room, then dashed across a narrow hall and through the doorway where he'd seen her disappear.

Moments later he entered a huge kitchen and saw

her on the other side of the room, standing at the door, fumbling with a lock. Increasing his speed, he caught her just as the door swung inward, grabbed her by the shoulders and spun her around, unaware that the grimace he saw on her face was one of pain, not fear.

"I'm sorry, I'm sorry," he said quickly. "I know you don't understand, but you can trust me. Please trust me. I won't let them hurt you."

It was all he had time to say before the other three burst into the room, still arguing and shouting.

Amalie felt herself losing focus and knew she going into shock. In her mind, it was the shooting all over again, only now there were four men trying to hurt her, not one. She covered her ears, trying to block out the shouting, but it didn't seem to help. The floor was beginning to tilt, and then the sounds were fading around her.

Suddenly Lou knocked a thick crockery bowl off the counter. It hit the floor with a loud crack, then burst into dozens of pieces.

In Amalie's mind, it was the gunshot she'd been waiting for. She dropped to the floor, rolled up into a ball and started screaming.

"Don't shoot! Don't shoot! Please, God…don't shoot me again!"

Her screams silenced them. When she started rolling back and forth, muttering and weeping, even Lou took a step back. He wanted a piece of ass in the worst way, but he didn't want anything to do with a bitch who was off her rocker.

Nick felt sick. Whatever was going on with this woman, they had just made it worse. He hit Lou's chest with the flats of both hands.

"Get your ass to the other side of the room and stay there!"

Lou balked. "I don't have to—"

Wayman grabbed him by the throat and slammed him up against the wall. "Do what Nick said."

It was the hand at his throat that got Lou's attention. Wayman had already threatened him once today, and Lou wasn't brave enough to even pretend to challenge him twice.

Satisfied Lou was momentarily penned, Nick returned his attention to the woman, who had crawled into a corner against the wall and curled back up into a ball.

Sorry for what was happening, he squatted down beside her. This was all his fault. He'd brought them into her life. But what was it she'd said?—"Don't shoot me again"? What the hell was up with that?

He moved a little closer, then rocked back on his heels. She was slim to the point of frail, with a translucent cast to her skin—like someone who'd been inside too long. He wanted to touch her but was afraid of making things worse.

"Hey…lady…we don't mean you any harm. My name is Nick Aroyo. That's Wayman French and his brother, Tug. Tug got hurt in the tornado, and we were just looking for help and shelter. Lou is the jackass who scared you, and I promise he won't do it again. We didn't think anyone was here. I'm sorry we frightened you."

Amalie heard him, but she wouldn't look up, and she didn't believe him. She kept waiting for more guns to go off and the blood to fly.

When she didn't react to what he'd said, Nick scooted closer and held out his hand.

"Come on. Let me help you up."

"Get away! Don't touch me!" she cried.

"Lady, look at me," Nick said. "It will be okay."

Amalie flinched, but the words sank in. She uncoiled herself from the corner and ventured a glance.

One of the men was on his knees beside her. He had a stubble of black beard, a gold earring in one ear, a square jaw, and the blackest eyes she'd ever seen. She felt pinned by his presence and the force of his stare, and needed to put some space between them.

She took a slow, deep breath and then made herself focus. Shelter. They wanted help—and shelter. Then her gaze slid to the man who'd tried to attack her. Lou. They'd called him Lou. She didn't care what this Nick said. She didn't trust Lou. She didn't trust any of them.

"I need you to move back, please," she mumbled.

Nick stood up and stepped back.

Amalie pushed herself up to her feet, then suddenly swayed.

Thinking she was about to pass out, Nick grabbed for her shoulder to steady her.

Pain ran down her arm and all the way to her teeth. She cried out and lurched sideways.

"Ow...God...let go! Let go," she begged, and hunched forward to ease the spasm rippling through her body.

Nick yanked his hand away, but it was obviously too late. Somehow he'd hurt her, though he hadn't meant to.

"I'm sorry. What happened? What did I do?"

Doubled over with pain, she began to sob. This couldn't be happening. Please, God, she begged silently, let me wake up now.

Wayman saw the way she was cradling her arm.

"It's her arm, Nick. Hey, lady...what's wrong with you?"

From across the room, Lou chimed in. "What's the matter, bitch? Cat got your tongue?"

Amalie flinched as if she'd been slapped.

Bitch? He'd called her a bitch?

So the nightmare was real. She'd tried escaping, but that hadn't worked out. Maybe being congenial would save her.

"My shoulder...it's still healing," she whispered.

"From what? Your old man rough you up?" Lou asked.

Nick spun, pointing a finger at the smaller man. "Shut up. You shut the hell up."

Amalie gasped. This man was so tall, and the anger in his voice was frightening. Still cradling her arm, she moved farther into the corner. But when he turned back to her, the tone of his voice shifted to one of concern—even kindness—which made no sense.

"What's your name?" he asked.

"Amalie Pope."

Nick nodded, repeating her name. "Ah-mah-lee… that's a beautiful name. So, Amalie, were you in an accident?"

She shook her head.

"No. I was shot."

It was the last thing he'd expected to hear. All of a sudden she'd moved from nameless female to a person who'd experienced some of the worst life had to offer.

Nick felt like he'd been kicked in the gut.

Son of a bitch…what were the odds of finding someone in such a fragile condition here?

He was reminded that it was his fault they were here. If only he'd checked the place out better before he'd led them here, none of this would be happening. He was trying to wrap his mind around where she could have been to get herself shot when Lou came out and asked.

"Who shot you?"

Nick saw her eyes go flat; then she started trembling.

"A student where I used to teach. It was the evening of the high school graduation. A lot of people were hurt. Some of them died. I was one of the lucky ones."

"Hell! I heard about that!" Wayman cried, eyeing her with something akin to sympathy. "In Oklahoma, right?"

"No. It was Texas. Jasper, Texas," Nick said softly, remembering the story he'd read over a month earlier. Remembering the photo. "They said you were a hero. You took a bullet meant for one of the kids."

Tug was in so much pain he could hardly think. The room kept going in and out of focus to the point that he could barely see the woman's face, but he'd been shot before and had gleaned enough of what she'd said to empathize.

"Leave her alone," he said, pointing in Amalie's direction. "Don't nobody mess with her. Just get her car keys and some food, and we'll be gone."

Amalie's heart sank as she realized she couldn't furnish what they needed.

"Um, my keys won't do you any good," she said, and pointed out the window.

When the men saw the car and the enormous limb that had fallen across it, they realized their immediate plan for escape had just been detoured.

"Son of a bitch!" Lou cried, and turned on her. "Don't you have something else to drive?"

Amalie shivered. "No."

"You got a husband who's gonna show up here around dark?"

She wished she could say yes. It would be comforting to know she wasn't in this alone. But there was no use lying. Time would inevitably prove her wrong.

"No. No one. My grandmother used to live here by herself, but she died while I was in the hospital. I inherited the property and just got here today."

Nick groaned inwardly. Their timing couldn't have been worse. He didn't want to consider revealing his true identity, but he would do whatever it took to keep her safe. However, if it came to that, he would need to be sure she wouldn't give him away. As desperate as these three were, they would kill both of them in a heartbeat to save themselves.

"Please," Amalie said. "Take what you need…food… my money…anything…just leave."

"So you call the cops the minute we walk off? What do you take us for?" Lou asked.

Amalie flinched. "The power is off. The phones don't work. I guess the storm knocked out service."

Nick sighed. This just kept getting worse and worse.

"It wasn't just a storm, it was a tornado," he said. "It went right down the middle of Bordelaise."

Amalie gasped. "Oh, no! I had no idea!"

All of a sudden Tug swayed, then dropped to the floor, unconscious.

"Tug! Tug!" Way screamed, and went down on his knees in an effort to rouse him.

Amalie groaned. Now they couldn't even leave on foot. The only thing she could do was try to ease the situation and hope they felt enough gratitude not to hurt her.

"There's a bedroom on the ground floor," she said. "If you can carry him, I'll show you the way."

Nick and Wayman got Tug on his feet and followed Amalie out of the kitchen. She led them through a maze of rooms and corridors until she finally came to a stop at the end of a long hallway.

"In here," she said, as she hurried inside the room and turned down the bedspread.

She wouldn't let herself think about that bloody, dirty man on Nonna's clean white sheets.

They laid Tug down, pulled off his boots and then took the bandage off his head. It was still oozing blood.

"This needs stitches," Nick said.

"Then sew him up," Wayman said.

Amalie shuddered. This just kept getting worse.

"Where's Lou?" Nick asked. "He had the sack with the first aid supplies."

Amalie looked out into the hall.

"I don't see him," she said.

"That's not good," Nick muttered, then pointed at Amalie. "Stay here. Way won't hurt you. I'll be right back."

Amalie darted a nervous look at the redheaded giant who was hovering over his brother's bed and decided not to argue the point.

"Uh...what was your name again?"

"Wayman. They call me Way. This is my older brother, Tug."

She nodded. "Okay, Way, see that bathroom?" She pointed to an adjoining door. "I'm going to go in there and get some stuff to clean your brother up a little. It will make him more comfortable. If you're going to…uh…do something to his injuries, they need to be clean."

"I thought you said the power wasn't on. How you gonna get water without electricity?"

"There are a few bottles of water under the counter. Nonna…my grandmother kept them for guests."

He frowned, then strode across the room and shoved the door open, making sure she hadn't been lying. As she'd said, it was a bathroom—and with no window or a way to escape.

"Yeah. All right," he said, and went back to his brother's bedside as she went inside and began gathering washcloths, a couple of bath towels, some alcohol, soap and a packet of gauze pads. She carried everything to the bed, then went back in for the water. There were a half dozen bottles under the cabinet—enough to fill a basin. She carried them out into the bedroom, then started toward the door.

Wayman looked up, then frowned and started toward her.

"What are you doing?"

Amalie shuddered as he approached, then pointed shakily to the ewer and basin on the old dresser top.

"I'm just getting this basin to pour the water in, okay?"

"Oh. Yeah. Okay."

Amalie's heart was pounding as she carried the basin back to the bed table. With shaking hands, she unscrewed the lids and emptied the water into the basin, then began to clean Tug French's face.

All the while, she kept looking over her shoulder, waiting for Nick Aroyo's return. It didn't make sense to trust any of them, but he'd promised he wouldn't let them hurt her, and until she had proof that he was lying, it was all that was keeping her sane.

Nick went through more than half the rooms on the ground floor before he found Lou in the library going through a desk. His pockets were bulging, and he was about to lift another piece of loot when Nick walked in.

"What the hell are you doing?"

Lou looked up, then grinned. "This house is full of valuables. I got a friend in Savannah who'll fence 'em for me."

Nick wanted to deck him where he stood, but he couldn't object to everything Lou kept doing. That would be bound to raise suspicion. If he could just keep the man away from Amalie, he would be satisfied.

"What? You gotta do all that now?" Nick asked. "We aren't going anywhere for a while. Put the damn stuff down and come help. We're gonna have to sew up Tug's head, and if he wakes up, it's going to take all of us to hold him down."

Lou paled. "Sew him up? What the hell?"

"His head is still bleeding. It's too deep to stop on its own. We've got to sew it up."

"Fuck! I'm not touching him."

Nick's voice dropped to a whisper as he put a finger right in the middle of Lou's chest.

"You are going to help hold him or you'll be the next one in need of stitches. And by the way, where the hell is the sack with the meds in it?"

Lou blinked. "Over there."

Nick grabbed it and glared.

Lou stared back. This was a side of Nick Aroyo he'd never seen, and he didn't think he liked it. Still, he wasn't big enough to challenge the man and come out on the winning end, so he unloaded his pockets, hunched his shoulders and stomped out of the room with Nick right behind him.

When they got back to the bedroom, Tug was lying on the bed in nothing but his underwear, and Amalie was carrying a basin of dark, bloody water into the bathroom.

Nick paused to watch her. This woman was a far cry from the one who'd been cowering on the kitchen floor a short while ago. Then he moved toward the bed where Wayman was drying his brother's body with a large white towel.

"She gave him a bath," Wayman said. "Cleaned him up real good, too."

"I see that," Nick said, as he set down the sack.

Amalie didn't know the men had come back until she heard Nick's voice. She paused inside the bathroom, watching him from a distance.

His height alone was menacing, and there was a purpose in his step. More than once she'd caught a gleam in his eye that didn't fit his demeanor. She was just as afraid of him as she was of the others, and yet when she got caught in his gaze, she couldn't look away. The men in her social circle didn't look like him. Unshaved faces and a gold earring did make a statement, but nothing reassuring.

She caught him looking at her and once again felt trapped. Trying to change the mood of the moment, she pointed to a door across the room.

"I think there's a sewing box in that closet. You'll need some kind of needle to sew him up, right?"

Nick hated that she was afraid of him, but this wasn't the time to worry about it. If Tug died, Wayman would freak out on the world, and then they would all be in trouble.

"Yeah. Great. Get it, will you?" Nick said.

Amalie did as he demanded, but as she entered the closet she was instantly assailed by the scent of jasmine that she associated with Nonna. For a moment she leaned her head against the door and closed her eyes.

"Are you all right?"

Amalie jumped. Oh, Lord. He was right behind her.

"I'm sorry. It's just… I was…"

She shrugged it off, unwilling to explain herself or to share something as precious as her Nonna with these men. She began poking through the clutter, moving clothes and shifting pillows and boxes until she found what she'd been looking for.

"Here it is," she said, and reached up.

But she'd forgotten about her shoulder. The muscles

pulled. "Ow!" she cried, and pulled back, wincing in pain.

"Let me," he said, and reached over her to the shelf above. "Is this it?" he asked, with his hand on the handle of a round woven basket.

"Yes."

She didn't like the feeling of being trapped, and quickly backed out and away from him.

Nick took the basket to the table and began digging through it, and found the pincushion, then the needles, but when he pulled them out one by one, he began to frown.

"These needles are too short. Are there any others?"

"There should be more in the bottom of the basket. Let me look."

He handed her the basket.

After a few moments, she held up two small flat packets.

"Will any of these do? Nonna used them to quilt."

Nick chose one of the longer, thinner needles and then turned to her again.

"Would you thread this one for me, please?"

Again Amalie did as he asked. Then she watched as he poured alcohol on the needle, then over his own hands, before moving back to the bed.

"Hold him," he ordered.

Wayman got on one side and Lou on the other.

Nick took a deep breath, pinched the gaping edges of the wound back together and pushed the needle through the flesh.

Four

A short while later Nick was tying off the last stitch, thankful that Tug had not regained consciousness. If he had to venture a guess as to the extent of the man's injuries, it would be broken ribs, the possibility of internal bleeding and maybe a fractured skull. Without medical care, his days were numbered.

But it wasn't whether Tug would live or die that bothered Nick the most. It was what their presence was doing to Amalie Pope. With every stitch he put in Tug's head, he'd heard a slight shift in her breathing. If blood suddenly gushed through the wound, she would gasp. He had a suspicion that the sight of blood was a trigger for PTSD after what she'd been through, and that she was fighting every instinct she had not to faint.

Every time Nick pushed her grandmother's quilting needle through the skin on Tug's head, Amalie thought she was about to pass out. The blood splatters on the pillow were vivid and ugly reminders of the night of the shooting. The memories that kept flashing through her mind were random, but impossible to forget.

Blood blossoming on the front of a man's white dress shirt.

The exit spray on the wall behind him turning into the vermillion version of a Rorschach blot.

Blood running out from under bodies in lazy rivulets.

The reflection of overhead lights on the glossy surface of a crimson pool on the gymnasium floor.

Then Tug moaned and reality surfaced, although the horror of what she'd experienced was still with her. When Nick tied off the last stitch, she closed her eyes, willing herself to a calm she didn't feel. All she knew was that if she fainted, she would be vulnerable to the whims of four strangers. She was so disconnected from what was happening, she didn't even know Nick was done until he spoke.

"Amalie, I need gauze and tape. They're in that sack at the foot of the bed."

She flinched, then opened her eyes, spotted the sack and went to get it, giving Lou a wide berth as she passed.

"Before I leave..." Lou whispered, and stroked his crotch, leaving the rest to her imagination.

Her stomach turned, but she refused to let him see her fear. She grabbed the sack, shakily opened the box of gauze pads and laid them on Tug's belly, then tore off several strips of surgical tape and hung them on the headboard.

Nick covered the head wound, then tossed the needle and remaining thread in the trash.

"That's all I can do for him, Way. He needs to get to a hospital as soon as possible."

"Where were you men when the tornado hit Bordelaise?" Amalie asked.

Nick hesitated. It was enough that they'd invaded her home. There was no need telling her that they'd been in jail, or that they were escapees on the run.

"In...uh...we were inside a building."

"Oh."

Lou snorted.

Nick gave him a warning stare.

"Then how did you get all the way out here?"

"The car we were driving broke down. We began walking, hoping to find help to get Tug to New Orleans."

"There's a good hospital in Bordelaise," Amalie said.

Nick thought fast. He said a mental apology for the fact that he was about to add to their lie.

"It was hit by the tornado, too."

"But—"

Wayman was tired of the conversation and interrupted.

"We're here now, and nothing's going to change that except a ride out."

Amalie felt the undercurrent of secrecy and could

only wonder what else they weren't telling, then caught a glimpse of herself in the mirror and quickly looked away. Her entire body was trembling, and she was white as a sheet.

Nick felt her panic. Damn Lou and the situation in general. He needed to change the subject, and thinking about the power being off and wanting a shower led him to his next question.

"I don't suppose your grandmother had a generator on the property?"

The shift in subject worked.

"Maybe," Amalie said. "If she did, it would be in one of the sheds."

"After that trek through the swamp, we could all use a shower."

She thought of the rainwater barrel at the corner of the house.

"If you're okay with the great outdoors and rainwater, there should be a barrel full of it out back."

"That'll work," Nick said. "Way…there's nothing else we can do for Tug. Lou and I are going to take the lady up on her offer. We'll be back in a few minutes."

Lou frowned. "I don't need to—"

"Yes, you do," Nick said. "You stink. We all stink. We've been wading through bayou country. At the least, I would think you'd want to check for leeches."

Lou's eyes widened as his lips went slack. "Check for what?"

"Leeches. You know…flat, bloodsucking worms. They latch onto your skin and suck the blood out of your veins. Leaves a hell of a sore when you pull them off."

"Hellsfire!" Lou cried, and bolted toward the door, pulling his shirt over his head as he went.

Nick could see the relief in the woman's expression as he added, "Way won't bother you, and we won't be long."

Amalie shrugged. She wasn't going to thank him. If they hadn't invaded her house, being bothered wouldn't be an issue. She was beginning to realize that there was a reason why they didn't just send someone for help for the man who was injured. They were hiding. But from whom? Lord. What kind of people had invaded her home?

There wasn't anything more Nick could say to reassure her. He made a quick trip into the bathroom, gathering up a couple of washcloths and towels, and a bar of soap.

"Be back in a few minutes, Way, then you can wash up."

"All right," Wayman said.

Amalie glanced at Tug French. He didn't look all that good. Her gaze shifted to his brother. They were both big men—tall and heavy-set.

She glanced at the phone. If the power would just come back on, she could slip away long enough to call for help.

She was still lost in thought when Wayman walked up behind her.

"You got anything to eat?"

Startled, she spun to face him, her heart hammering so hard that she nearly passed out.

Wayman frowned. "I didn't mean to scare you. Thanks for helping with Tug."

Amalie struggled with the urge to cry. *But you* did *scare me*, she accused him silently. *You continue to scare me.* She wanted to hide. Instead she was forced to interact.

"I guess I can make sandwiches."

He grinned. "Yeah...good."

Amalie pointed toward the door. "I'll have to leave the room."

"Uh, yeah, okay." Way glanced at his brother. "I guess I can come with you."

Amalie shrugged. "Whatever..."

They left the room together, their footsteps echoing on the old wooden floors as they made their way down the hall. Amalie wanted to run, but she knew she would only get caught.

God...where are You? Why is this happening to me again?

She'd had so many expectations when she'd decided to come back to Louisiana, but none of them had involved being held hostage in her own home.

As soon as she got to the kitchen, she began assembling the ingredients for sandwiches, making two each for the three men. She banged drawers and slammed cabinets, venting her fear and frustration on the furniture, and hoping the men got the message. She grabbed a bag of chips from the pantry, added a handful to each plate, then handed a plate to Wayman, who immediately began eating.

"Got anything to drink?" he asked.

"Dr. Pepper and Pepsi, but the ice is melting."

"That's all right," he said.

Amalie handed him a glass and a two liter bottle of Pepsi.

"Knock yourself out," she muttered, and then moved to the other side of the kitchen, putting as much distance between them as possible.

Moments later footsteps at the back door signaled that the other two were returning. She looked up just as Nick and Lou walked in. One look at Nick's bare chest and hard belly, and her heart skipped a beat. She had to remind herself that a stunning body did not compensate for being bad—although, if it did, Nick would have qualified for sainthood.

Despite her best efforts, she didn't look away, then told herself it wasn't a crime to look. He was just a man without a shirt, and she considered herself a normal twenty-six-year-old woman. Although she'd seen men in various stages of undress over her lifetime, she hadn't seen a one who could hold a candle to him.

Water was dripping from his jeans, and she guessed he'd doused them in the water, too—obviously to remove the mud. She couldn't blame him for the effort, but the wet denim clung far too suggestively for her peace of mind. She noticed his boots were also clean, and the shirt he was carrying appeared to have been scrubbed clean, as well. Water was beading on his hair and chest as he draped the shirt across the back of a metal stool to dry.

All of a sudden he looked up and caught her staring.

Rats. She looked away, but it was too late. He'd seen her. Lord only knew what he would make of that, but it couldn't be good.

Lou wasn't nearly as wet, which meant he wasn't nearly as clean, but for once he was focused on something instead of her.

He pointed to the food.

"Hey! Gimme some of that."

Amalie handed him one plate and Nick the other. As they began to eat, Nick glanced at the battery-powered clock on the wall. It wasn't long before sundown.

"I don't suppose you have a chain saw, or even a hand saw?"

She shrugged. "If I do, it will be in one of the sheds out back."

"Why do we want a saw?" Wayman asked.

"To cut that tree off her car."

"But the top's mashed in," Lou said.

"One thing at a time," Nick said. "If we can clear the debris, we might be able to pop the roof back up enough to drive it."

Wayman grinned, but Lou's reaction was a frown.

"Why go to all that trouble? As soon as the power comes back on, we'll just make a phone call and have someone come get us."

Nick frowned. "And if the power doesn't come back

for a week, are you willing to sit here and wait to see how long it takes Tug to die?"

Wayman's face turned as red as his hair. He slapped his hand on the table, making the dishes rattle.

"Like hell! Tug's not gonna die. Stop saying that."

"Wishing won't keep it from happening. He needs a doctor," Nick said.

Way didn't comment, but Amalie could tell he hadn't liked being corrected, especially by Nick.

Nick finished his food, then carried his dirty dish to the sink, while the other two got up, leaving theirs behind for her.

Once again Amalie was struck by how different Nick seemed from the others, and she couldn't help but wonder how they'd all hooked up.

"I'll be with Tug," Wayman said, and left the room.

When Nick started out the back door, Amalie panicked. They were leaving her alone with Lou, and from the expression on his face, he was ready to take advantage of the situation.

Suddenly Nick stopped.

"Lou, there are two sheds out back. Go see if you can find a saw."

Amalie went weak with relief.

Lou frowned. "I thought you were going."

"I changed my mind."

"Bossy son of a bitch," Lou muttered, and slammed the door behind him as he left.

The sudden silence in the kitchen made Amalie

uncomfortable as it dawned on her that now she and Nick were the ones alone. Nervously she began clearing the table of the other dirty dishes, aware that the man was watching her every move. She kept telling herself it meant nothing, and still her stomach knotted and her palms grew clammy. She had accepted the fact that, if they jumped her, she would not be able to fight them. Whatever fate had in store for her next was beyond her control.

Nick could tell she was struggling with her emotions. She kept biting her lip and blinking back tears. Then she slumped, as if the weight of the world had just settled on her shoulders, and Nick found himself struggling with the urge to take her in his arms.

"Sit down, girl, before you fall down," he said softly.

The tenderness in his voice caught Amalie off guard. Her eyes welled. She hesitated, then moved to the kitchen table and sat down.

Now Nick was waiting on her. He made her a sandwich and poured her a glass of Pepsi.

"Eat," he said, as he slid the plate in front of her, then took a seat on the other side of the table.

Amalie's voice was shaking as she blinked away tears.

"I don't think it will go down."

"Just try."

She took a small bite, then stared at her plate as she chewed.

"So…a teacher."

She nodded.

"What do you teach?"

She took a drink before she answered. "Art."

"You're an artist? That's a gift."

She shrugged. "I guess. I don't paint for myself anymore."

"Why did you quit?"

"I don't know…. Caught up in the job, I guess."

"So you could take it up again now that you're here."

"Maybe," she said, and took another bite.

She eyed him curiously as she chewed. He was such an anomaly—a bad guy with a handsome face, a hot body and what passed as a conscience.

"Can I ask you something?"

He nodded.

"Are you going to hurt me?"

Nick hated what she was thinking. In that moment, it took every ounce of resistance he had not to reveal himself.

"No. I told you we wouldn't hurt you."

"No. You said you wouldn't let them hurt me. What about you?"

Her response made him angry, which lowered the timbre of his voice. "I'm not in the habit of hurting women. Bear with us, and we'll be gone before you know it."

Amalie wanted to believe him, but she finished the rest of her sandwich in silence.

Frustrated with the situation, Nick pushed away from

the table and strode to the door. Lou was coming back toward the house carrying some tools.

"Looks like he found a couple of saws," Nick said. "Maybe we'll be out of your hair by nightfall."

"When you leave, are you going to kill me?"

Nick spun, his expression hard and angry. "Hell, no."

Amalie stood, her voice still trembling. "I'm sure you'll understand when I say I don't believe you."

"Believe what you want, but I meant what I said. I won't let them hurt you. You just have to trust me."

Amalie's chin quivered as she struggled to maintain her emotions. "I want to believe you."

Nick felt sick for what their presence was doing to her.

"I know." Then he glanced back out the window. "I need to go out and help. Please come sit on the porch where we can see you."

The request was all the proof Amalie needed that she was a hostage. Whatever story they tried to spin about how they'd come to be at her house, it was obvious they didn't want her to get away and reveal their whereabouts. But who were they running from, and why?

She followed him outside, then took a seat in one of the old wicker chairs as he moved down the steps and toward her car.

Shadows were creeping across the yard. In a couple of hours it would be dark. What would happen to her then? She closed her eyes and said a quick prayer, then focused her attention on the men. If something happened to change the status quo, she didn't want to be taken unaware.

When Lou saw Nick coming, he handed him a handsaw, then chose the chain saw and started it up. Without caution, he swung it wide, then aimed it toward the debris on top of the car.

"Careful," Nick said.

"I know what I'm doing," Lou insisted, and lowered the spinning chain onto a minor limb jutting down toward the ground.

He was still exerting pressure on the chainsaw when it severed the limb. Before he could pull back, the saw cut into the toe of his boot, spitting out bits of leather and then a shower of sparks.

"Son of a bitch!" Lou yelled, and let go of the switch, shutting down the saw.

Amalie jumped up from the chair, expecting to see a gush of blood.

Nick's heart was racing as he rushed forward. "Did it go all the way through? Are you bleeding?"

"I don't know!" Lou screamed, and dropped to the ground to examine his foot. Within seconds he was grinning. "These boots I lifted got steel toes. Who knew?"

Amalie gasped. Lifted? That meant he'd stolen them. Her opinion of these men continued to slide into the toilet. What else were they capable of—besides home invasion and theft? She wasn't sure she wanted to know.

Nick eyed Lou's boot and the shiny metal beneath the

layer of leather that had been removed, then shivered. It could just as easily have been someone's arm or leg.

"I'll saw, and you drag away the debris, okay?"

For once Lou wasn't arguing. "Whatever."

Nick looked back toward the house. Amalie had curled up in the seat of an old wicker rocker with her knees beneath her chin, hugging her legs. From where he was standing, she appeared to be battling a fresh set of tears. He wanted to make it all better, but the best thing he could do for her was get them off her property. And the best way to do that was to free this car.

He was about to restart the chainsaw when Lou looked up and pointed.

"Chopper coming over the trees!"

Nick stopped. His first thought was, thank God. Logically the smartest thing they could do was get themselves caught, get Tug in a hospital and finally face arraignment. The judge would set bail, and his troubles would be over.

But his agenda was not on Lou's radar. When Lou started running toward the house, Nick had no choice but to follow. He could hardly stand out in the yard and wave down the pilot. Way and Lou would kill him and the woman before the police could ever arrive.

When Lou grabbed Amalie's arm and yanked her into the house, she was more confused than ever.

"Why are you running? What's wrong? We need to flag down that chopper and let them know there's an injured man in here."

Lou shoved her up against the wall. "You ask too many fucking questions, bitch."

Amalie's heart began to hammer as her legs went weak. She tried to push him away, but her arms felt like lead. Suddenly his hands were on her breasts, then her belly—pulling at her shirt and the waistband of her jeans.

"Oh, God…stop…don't!" she begged.

When Lou's hand cupped her crotch, she felt the room tilt beneath her feet.

She didn't see Nick come flying into the room, or know when he grabbed Lou by the back of the neck and yanked him halfway off the floor. She had already fainted.

"What?" Lou yelled, and pulled away angrily. "You don't have any claim on her, and I want a piece of tail."

Nick shoved his forearm under Lou's chin and pushed him against the wall.

"If you touch her like that again, I'll kill you."

Lou wanted to argue, but the matter-of-fact tone in Nick's voice caught him off guard.

"Go to hell," Lou muttered, and stomped out of the room.

Nick turned back to Amalie. She was lying in a crumpled heap, right where she'd fallen. He scooped her up and carried her into the living room, then laid her on the sofa. Outside, the chopper had passed over the house, but he could still hear it and knew it had not left the area. If it was part of a search party, they would be flying a grid, which meant he couldn't go back outside. Time was wasting.

He quickly turned his attention to Amalie. Although he saw no new injuries on her, he was overcome with guilt. He'd promised they wouldn't hurt her, and then the first chance Lou had, he went at her like the animal he was.

Nick touched her cheek, then her forehead, making sure she wasn't feverish. She was thin—almost too thin—likely because of the trauma she'd suffered. Her skin was pale, and there were shadows under her eyes—yet another symptom of suffering.

Her eyelids began to flutter. She was waking up. He took a couple of steps back, making sure he wasn't too close when she woke. He watched as her eyes began to open, then saw her cognizance shift to panic as she remembered what had happened.

"You're okay. He's gone."

She sat up, grabbing at her clothes as if someone was still trying to tear them off.

"I'm sorry that happened," Nick said. "I promise you it won't happen again."

Amalie stood abruptly, then combed her fingers through her hair. Her chin was quivering and her vision kept blurring, but it was building anger that kept her from breaking down.

"You can't promise me anything I'll believe," she spat out.

Her words were sharp and uncompromising, but Nick

understood. Before he could answer, Wayman came running.

"Nick! Tug's awake. He wants to talk to you."

Nick nodded, then pointed at Amalie. "After you."

She took off down the hall with an angry stride and didn't look back.

Sunday afternoon—Washington, D.C.

It was his day off, and he was supposed to be relaxing at home with his family, but Stewart Babcock's life as deputy chief of the DEA was anything but relaxing, and today was no exception.

He was worried. One of his best agents, a man named Nick Aroyo, was five days late checking in. When any of his undercover people broke routine, it was time to worry.

The last time they'd spoken, Nick had been both antsy and elated, claiming that within a week he would have all the evidence they needed to take down the gang he'd been running with. But that had been twelve days ago, and Babcock's gut was in knots. He wanted the goods on the pushers, and he wanted his agent. So far, he had neither.

He glanced out the library window, pausing to watch his two grandsons playing catch with a football. Just as he was telling himself to go out and join them, his cell phone rang. He dug it out of his pocket and grunted when he saw the caller ID.

"Babcock."

The agent on the other end of the line cleared his throat, then delivered the message.

"Sir…just checking in. Nothing yet on Aroyo."

Babcock sat down with a thump. "Damn."

"We've been running his name through hospitals and morgues, as well as arrest records."

"Morgues?"

"Just being thorough," the agent replied.

Babcock sighed. "Right. If you get a hit, get back to me."

"Yes, sir."

Babcock was just hanging up when he heard a cry from outside and turned to see his youngest grandson bleeding profusely from his nose.

"Oh, shit."

He dropped the phone in his pocket and hurried out.

It was after dark before he and his wife left the emergency room. The boy was sporting a broken nose and working the pity party for all it was worth, while his older brother continued to feel guilty for having thrown the football too hard.

It was nearing midnight by the time they got home. Worn-out and worried, Nick Aroyo's whereabouts had finally slipped his mind.

Candlelight was supposed to be romantic, but for Amalie, the scene around Tug French's bed was like something from a horror movie.

She kept thinking it was like sitting at a wake,

keeping the deceased company until the body could be interred. Only the man in the bed had yet to die; he was only drifting in and out of consciousness. The shadows cast by the weak flickering lights gave the other men's faces a skeletal appearance, adding an eerie note to the scene. As she sat, she realized it was raining again—a sign that the hurricane-spawned weather pattern wasn't over yet.

Wayman kept pacing the floor, moving from one side of the bed to the other, wiping his brother's face with a wet cloth and asking the same questions over and over.

"Nick. What should we do? Do you think he's getting worse?"

"I've already told you what I think," Nick said. "If it was my brother, I'd have him in a hospital."

"But Tug said—"

"Tug's got a hole in his head," Nick said. "His judgment is not the best."

Wayman frowned, then moved to the other side of the bed. "Tug's the boss. We do what Tug says."

Amalie frowned. That didn't make sense.

"Why doesn't he want to go to the hospital?" she asked.

Lou snorted, then laughed loudly.

"Shut up," Nick said softly.

"I didn't say a fucking thing," Lou snapped.

Amalie glanced from one man to the other. It was obvious they didn't like each other, so how had two people with so much animosity toward each other wound up together?

Lou caught her watching them and blew her a kiss.

She shuddered.

"If it quits raining, maybe we could try to saw that tree off her car," Wayman suggested.

Nick shook his head. "We're not starting up a chain saw in the dark. Not after Lou sawed the toe of his boot in broad daylight."

Lou glanced at his boot. For once, he had to agree.

Conversation lagged.

Lou drifted off to sleep sitting up, and began to snore.

Wayman left Nick in charge and, rather than use a toilet that wouldn't flush, went outside to relieve himself, leaving Amalie and Nick the only two people in the room who were still awake.

She was exhausted, and her shoulder was throbbing.

"I need to take a pain pill," she said.

Nick stood. "As soon as Wayman comes back, I'll go with you."

"But there's a problem," she said.

Nick frowned. "Like what?"

"I won't be able to stay awake."

"So?"

She resisted the urge to roll her eyes as she pointed at Lou.

"You're not seeing this situation from my perspective. I can't even turn my back on him without fearing for my safety. What do you think is going to happen if I fall asleep?"

"Oh."

Exhaustion prompted her to beg. "Please…just let me go up to my room. The windows are two stories high. I can't fly, so there's no way I can get out from inside that room. I just need to rest."

When Wayman came back, Nick stood up and pointed to Amalie.

"She's in pain. She needs to take a pain pill and go to sleep. I'm going to walk her up to her room."

Wayman frowned. "We need to stay together."

"No, we don't," Nick said. "But if you're that concerned, I'll bunk down outside her door."

Lou had roused when he heard the words "go to sleep."

"If she's going to bed, I'm—"

"Don't say it," Nick warned. "She's off-limits."

Lou's voice got louder as he began spoiling for a fight. "You just want her for yourself."

All of a sudden Tug French rose up on one elbow.

"Shut the fuck up! All of you. Nick, take the woman up to her room and stand guard. Lou, shut the fuck up. It's your damn fault we got arrested in the first place."

Then he lay back down and closed his eyes.

Amalie was quietly absorbing the latest bit of news. It was just as she'd feared. They'd been in jail. And since they were so desperate to get a ride and get away, it stood to reason that they had escaped—probably during or just after the tornado. It was hard to believe, but this day had just gotten worse.

Five

Nick watched shock spreading across Amalie's face. The proverbial cat was finally out of the bag. Now that she knew they'd been arrested, she also knew they were on the run and why they'd rushed to hide from the police helicopter. This mess kept getting worse and worse, and the only thing he could do about it was try to keep her in one piece until they were gone.

Amalie stifled a new set of fears as she made herself look at Nick. To her relief, he didn't seem any more dangerous than he had before.

"I still want to go to my room," she said.

He nodded.

But Lou couldn't leave it alone.

"I don't see why Aroyo gets the woman to himself. She's here. She should be available to anyone who's interested, and I'm—"

Tug sat back up. Sweat was beading on his forehead and his hand was shaking as he pointed it at Lou, but the words coming out of his mouth were loud and clear.

"Wayman. Get yourself a blanket and a pillow, and bunk out at the foot of the stairs." His gaze shifted to Lou as he continued. "If anyone tries to get past you, kill him. I mean it. I've heard all the crap I want to hear over who fucks the woman. Do I make myself clear?"

No one moved. No one spoke. Then he looked at Amalie.

"Get the hell out of my room so I can rest." Then he eased himself back down and closed his eyes.

For Amalie, it was the last straw in a day of hell.

"It's not your room or your house," she snapped. "It's mine, and no one wants to be out of this room more than me."

Her chin was up and her hands curled into fists as she strode past the foot of the bed.

Tug rose back up on his elbow. A woman with the guts to talk back could cause trouble. "Nick, if she runs...get rid of her. Understand?"

Nick hesitated, then nodded. No need to mention the fact that he'd already made Amalie a promise that he would keep her unharmed and alive.

Amalie swallowed a spurt of panic at Tug's threat and pretended she didn't care. She just kept walking toward the door, where Nick waited with a flashlight.

"Lead the way," he said, and then took her by the elbow.

Amalie flinched at his touch, but when she realized it was nothing more than a steadying gesture in a darkened house, she led the way upstairs.

The beam from the flashlight was pencil thin, but it

didn't matter to Amalie. She knew the place by heart—
from the hole in the floor of the entrance hall made by
a mini-ball, when a Yankee soldier had made the mis-
take of thinking he could come in without an invitation,
to a rafter in the attic where a servant had supposedly
hanged himself. She also knew that the left newel post at
the foot of the stairs was not original to the house. The
original had to be replaced during the mid 1800s, when
the Pope in residence at the time came home drunk,
rode his horse into the house and tied it to the newel
post before going up to bed. Early the next morning, a
slave came through the house to begin her chores, saw
the horse and the manure it had dropped on her gleaming cypress floors and screamed. The scream spooked
the horse, who reared up, ripping the newel post from
the staircase, before racing off down the hall at a frantic
clip.

Amalie sighed, remembering how she'd loved to hear
Nonna retelling those stories, and realized that it was
now up to her not to let that history die. But there was
a lot more than the possibility of lost history riding on
the next few hours.

"Watch your step," Nick said, and angled the flashlight down onto the stairs so they could see where they
were going.

Amalie didn't bother to look down. She knew the
depth and width of each step, from the first floor to the
third. She knew that the fifth step squeaked no matter
where you put your foot, and that under the carpet

runner on the eleventh step was a bloodstain that no amount of time and scrubbing could remove.

When they reached the landing on the second floor, she reoriented herself by the faint ticking of the grandfather clock at the far end of the hallway. She wasn't afraid of the Vatican, or of the dark. Only those who had come in unannounced.

As they paused in the dark, she played with the notion of escape. All she had to do was knock the flashlight out of his hand and slide back down the banister. In a matter of seconds she could be out of the house and making a run for it in the dark. It was what came afterward that left her in doubt.

Where could she go should she actually make it outside? With nothing to drive, and the swamp less than a half of a mile behind the house, that left the wide-open space between the road and the front of the house as her escape route, and with his long legs, he would eventually catch her.

She sighed. If only she wasn't still recovering from the gunshot she would take her chances in the bayou, but she didn't have the stamina. And making a break for it and getting caught scared her even more than staying put. Right now they were giving her some leeway. If she pissed them off, Tug had made it clear what her fate would be.

Nick felt the tension in her body. He thought about telling her now, while they were away from the others, that he was an undercover agent, but his training and experience prompted him to keep quiet. As long as he could juggle her safety and his identity, he wasn't going to take the chance.

He swung the flashlight down the long hallway, then swept the light back up the stairs that continued to the third floor.

"This is quite a place. What's up there?"

"It used to be the servants' quarters. Now most of the rooms are empty, or used for storing furniture from past generations…nearly two hundred years' worth."

Nick absorbed the matter-of-fact tone of her voice, marveling at what she took for granted.

"Your family has owned the place that long?"

"From the time the land was first purchased, it's belonged to a Pope. Unfortunately I'm the last."

Nick swung the flashlight back at her, highlighting her face.

"Why so sure of that?"

She grimaced and pushed the flashlight to the side. "Because I'm a woman. No male heirs left to carry on the Pope name."

"So…when you marry, just don't change your name," Nick said.

The answer was as out of sync with her expectations as the man himself. He was so tall Amalie had to tilt her head back to see his face; then, when she did, she couldn't see his expression past the flashlight's halo. All she could see was his looming silhouette, and the occasional glimmer of light reflecting from his eyes. The image of a cougar crouching in the dark flashed through her mind, and then she shoved it aside.

"That's a remark I would have associated with something of a liberated man, not a...a..."

She stammered, then stopped.

Nick's eyes narrowed. "What? A criminal? Are you saying only forward-thinking men wear white shirts and ties?"

Amalie wasn't going there with him. "I'm not saying anything," she muttered. "I just want to get my pain pills and rest." She headed for her bedroom, as sure of her footing here as she had been coming up the stairs. "This was Nonna's room. Now it's mine," she said, wondering why she was telling him something that couldn't possibly matter to him, and walked inside, leaving him to follow.

Nick swept the flashlight around the room, taking quick note of the setup. There were two large windows with the drapes still open. He crossed the room and looked out. It was a long way down, with nothing to climb out on. He quickly checked the bathroom and the huge walk-in closet. He didn't see any obvious means of escape and decided she should be secure enough in here.

He turned just as she was shaking a pill out into her hand. The dejection in her manner was obvious. Even without the stress of their intrusion and her recent injury, it dawned on him that she would still be grieving the loss of her grandmother.

"I take it you and your grandmother were close."

Amalie bit her lip. She wasn't talking to him about Nonna. She wanted him out of her room and all four men out of her house, and because she was at her wits' end, she snapped.

"My parents died when I was younger. She finished raising me." Then she turned on Nick. "I never thought I'd say something like this, but I'm glad she's dead. At least she isn't having to suffer the fear of having her home invaded."

Surprised by the unexpected anger, Nick realized the best response to what she'd said was silence.

Amalie was shaking, both from exhaustion and rage, when she turned her back again and reached for the box of matches next to a candle she left here earlier in the day. The sharp rasp as she struck the match was followed by a fleeting scent of sulphur. The flame flared, then settled into a small, flickering tongue of light, casting ominous shadows into the corners of the room. She picked up the candle, then turned to face him.

Nick found himself drawn to this woman in ways that were anything but wise. He was in one hell of a mess right now, and a woman, no matter how pretty or interesting, had no place in his life. When he realized she hadn't moved, he fidgeted beneath her stare.

"Aren't you going to lie down?" he asked.

"Are you going to stand there and watch me?"

The fear was back in her voice.

"No. Sorry. I'll be outside the door. If you need anything, just call out. Okay?"

Amalie still didn't trust him to do what he said. "Look. If you're going to wait until I'm asleep to pull something, do us both a favor and do it now while I'm awake. It's apparent I could never fight you off."

The tremor in her voice was his undoing. He cursed beneath his breath and then strode toward the door, pausing on the threshold to look back.

"Just go to bed, woman. I told you I'd keep you safe, and I meant it."

With that, he shut the door with a solid *thunk*.

Amalie blinked. The knot in her belly was still there, but he'd surprised her. She began moving around the room, getting herself ready for bed. She used the toilet, although she couldn't flush, and she had enough bottled water to wet a washcloth and clean her hands and face.

When she came out of the bathroom, she thought of the nightgown she'd brought with her. It would be wonderful to get out of these clothes and into something comfortable, but she discarded the notion. No way was she taking off a stitch. She'd slept in her clothes before. It wouldn't hurt her to do it again. She glanced at the door, then kicked off her shoes, pulled back the covers and lay down.

The air outside was still and sultry, heavy from a lack of wind. And it had quit raining again. Without air-conditioning, the air in the house felt too thick to breathe. She thought about opening up a window but knew from experience that all she would get was an influx of mosquitoes—something she could do without.

She closed her eyes, then found herself listening intently, trying to figure out what Nick was doing outside her door. She kept hearing thumps and dragging sounds, and tried to imagine what could be causing them, then decided that as long as he wasn't coming inside, she didn't care.

Nick had gone across the hall into another room and dragged the mattress off a twin bed, then across the hall to her doorway.

He was exhausted, both mentally and physically, and would have liked nothing more than to close his eyes and sleep for at least a week. But he knew his running buddies too well. If Lou Drake thought he could get away with it, he would come up the stairs and slit Nick's throat just to get at the woman, and that was something he couldn't let happen.

He lay down on the mattress, pulled off his boots, then rolled a pillow up beneath his neck to elevate his head. From where he was lying, he had a straight line of vision to the landing. Coming up, he'd counted the steps. He knew the ones that squeaked. And he'd learned long ago that being a light sleeper on the job was a good way to stay alive. Despite Wayman supposedly standing guard at the bottom, if someone started up the stairs, he would know it, and when they got to the top, he would be waiting.

Nick was dreaming. In his dream, he was running. Somewhere behind him, he could hear the scream of sirens and the sound of thunder.

Then all of a sudden his eyes flew open, and he

realized someone was running up the stairs and that it wasn't sirens he'd been hearing, it was screams—coming from inside Amalie's room.

He rolled off the mattress just as Wayman and Lou came flying down the hall, the lights of their flashlights bobbing as they ran.

"What the hell's going on?" Wayman asked.

Lou pointed at Nick. "He did her, that's what!"

Wayman backhanded him, knocking him against the wall.

"Shut up, stupid. You saw Nick lying on that mattress at the same time I did. He wasn't inside her room. He was asleep."

"I dreamed I was hearing sirens," Nick muttered. "I didn't know it was her." He kicked the mattress aside and pushed the door inward.

The screams had stopped. Amalie was sitting up in bed with her hands over her face, sobbing quietly. When the door opened, she looked up. Even though she was still dressed, it was instinct that made her pull the sheet up in front of her. She pointed toward the door, her voice shaking as she spoke.

"Get out of my room."

"You were screaming your head off, lady," Wayman muttered.

Amalie took a quick breath when she realized they weren't leaving. When Lou took a step closer to the bed, her fear rose.

"I was dreaming. I'm sorry I woke you up. Now get out."

Ignoring her demand, Lou took the opportunity to check out her room, fingering all the knickknacks, going through drawers, looking for valuables and the possibility of another way into the room. He saw neither. And since she was still in her clothes, it appeared he'd been wrong about Aroyo nailing her, too. He stopped at the foot of her bed, making sure she felt threatened, then stomped out of the room and back down the stairs.

"Shit, lady, you need to keep it down," Wayman said. "You might wake up my brother."

Amalie was still shaking from the dream and then the invasion into her room, but his indignant tone turned her fear to disbelief. What the hell? She was the one who'd been shot, taken hostage, scared half out of her mind, and they were worried about waking someone up?

She laughed once—a sharp, strident sound that did not fool anyone into thinking she was happy.

Nick's gut knotted. She was on the verge of losing it, and Wayman didn't have a sense of humor.

"What the fuck's so funny?" Wayman asked. "Tell her to shut her trap or I'll do it for her."

Nick shook his head as he eased the big man out of the room.

"You go check on Tug and keep Lou off the stairs. I'll take care of this."

Wayman nodded grudgingly, glared at Amalie, then stomped out the door.

As soon as he was gone, Nick closed the door and then walked over to the bed.

Amalie's momentary spurt of rebellion ended when the door shut. At that point, tears resurfaced, and once they started, she couldn't seem to make them stop.

Nick couldn't stand it. His first instinct was to take her in his arms, but that would only freak her out again. Instead he sat down at the foot of the bed, careful not to touch her.

"What can I do?"

Amalie swiped at the tears on her cheeks. "You're kidding me, right? You want to know what you can do? Take your friends and get the hell out of my house. Just go and leave me alone. I can't call anyone. I can't drive anywhere. You would be long gone before I could get help."

Guilt pushed hard at Nick's conscience. He reached toward her, but she saw the motion and yanked her knees up beneath her chin.

He stifled a sigh. "I wish that I could make that happen, but Tug isn't able to walk anywhere, and without a telephone to call for help or a car to drive, we're stuck."

"God," Amalie groaned, and rolled out of bed and strode to the window, staring blindly into the dark.

Nick followed her.

"I'm sorry."

Her shoulders slumped as she leaned her forehead against the window, her voice little more than a whisper when she said, "Just go away."

"I can't," Nick said softly, and then took a chance and slid a hand across her back before stopping at her nape.

He felt her jump, then the tension in her body as she waited for an assault that never came.

"Talk to me," he whispered. "Remembering good times is the best way I know to get past the bad ones."

Amalie turned, only to find herself mere inches from his face. His features were shadowed, but she could see strength in his gaze and what appeared to be tenderness in the curve of his mouth. She'd always prided herself on being a good judge of character, but this man was an anomaly. She should be as disgusted by his presence in her home as she was by the others, but that wasn't the case. In spite of everything she knew about him, he was intriguing.

Nick cupped her elbow. "Come on…go back to bed and get comfortable first."

Amalie sighed. "I don't want to sleep. All I'll do is dream about the shooting all over again."

Nick frowned. That explained the screams.

"But if you lie down, at least you can rest…and we'll talk. Okay?"

"I guess," Amalie said, and got back into bed, then pulled the sheet up over her breasts.

As soon as she stretched out, her gaze slid to his face, making sure he wasn't going to put a move on her when she was at her most vulnerable.

Instead he sat down at the foot of her bed again and stretched his legs out in front of him. He was so close that if she extended her arm, she could touch his bare feet, and yet he didn't move. He just leaned against the footboard and crossed his arms.

"Where did you graduate high school?" he asked.

Amalie rolled her eyes. "We skipped right past the first eighteen years of my life."

He grinned. "Yeah…birth, diapers, teething and potty training. I've got the picture. And I already know your parents died and your grandmother finished raising you, so where did you graduate high school?"

Amalie didn't want to like him, but his humor surprised her. It appeared he could be charming when he wanted to be.

"I graduated in Bordelaise. Then I went to college at Louisiana State. I began teaching art in Dallas within a year of graduation, then moved to Jasper about five years ago."

"Did you always want to teach?"

Amalie shook her head, unaware that she was smiling. "No artist dreams of teaching first. The dream is always about being discovered and getting famous, whether your style is Warhol, Wyeth or Picasso."

Breath caught in the back of Nick's throat. Her smile lit up her face, turning her from pretty to beautiful. The urge to kiss her was strong, but he ignored it.

"So, Amalie Pope…what is your style?"

Her eyes narrowed as she shoved her hands behind her head.

"I would say it's more in the vein of Andrew Wyeth. I like the reality of a subject to come through in a big way, but with the focus on something you might otherwise overlook."

Nick frowned. "How so?"

"Oh…you know…say the subject was a little boy and his dog sitting under a tree. You'd think it was an appealing scene until you realized the dog was old and at the end of its life, while the child's was just beginning."

His eyes widened. "If you can paint with oils as well as you paint with words, you must be pretty darned good. That was an amazing analogy."

Again Amalie smiled, reacting to the praise without thinking.

"Ah…the dreaded 'if.' Obviously I can't, or I would be painting, not teaching."

"Maybe you didn't give yourself enough time. It's my understanding that everything gets better with age."

"That's wine. Time does change everything, but not always for the good. People get old and die."

And just like that, the light was gone from her eyes and the talk was over.

"I want to sleep now," she said.

Nick knew when to make a graceful exit. He got up and walked out of the room without another word.

Once again, he'd taken Amalie by surprise.

She'd expected an argument, or at the least another warning.

Instead she found herself alone. She rolled onto her side, remembering the times when she would sleep curled up in Nonna's arms. Only Nonna wasn't here anymore, and the devil was in the Vatican.

Nick resumed his post on the mattress, tossing and turning, trying to get comfortable. Finally he gave it up as a lost cause and sat up, his back against her door, and thought about a little dark-haired girl with green eyes who'd once laughed and played within these walls.

Six

Amalie woke up to sunshine streaming into the room, but the promise of a sunny day was marred by circumstance. She cast a nervous glance toward the door, half expecting the men to come charging in again like they had last night.

Curious as to why it was so quiet, she got out of bed and tiptoed to the door to listen. The silence was comforting as she slowly stretched to ease sore muscles, then went into the bathroom. Out of habit, she tried the light switch to see if the power had been restored, and to her delight, the room was instantly bathed in light. That meant she would have running water again, as well.

She ran back into the bedroom, grabbed a change of clothes and underwear, and then locked the bathroom door behind her as she went in. A couple of minutes later she was in the shower. The steady flow of warm water against her healing shoulder wound went a long way toward easing the morning aches. After soaping her body, she shampooed her hair, but she didn't linger in the shower as she liked to do. She grabbed a towel and quickly dried before putting on fresh clothes. Once she was dressed, she began looking for the hair dryer. By the time she came out of the bathroom, she felt better prepared to face the day.

She was straightening up the bed when it hit her. If the electricity was on, maybe the phones were working, too! She made a dive across the bed and grabbed the receiver. The lack of a dial tone put a damper on her mood. Reluctant to leave, she straightened her bed again, then reached for her sandals. Moments later she changed her mind and chose tennis shoes instead. Without knowing what lay ahead, being able to run swiftly might be the difference between life and death.

Completely clean and completely dressed, she still hesitated. In here, she felt safe, even if it was a false sense of safety. Beyond the door, uncertainty awaited. Hopefully today would be the day the injured man got well enough for them all to leave.

Suddenly there was a knock on her door, and before she could answer, it swung inward. Nick entered, barefoot and bare above the waist, his devil-black hair still gleaming with droplets from the shower he must have taken in the room across the hall.

"Wayman wants your phone."

Wayman pushed past Nick and strode toward Amalie.

"The phones are still out, but at least your electricity is back on," Nick said.

"I know. A great reason to rejoice," she drawled, then

watched as Wayman reached for the phone and started to rip it from the jack.

"Wait! For God's sake, wait!" She ran toward him, then quickly unplugged it from the wall. "There's no need for destruction," she muttered, as she set the phone firmly in his hands.

Taken aback by her reprimand, Wayman flushed, then left the room cursing under his breath.

Nick was grinning. "That doesn't happen often," he said.

Amalie's focus shifted, and it was all she could do to keep her gaze on his face instead of his body.

"What doesn't happen often?"

"A woman getting under the French brothers' skin."

She rolled her eyes. "All he had to do was ask. I wasn't going to wrestle him for it."

Nick grinned.

Amalie frowned. "You're missing a shirt."

"I'm also missing underwear. When the power came back on, I hand washed them, then tossed them in your dryer, and…until the timer goes off, this is what you're going to get."

A bright flush spread up her neck and across her face.

Damn the man. He knew he was getting to her.

Her eyes narrowed. "I suppose you men are expecting breakfast?"

He was studying the faint blush under her skin, wondering what had possessed him to taunt her.

"I suppose," he said.

"Fine," Amalie muttered, then strode past him, descending the stairs with her nose in the air and the man at her heels. To her disgust, Lou was digging through the refrigerator when she entered the kitchen.

"I was told to prepare breakfast," she announced.

He jumped like a kid caught with his hand in the cookie jar, then slammed the door.

Amalie pointed at the lunch meat in his hand.

"You do know that when that's all gone, there won't be any more."

He glared, then, out of spite, stuffed an entire slice into his mouth and chewed loudly as he went out the back door.

Nick walked in just as Lou walked out. He took one look at Amalie's face and frowned, wondering what had just happened.

"What?" he asked.

"Nothing. I just caught your friend going through the refrigerator and reminded him that when the food was gone, there wasn't any more and no way to replenish it. I don't think he cared."

Nick's face lost all expression. "He's not my friend, and you're right. He doesn't care…not about anyone but himself."

Amalie threw up her hands in frustration.

"Then why do you hang out with him? Why do you hang out with *any* of them? What did you do for a living before you started your life of crime?"

Answering this with anything but a lie would get

into dangerous territory, and he wasn't ready to add to the lie already in place.

"What makes you think I knew anything else?"

Amalie was disappointed that he didn't defend himself and reminded herself that just because he was good-looking, that didn't mean he had an ounce of goodness in him. Still, she couldn't let it go.

"You have a conscience, something the others are lacking. I just assumed there was more to you. Obviously I was wrong. So, unless you want to make yourself useful, stay out of my way."

She banged a couple of cabinets as she got out some plates, then started the coffee, well aware that Nick was watching her every move. She glanced out the window and saw Lou with the handsaw, trying to remove some more of the limb. At least they were trying to get the debris off her car again. The sooner the better.

It wasn't long before the scent of frying bacon and freshly brewed coffee filled the air. As soon as the bacon was done, she began scrambling eggs and making toast. Within a couple more minutes, the meal was finished.

"Breakfast is ready," she announced, without turning around.

Nick called Lou into the house as Wayman entered the kitchen.

"I smelled food," Wayman said.

Amalie pointed at the table, where she'd carried their plates.

"I want sugar in my coffee," Wayman said.

Amalie pointed. "It's on the table."

Still smarting from her earlier put down, Wayman's hands curled into fists.

"Don't get smart with me, lady. You're not the one in charge."

Nick heard the tone of Wayman's voice and knew he was only seconds from exploding. He strode to the table and shoved the sugar bowl toward Wayman.

"Help yourself," he said softly.

Wayman blinked. He'd seen that expression on Aroyo's face before, and while he was confident in his ability to beat the holy shit out of Lou, Nick would be a different story.

"Yeah…whatever," he muttered, and dumped two huge spoonfuls of sugar into his cup before stirring.

Amalie's stomach was in knots. When Lou's footsteps sounded on the back porch, the knots grew tighter. Refusing to let them see her fear, she lifted her chin and turned her back. With shaking hands, she reached for a piece of toast, buttered it, then took a bite and began to chew. Maybe if she treated them like she did her recalcitrant high school students, she could gain a little leverage. At the least, they wouldn't know she was scared out of her mind.

Nick ate quickly, then carried his plate to the sink. The limb they were trying to remove was closer to the size of a small tree, and they still had a lot of cutting to do. Even when it was finished, there was no guarantee they would end up with a car they could drive. He had no idea how they were going to pop up the roof, or if they did, that the doors would open or then shut again.

All they could do was take it one step at a time, and, hopefully, leave Amalie and her home intact when they left.

"Thank you for breakfast," he said quietly.

She shrugged. "I made some for the other man, too."

Wayman looked up from the table. "You made breakfast for Tug?"

"Yes. Do you think he can eat it?"

Wayman's attitude took a one-eighty shift. Doing something nice for Tug was like doing something nice for him.

"Yeah, yeah...he'll eat it. Thanks," he said, then got up, grabbed the plate and a cup of coffee, and quickly left the room.

Lou banged his coffee cup on the table. "I need a refill."

Amalie grabbed the coffeepot, and before Nick could intervene, she was at the table. The moment she leaned forward to refill his cup, he palmed her breast, then squeezed it hard—hard enough to cause pain.

But she'd been expecting it. She pretended shock and reacted by pouring coffee into his lap instead of the cup.

"Shit!" Lou yelled. He leaped up from his chair and grabbed at the front of his pants, trying to pull the hot, wet fabric off his skin. "You bitch!" he cried, and swung his fist.

Suddenly Nick was between them, his hand curled around Lou's forearm.

"Don't even think about it," he said, and pushed Lou away. "I saw the whole thing. It's your own fault for grabbing her. You knew she had a pot of hot coffee, and yet you couldn't keep your damned hands to yourself. All she did was react when you hurt her."

Lou stomped out of the kitchen without looking back, slamming the door behind him.

Nick spun toward Amalie.

"You did that on purpose. Are you crazy? Next time I might not be close enough to save you."

Amalie turned on him, her voice shaking with rage. "Save me? From what? Dying? I've already faced that. And guess what, mister? I'm not afraid to die. I'm still trying to wrap my mind around why I survived a massacre to come home to this! It would be easier to be dead. My biggest problem now is finding the courage to live."

Nick was speechless. He didn't know how to counter such rage and despair.

Amalie began clearing the table, and when she had finished, she went into the utility room to get a mop to clean up the floor.

"Let me," Nick said, and took the mop out of her hands.

"Fine," Amalie said, and started stacking dishes into the dishwasher, too aware of the man behind her.

Wayman came back into the room as she was rinsing out the sink.

"Tug ate almost all of it," he said. "Thank you."

Amalie sighed. She understood family loyalty. "You're welcome."

Wayman glanced around the room. "You got any more coffee?"

She rolled her eyes as Nick interjected.

"Lou spilled it."

Wayman shrugged. "Tug's asleep for now. I'll go help Lou," he said, and headed out the door.

Nick turned to Amalie, hoping to lighten the moment.

"Alone at last."

Her lips thinned. "Surely you jest."

"Yes, but obviously not too well."

"Oh. That was a joke? Sorry. It appears my funny bone is still healing, too."

Nick grinned. Damn the woman, but she was something—and she was getting under his skin.

Breath caught in the back of Amalie's throat. What that smile did to his face should be illegal.

Then the moment was shattered with a cry of alarm.

Nick's first thought was that Lou had actually hurt himself this time, and he headed out the door as Lou and Wayman came running toward the house.

Nick stopped on the porch, then heard the helicopter and knew why they were running. The search for the missing prisoners was still ongoing.

The pair flew up the steps and into the house, tracking mud as they went.

"Son of a bitch!" Lou said, as he slammed the door

behind them. "There's another chopper coming over. They're gonna find us. *They're gonna find us.*"

"Not if we stay out of sight," Wayman said. "I say we wait until dark. We got power again. We can string some lights and work outside then."

"There aren't any to string," Amalie said.

"You got extension cords," Lou said. "I saw them in the pantry. We'll by God drag out some of your fancy lamps if we have to."

Amalie refused to react.

"Whatever. But you should know that the bayou is the first place the authorities go to look for missing people. It's not hard to figure why the chopper is flying low over the house. The swamp starts less than a half mile from the back of this property. I'm sure they're flying low over lots of people's houses."

"We can't take any chances," Wayman said. "Damn it. This place is driving me crazy. We're trapped here just like we were back in Bordelaise. I'm going back to be with Tug."

Amalie pointed at Wayman's feet. "Would you mind wiping your feet first? Your shoes are muddy."

Lou sneered, but without a comment, Wayman wiped the soles of his shoes. Lou wasn't in the same frame of mind. He started to step off the mat.

"Wipe your feet," Wayman said.

Lou cursed, but he wiped the mud from his shoes.

"Thank you both so much," Amalie said.

Wayman was not a man who understood sarcasm.

"You're welcome," he said, and left the room.

Lou was still standing on the mat with his hands curled into fists and a look of rage on his face.

"You think you're something, don't you, bitch? That's fine. You just keep on dreaming. Just know that before we leave, I'll wipe that smirk off your face—permanently."

Amalie flinched. There was no mistaking the threat, but it wasn't anything new. She'd known from the beginning that this man was the one who posed the most danger. Still, she wasn't going to give him the satisfaction of knowing that he'd scored.

Nick stepped between them.

"You through talking?"

Lou's anger was a living thing, infesting his thoughts to the point that he physically shuddered. He tried to shift focus but couldn't make it happen. He wanted to watch her die, and that was a fact. The moment would come, and when it did, he was going to be the one to take her down. He pointed at Amalie, aiming his hand like a gun, and then pulled the trigger.

"I'm going back out to the car," he said.

Nick pointed out the window.

"The chopper is making another pass over the house."

Lou hit the wall with his fist.

"Shit! We're never gonna get out of here. Anybody checked the phones to see if they're working?"

"They're all under Tug's bed," Nick said.

"Then I'm gonna get one and plug it in to see if there's a dial tone."

He blew a kiss at Amalie as he passed, then made a smacking noise with his lips, as if he'd just tasted something good.

Amalie glanced at the clock. It was a little bit after 10:00 a.m., with the entire day stretching out before them. The possibility of being stranded inside did not bring them any closer to leaving than they'd been the night before. Frustrated, she turned to Nick, her hands on her hips.

"Now what?"

Nick sighed. "I wish to hell I had an answer for that."

"So while you're looking for answers, I'm going to get a book from the library and go back to my room. It's not like I can garden, or sit on the porch and enjoy the day. I didn't sleep so well last night. I might take another nap…really live it up."

Nick was just as frustrated as she was. He was sitting on vital information that needed to be relayed, and instead he was trapped in a house with three thugs and a pissed-off woman.

"I'm really sorry," he said again, and realized he was also sick of apologizing.

The chopper buzzed the house again as it flew over, drowning out most of his words, but it didn't matter. Amalie was already on her way out of the kitchen.

He followed her to the library, pausing in the doorway to watch what she was doing.

The tension in Amalie's body eased as she ran a finger along the spines. She felt as if she was saying hello to old friends, because each title brought back so many childhood memories. Then it hit her. Memories were all she had left. She grabbed a book without looking at the title as her eyes filled with tears, then tucked it under her arm and headed for the door.

Nick saw tears on her cheeks. His stomach knotted. Damn, but he hated to see a woman cry. Then their gazes met, and he realized her tears did not diminish her anger.

"Don't ask. Don't talk to me. Just leave me alone," she muttered, and headed for the stairs as fast as she could walk.

Nick followed at a slower pace, knowing there was nowhere she could go but up. By the time he got to the second floor landing, she was already in her room with the door shut. He paused outside the door to listen.

At first he heard nothing; then the springs on the bed suddenly squeaked, followed by the muffled sound of sobbing.

"Son of a bitch," he muttered. This was one seriously effed up mess.

With Amalie safe in her room, he spun on his heel and went back down the stairs two at a time. Lou was digging through drawers in the library they'd just exited.

"Hey!" Nick yelled. "Put that stuff down and come with me."

Lou pocketed the gold pen he'd found on the desk, then exited the room behind Nick as they headed for Tug's room.

"What's going on?" he asked.

"Nothing," Nick said. "And that's the trouble."

Lou grinned. He liked conflict, and he could feel it coming.

"I vote the two of us strike out on our own and leave the French brothers on their own."

"That's not happening," Nick said, and kept on walking.

Lou hit his fist against the side of his leg.

"I don't get it! Since when did you get a hard-on for the French brothers? This is our chance to get away."

Nick stopped and turned, catching Lou by surprise.

"I don't know everything," Nick said. "But I do know that it's a damned small world, and when you betray someone's trust, it gets even smaller."

Lou frowned. "What the hell's that supposed to mean?"

"You fuck with Tug... Wayman won't stop looking for you, that's what that means."

Lou paled. "Shit."

"For once, just keep your mouth shut and let me do the talking," Nick said.

Lou didn't agree, but he wasn't arguing. He decided to wait and see what happened before he made another judgment call.

Nick reached the room, knocked once on the door, then walked in without waiting for permission.

Tug was sitting up in bed. His carrot-orange hair was poking up between the bandages on his head like grass growing through the cracks on a sidewalk, and he was pale and sweaty.

Nick grinned. "Hey, it's good to see you sitting up. How do you feel?"

"Like shit," Tug said.

"Where's Wayman?" Nick asked.

Tug pointed toward the closed bathroom door.

Nick nodded.

"Where's the girl?" Tug asked.

"She took a book up to her room. Said she might take a nap. She didn't get much sleep last night."

"Yeah, and neither did anybody else," Lou snapped.

Tug frowned. "What do you mean?"

"She freaked out, man. Screamed her damned head off, that's what. We all thought Nick was stickin' it to her, then me and Wayman caught him on his mattress outside her door."

"She had a nightmare about the shooting," Nick said.

Tug rubbed a hand lightly over his head, then winced. "Whatever... Damn, my head's killing me. Hand me another one of those pain pills, will you?"

Nick picked up the bottle. There weren't very many left inside.

"When did you last have a pill?"

Tug cursed. "Shit! I don't know! I hurt. Give me a damned pill."

Nick tossed the bottle in Tug's lap. "Help yourself. That way, if you OD, then you've offed yourself."

Tug groaned, then eased back down onto the pillow. "So what'm I supposed to do? I can't take this pain."

"You need to be in a hospital," Nick said. "For all we know, you're still bleeding…maybe even into your brain. It's for damn sure you have a concussion, which means your brain is swollen. If it doesn't go down and keeps swelling, you'll die."

Tug's expression shifted from pain-filled to horrified.

"Well, hell, Aroyo. Don't sugarcoat the news or anything."

Nick moved to the foot of the bed to emphasize his point.

"I'm not trying to scare you, man. I'm trying to save your life."

"The phones are still out," Tug said. "But Wayman said the woman has a car."

"It's under a small tree with the roof caved in," Nick said.

"And there's a damned police chopper that keeps flying over the area," Lou added. "It's buzzed the house a couple of times already."

Tug flinched, and tried to swing his legs off the bed.

"Wayman didn't tell me that. We gotta do something. Someone hand me my pants. We gotta get out of here. I don't want to go back to jail."

"None of us do," Nick said. "But you can't walk, and so far, we haven't been able to work on clearing the car long enough to know if we can drive it."

"Wait until dark," Tug said. "Work through the night. You hear me? We gotta get out of here."

The bathroom door opened. Wayman was zipping up his pants as he strolled into the room.

"You heard Tug. When it gets dark, we'll go to work. If we have to, we'll work all night."

Nick gave up. There was no way he was going to be able to talk them into surrendering.

Then the floor creaked above their heads, which meant Amalie was on the move.

"I'll talk to you later," he said, and hurried out the door.

Seven

Nick raced up the stairs, certain that the footsteps he'd heard when he was in Tug's room had been Amalie's. Except her room wasn't directly over Tug's, so he shouldn't have been able to hear her walking. If she was trying to run and they caught her at it, her life wouldn't be worth a dime. And without a weapon, he couldn't save her.

As he burst into her room, his anxiety quickly grew. She was nowhere in sight. Cursing himself for leaving her on her own, he wasn't sure what to do. Calling out for her would only alert the others. He ran to the window, but it was still shut and locked. The bathroom door was open, but she wasn't inside. Then he noticed the closet door was ajar.

His heart was pounding as he yanked it open.

"Amalie! Are you in here?"

His hopes fell when she didn't answer. The light was on, but she was nowhere in sight.

"Damn it, Amalie…you're going to be the death

of me," he muttered. He turned to leave, then heard what sounded like someone falling to the floor, followed by a muffled groan. Convinced she was hiding somewhere inside, he began shoving clothes aside and moving deeper into the closet.

Amalie was at her wits' end. Nick had been on the stairs behind her, but she'd refused to wait or look back. She didn't owe him any courtesy. By the time she reached her room, she was verging on a meltdown. She slammed the door, tossed the book on the bed and burst into tears. The hope she'd had that these men would be gone by tonight had ended with the return of the search party. Now what? Would their frustration and fears morph into a bigger threat to her? This constant state of panic and indecision was pushing her to the brink.

She cried until her head was throbbing and her stomach was in knots. Finally the tears came to an end, but her misery did not. She rolled over onto her back and stared up at the ceiling, too numb to think. When she finally got up, she moved to the window overlooking the south end of the property, her steps dragging.

"Nonna, Nonna…what do I do? I'm afraid to run for it, but if I don't try, there's no guarantee they'll leave me alive when they go."

Unfortunately there were no answers from Nonna, and nothing Amalie knew had prepared her facing this kind of trauma. She braced her hand against the windowsill, and as she did, she felt the imperfection beneath the paint and remembered what had been carved into the wood.

We are alive—1864.

Amalie shivered, remembering that the war had been raging for three years at that time and had not ended until the following year.

She leaned her forehead against the glass and took a slow, deep breath. It was the reminder she needed that worse things had come to pass on this land and Popes had lived through them. Just because she was the last, that didn't mean she was lacking in strength.

She watched the chopper make another pass over the far end of the property before banking and heading back out over the bayou. Never had she needed a cell phone as much as she needed one now. Here she was, living in the time of übertechnology, stranded in a two-hundred-year-old house without the ability to connect with the outside world. Time warp. That was what this was. A freaking time warp.

She didn't know if Nick was standing guard outside her room like he had last night, but she wasn't going to rattle the tiger's cage by going to look. And if she was going to spend some time in here, she was going to get more comfortable. She headed for the closet with one thing in mind: changing into her favorite but faded, oversize and ragged LSU T-shirt.

She turned on the light in the walk-in closet, trying to remember where she'd put the shirt when she'd un-packed. There was a small chest of drawers at the back of the closet, and she remembered putting some of her things in there.

Her grandmother's clothing was still hanging on the rods, and as she walked toward the chest she caught a whiff of perfume and paused to bury her face in the fabric of Nonna's favorite Sunday dress. It smelled of jasmine, too. Everywhere she turned, she kept coming in contact with her grandmother's favorite scent.

Amalie blinked back tears, trying not to think of the things that had gone undone when her grandmother died. This was Nonna's favorite dress, which begged the question, what had they buried her in? It made Amalie sad, wondering if her grandmother's funeral had been less than it should have been because she had not been in charge of making the arrangements.

"Sorry, Nonna," she said softly, then stepped away from the dress and reached for the chest of drawers.

The first thing she saw when she opened the top drawer was an LSU logo. Bingo. She grabbed the shirt, then, before she could close the drawer, dropped the shirt on the floor.

"Drat," she muttered, as she bent over to get it.

As she did, her gaze fell on the back of the closet, and all of a sudden she was a child again, playing hide-and-seek with her father and scooting as far back into Nonna's cedar-lined closet as she could get.

In doing so, she'd accidentally leaned against a spot on the wall that triggered a hidden latch. The hair rose on the back of her neck as she remembered a small section of the wall swinging inward. Thinking that she'd broken something, she quickly pulled it shut without ever saying anything about it, and over the years, she'd completely forgotten the incident had ever occurred.

But now she was old enough to understand the implications, and the location of a secret door was something she wanted to investigate.

She ran back into her bedroom, tossed the T-shirt on her bed, grabbed a flashlight and then ran back inside the closet. Within moments she was on her hands and knees, crawling beneath the clothing to the farthest corner. Then she sat back against the wall, just as she'd done when she was little, and began pushing against the panels. It took a few tries before she hit the right spot, then all of a sudden the door swung inward without making a sound.

"This is so cool," Amalie said, as she rolled over onto her hands and knees, and swung the flashlight beam into the darkness.

The air inside was musty but otherwise lacking any identifiable scent. It occurred to her that there could be anything from spiders to rats inside, and she winced as she swept the interior with the small beam of light. To her surprise, except for a slight film of dust, it appeared void of critters, crawling or otherwise.

She inched her way a little farther inside, again sweeping the low ceiling and dark corners with the flashlight before crawling the rest of the way in.

The room was small, but once inside, the ceiling was just high enough that she could stand. Testing the floor gingerly with each step, she moved deeper inside, constantly sweeping the walls and floor until she was in the farthest corner.

She swept the light across the wall and then suddenly stopped.

"What in the—"

She moved closer, aiming the light at one specific spot. A name had been written on the unpainted wood. It was faded and faint, and she'd almost missed it.

Polee.

That was an odd name. She aimed the flashlight again, looking to see if there was a surname to go with it, then froze. There were more names—all kinds of names, all over the wall—written in pencil, some carved into the wood, a few written in something that had left thick, dark smudges, something like blood.

But the longer she looked, the more certain she was that the names had nothing to do with the people who'd lived here. There was not one name on this wall that ended with Pope.

As she stood staring at the names, the hair on the back of her neck began to rise.

Most of the names were misspelled, while in other cases all she saw was an X. She began to read aloud.

"Sarah—Big Joe—X—Jude—Rufus—X X X—Ol Mamy—Litl Pete—Markus—Zeb—Polee—X X X X—Abel—Huney—Babe Gurl… "

Name after name, mark after mark—like a roll call from the past. There were dozens upon dozens— maybe as many as one hundred. She knew for a fact that the early Popes had been slave owners. But this defied understanding. It would seem that, over time, their mind-set might have changed.

These names on the wall—all written in different hands, in different mediums—were hard to explain away by any means other than the obvious. This hidden place was all that was left to show that at one time in history, the Vatican had been a stop on the Underground Railroad.

It was staggering to know that her ancestors had cared enough to risk their own lives and well-being to give others a chance at a better life.

Amalie laid her hand on the wall, imagining these people's terror and, at the same time, their strength of purpose. Desperate to escape the bonds of slavery, they had risked it all. She didn't want to think about the ones who hadn't made it. It was enough to know that they'd taken the chance, and for however brief their time on the run, they'd been running free. When she finally stepped back, she was crying again, but this time it wasn't for herself. It was for them.

And in a strange way, finding out what her ancestors had risked, as well as knowing what the runaways had endured to even get this far, gave her a newfound strength to deal with what was happening to her now.

If she lived through this mess, she was going to make sure that the proper authorities learned of this room. As a teacher, she could not overlook the value of such history. It needed to be shared. And as the last living descendant of the Popes, it was up to her to make that happen.

Just as she was about to leave, she heard the door to her room open, then close. She froze, listening to the sound of approaching footsteps.

God help me...don't let it be that pig Lou.

She thought she heard someone talking, but from in here, could not identify the voice. In a panic, she pushed the door shut. Then suddenly the footsteps were inside the closet. Her heart was pounding, her palms wet with sweat.

Then she heard a man's voice and breathed a quiet sigh of relief. It was Nick. He wasn't her knight in shining armor, but at least she wasn't afraid of him. Without caution, she knelt down to trigger the latch, but in the dark, dropped her flashlight and fell instead, ramming her shoulder against the wall. The pain was so sudden and so sharp that she jerked backward, holding her shoulder and groaning aloud.

Nick was frantic as he dug through the clothes. He needed to find her before the others knew she was missing, and although the groan he'd heard was definitely nearby, there was no one inside this closet but him.

"Amalie! Amalie! Where the hell are you?" he whispered.

"In here," she said, and then groaned again.

She couldn't find her flashlight, but she could feel the wall by the door. In the dark, she found the latch and tripped it, opening the door wide enough to let in some light. She saw her flashlight and picked it up, but when she tried to crawl out, her shoulder gave way.

When a portion of the closet wall suddenly swung inward, Nick's eyes widened with surprise.

"I'll be damned," he said, and got down on his knees to look in.

Amalie was sitting against the wall with a flashlight in her lap and cradling her shoulder.

"What in hell are you doing in here?" he asked, as he crawled toward her.

"Revisiting my childhood," she muttered, and rested her forehead on her knees, trying to psych herself up for the painful crawl back out.

"You're hurt," Nick said, as he laid a hand gently at her nape. "What happened?"

"I fell and bumped my shoulder," she said, then moaned again. "Lord have mercy, I have to crawl to get out, and my shoulder won't bear the weight. Could just one more thing go wrong today?"

Her sarcasm was impossible to miss, but so was her misery.

"I know I keep saying this, but it's the truth. I'm sorry. I'm so sorry," Nick said softly, then slid an arm carefully around her shoulder.

Without thinking, Amalie turned toward the comfort and buried her face against the curve of his neck.

Nick flinched. *Damn it. I don't want to feel like this. I can't afford to feel anything for her.*

But his emotions seemed to have a different agenda.

Amalie was in too much pain to think about how

perfectly she fit within his embrace. All she knew was that his voice was soft and his touch was tender.

"Will you help me get out?"

Nick rested his cheek against the crown of her head and closed his eyes.

Help her? I'm the one who's in trouble.

"You know I will. But just for the record, what the hell were you doing in here? Planning to hide?"

"No. I just remembered finding this place as a child and wanted to see it again. Only this time I went inside and found something I didn't see before."

Nick glanced around the space. It was dark and dusty, but there was still enough light to see it was empty.

"I don't see anything. What did you find? Ghosts?"

"In a manner of speaking," Amalie said, and aimed her flashlight at the back wall. "Have a look."

Nick took the flashlight and stood, immediately bumping his head on the low ceiling.

"Damn. Who built this room? Elves?"

"Sorry," Amalie said.

"It's not like this hasn't happened before," Nick said, and rubbed his head as he moved toward the wall in a crouch.

Amalie watched as he moved the flashlight beam across the names. When he came back to her, she could see the awe on his face.

"Those aren't your ancestors' names, are they?"

"I doubt it," Amalie said. "I never knew about this, and no one in the family ever talked about it to me, but

I'm thinking this house might have been a stop on the Underground Railroad. I can't wait to contact the historical society and have them come check it out."

"Weren't your people slave owners?"

"Yes, at one time for sure, which makes this all the more amazing."

Nick smiled, then cupped the side of her cheek.

"You're very beautiful when you smile."

Amalie froze. It wasn't like she'd never had a compliment before. And it wasn't like she'd never been attracted to someone the way she was attracted to Nick. But this was someone who had invaded her home. She'd heard about the Stockholm syndrome—the hostage becoming attached to their captor. This was getting too personal, and it needed to stop.

"Uh…like I said…I need help getting out, and I don't think my shoulder will bear my weight."

Nick dropped his hand and stifled a sigh. He got the message. Don't touch.

"No problem. I'll pull you out backward. You just sit flat with your legs out in front of you and let me do the work."

Amalie sat down, then stretched out, bracing herself as Nick crawled up behind her, slid an arm beneath her breasts and tightened his grip.

Her pulse kicked.

"Am I hurting you?" he asked.

Anything but. Then she frowned. Where the hell had that come from?

"No."

"Okay, here we go, and remember…let me do the work."

"Okay."

She heard him inhale, then felt him leaning backward, using his weight as leverage to move her along. And it worked. A few more tugs, and he'd pulled her out of the secret room and back inside the closet.

"I'm out," Amalie said, as her legs cleared the threshold. Then she shut the door. Before she could move, Nick was on his feet, pulling her up with him.

Amalie groaned, then winced as she found herself upright.

"What a mess that was."

Nick turned her around until they were eye to eye. Her forehead was furrowed in pain, and her curls were even more tousled than ever.

She'd already made it clear there was to be no touching, but there was a smudge of dust on her cheek.

"You have a little…uh, there's some…oh, what the hell," he muttered, and wiped away the dust with the flat of his hand.

"Oh…uh…thank you," Amalie said, then reached up just as he dropped his hand and bumped into him.

"Sorry," they said in unison, but neither of them moved.

Amalie stared up into his face, wanting him to be something he wasn't.

He was too close, and she was too tempting. He cupped her face with both hands, then slowly, slowly, lowered his head.

She knew what was going to happen, and she wanted it—as much as she'd ever wanted anything in her life. Giving herself up to the inevitable, she leaned forward, then closed her eyes.

At the same time, Nick was telling himself to step back, not to go there—but her lips beckoned. Then she sighed. He felt her breath against his face, and before he knew it, he was kissing her.

It was comfort where there had been chaos, pleasure where there had been pain. Amalie was lost in the moment and falling deeper when she suddenly heard Nick groan. That was when it hit her. She was kissing him back—and bordering on serious lust. What in hell was she thinking?

She panicked and pushed hard, trying to get away, which only aggravated her shoulder. It was the fresh wave of pain that ended the moment between them.

All of a sudden they were staring into each other's eyes, afraid to speak—each of them afraid to be the one to make the next move and have it be the wrong one.

Nick's heart was pounding. He wanted to carry her back to that bed and bury himself inside her. But from the look in her eyes, she wasn't on the same page.

"I refuse to apologize for that," he muttered.

Amalie hoped she was giving off indignant vibes. She didn't want him to know how much the kiss had rattled her.

"Did you hear me asking for one?"

"No, but—"

She rolled her eyes. "Nor do I want to hear a 'but'

come out of your mouth. How about we just pretend that didn't happen?"

Nick glared. "You do what you want with your memories. I'll do what I want with mine. Where are your pain pills?"

"In the bathroom."

"I'll get one for you," he said, and strode out before he made a bigger fool of himself.

Amalie watched the play of muscles across his back and hips as he walked away, and tried not to think of what he would look like naked. In another life, he would have made a perfect model for a nude study—and, if she was lucky, maybe her lover. But in this life, he bordered on scary. Falling for the bad boy might have been okay in high school—even college. But falling for a bad man just wasn't done.

Still cradling her arm, but refusing to admit that what just happened was as much her fault as his, she stomped out of the closet.

Nick was standing by the bed with a glass of water in one hand and a pill in the other.

She took the pill and downed it neat.

"Thank you."

"You're welcome."

"I'm going to lie down now."

Nick nodded and then headed for the door. "I'll be nearby. Rest well."

"Easier said than done," she muttered.

Nick paused at the doorway. "I'm sorry. What did you say?"

"Nothing," she said, and then held her breath, afraid he would come back and she wouldn't have the good sense to resist him.

He didn't believe her, but he'd already stepped over a line and knew better than to press the issue.

Amalie didn't breathe easy until the door closed behind him. Her LSU T-shirt was on the bed where she'd tossed it an eternity ago.

Determined to get comfortable before she lay down, she managed to get her shirt off, then put on the old shirt, wincing slightly as she thrust her arm through the sleeve. Then she pulled back the duvet, kicked off her shoes and crawled into bed.

The central air was on, and the ceiling fan above the bed was stirring the air just enough to lull her. Her eyelids grew heavy as the pain pill began to take effect, and she soon fell asleep.

Nick waited outside her door for a few minutes, then peeked inside long enough to assure himself that she was out. Confident that he had some time before she came to, he hurried downstairs. If the chopper had moved on, then maybe they could get in some more work time. As he reached the first floor, he heard a television and followed the sound.

Lou was in the living room with his feet up on the coffee table and the remote on the sofa beside him. He was finishing off a sack of potato chips and another liter of Pepsi, and from the amount of crumbs on his belly, he'd been at it for a while.

"If we run short of food, you're the first one who's going to be cut off," Nick said.

Lou jumped, scattering crumbs and almost spilling his drink.

"Damn it! Stop sneaking around!" he yelled.

"I heard the TV from the other side of the house. If someone shows up at the door, we won't know it until it's too late," Nick said.

Lou glared, but lowered the volume. He didn't want to go back to jail, no matter what. "I'm thinking that hanging around here like this is a waste of time."

Nick pointed. "There's the door. Don't let it hit you in the ass on your way out."

Lou's glare deepened. "You'd like that, wouldn't you?"

"Would I like not having to listen to you bitch? What do you think?"

Lou vaulted up from the sofa, so angry he was shaking.

"You bastard! Everything was fine between me and them until you came along. You better watch your back, asshole. Someone might shove a knife in it."

All of a sudden Nick was in Lou's face, pushing a finger against his chest as he fired back a warning of his own.

"I didn't fuck up your love affair with Tug and Way. You're the one who got drunk and busted up the bar. You're the reason we all got arrested. You're also the one who left the meth and paraphernalia in the car. And you're the one who wanted to leave the two of them behind in Bordelaise. You watch your back, too, little man. That bayou is full of big bull gators that could roll you and drown you, then rip the flesh from your bones within minutes. And just so you know…that's a hell of a way to die."

Lou shuddered. The swamp and its inhabitants were his nemesis, and everyone knew it. He couldn't imagine anything worse than dying from a snakebite or being eaten by a gator.

"Whatever," he muttered, and stomped out of the room.

Nick watched him go, making sure he was moving in the opposite direction to the staircase, then glanced at a clock.

It was almost noon, and the others would be getting hungry again. He headed for the kitchen to see if Lou had left them anything to eat.

Eight

The day continued to pass with helicopter flyovers from the Louisiana Highway Patrol, as well as an occasional small plane, amping the tension as the sun began to sink into the west.

Lou kept monitoring the television for updates that might explain what was happening, but as far as he could tell as he wandered in and out, the media seemed to be focusing more on the structural damage to the city, rather than what was going on with the residents.

Later they gathered back in Tug's room to see if phone service had been restored. Wayman pulled a phone out from under the bed and plugged it into a jack in the wall, but the absence of a dial tone sent him into a meltdown.

"Damn things still don't work," he said as he slammed the receiver back on the cradle, then kicked a chair against the wall.

"Don't break shit," Tug muttered. "We might need to use it later."

Way blinked. "Oh. Yeah, sure, Tug. I'm sorry. I was just worried for you."

Sweat beaded on Tug French's forehead—a sign of his excruciating pain. His belly hurt. His head felt like it was going to explode, and the room kept going in and out of focus.

Nick was pacing at the foot of Tug's bed, still trying to make the point that turning themselves in might be the only way to save Tug's life. The bonus to that would be getting them away from Amalie Pope before something bad happened.

"You have a fever," Nick said. "That means infection has set in. I'm serious, Tug. I don't want to go back to jail, either, but hellsfire, man, we hadn't even been arraigned. You know we would have bonded out. They didn't catch us with anything that would solidly link us to distribution. A smart lawyer would have cleared this all up in a matter of days."

"But we ran," Tug said, and then groaned as the room began to spin. "Damn it. I think I'm gonna be sick."

Way grabbed a trash can just in time. Tug vomited until he was gray and shaking, then fell backward on the pillow.

Wayman hurried into the bathroom to clean up the mess, leaving Nick and Lou at the bedside.

Lou shoved his hands into his pockets. For once, he was lacking a comeback.

Nick felt Tug's forehead. It was dry and hot to the touch.

"Tug…Tug…?"

Tug didn't answer. He had passed out again.

Wayman came back in the room, saw Tug and panicked.

"What happened?"

"He's unconscious again. Damn it, man…this is your brother. He's in no shape to make a decision, and you're letting him play Russian roulette with his life."

Wayman sat down on the side of the bed, helpless to act. He was scared out of his mind, but all his life, Tug had been the one in charge, and nothing had changed. As long as his brother drew breath, his word was law.

"Tug says he's not going back, so that's that," Wayman muttered.

"I give up," Nick said, and strode out of the room, slamming the door behind him.

Lou stared for a few moments, wondering how he could play this to his advantage, but without a getaway car or the means to contact the outside world other than to give himself up, he couldn't come up with a plan.

Frustrated, he left the room, as well.

When Way heard the door open and close again and realized he and Tug were alone, he started to cry.

"Tug! Tug! You need to wake up now," he said, and shook his brother by the shoulder, then by the leg.

Tug wasn't moving or talking, and the silence was frightening. Wayman French had finally met a situation he couldn't conquer with his fists.

The day dragged out, leaving the men in a constant state of frustration, but until the aerial search was abandoned, they were trapped.

It was later in the afternoon before Amalie came back out of her room and headed for the kitchen. She was stunned by the dwindling food supply and worried that they would run out long before the men were able to leave. Hungry men meant dissatisfied men, and that could mean trouble for her. She went through the motions of making a meal, dumping cans of vegetables together in an old pot until she had a passable soup simmering on the stove.

Nick continued to appear in the doorway every few minutes, as if he expected her to make a run for it. She ignored his hit-and-run presence for more than an hour before she lost her patience. She turned angrily, waving the soup spoon in his face.

"Yes, I'm still here! No, I didn't try to make a run for it. Yes, my shoulder is still sore. No, I didn't dope the soup. Yes, supper is nearly ready, although why I felt obligated to feed the lot of you is still beyond me."

Nick blinked, then grinned.

It wasn't the reaction she'd expected.

"There's nothing funny about any of this," she yelled, and waved the spoon again.

"You're absolutely right."

His straight-faced answer was also unexpected.

"Then what the hell is it you're hoping to accomplish by popping in and out like a jack-in-the-box? What do you want?"

For a fraction of a second Nick thought about telling her what he really wanted, then decided she wasn't ready to hear it. *She* was what he wanted—and in the most basic of ways.

He shrugged. "I just came to make sure you're okay."

"But that's just it!" Amalie cried. "I'm not okay. I won't be okay until you all are out of my house."

"Then can we look at the possibility that I'm just trying to keep my promise to make sure you stay safe?"

Amalie shoved the spoon into the soup, muttering beneath her breath, and didn't answer.

"Well?" he asked.

Amalie spun, her eyes blazing, her face flushed from the heat of the stove, but the words out of her mouth were in direct opposition to her mood. As her Nonna would have said, butter wouldn't melt in her mouth.

"You're absolutely right. I can see how I misunderstood your behavior, and I apologize."

Nick's eyes widened. Damn, but she was a handful. If only they'd met under different circumstances….

"Then we're good?"

Amalie folded her hands at her waist and smiled primly.

"We're just ducky."

"You are so full of it," he muttered, then pointed at the stove. "Is that done?"

"Why yes…I believe that it is," she said. "Would you care for a bowl?"

His eyes narrowed. "Don't push your luck, lady. I'm the only one with a sense of humor."

"Do you see me laughing?" Amalie snapped. "Go tell your goon friends their supper is done. I'll be eating in my room."

She turned her back on him as she reached for a bowl. All of a sudden he was at her back. She froze. Had she pushed too far? Was he finally going to show his true colors and hurt her?

But he didn't touch her. Instead he reached over her head, grabbed the bowl and then handed it to her.

"Just so you don't strain your shoulder."

She felt the breath from his words on the back of her neck, and then he was gone. Refusing to admit that he was getting deeper and deeper under her skin, she filled her bowl, grabbed a handful of crackers and a spoon and left the room, well aware he was watching her go.

It didn't hit her until she'd closed herself inside her bedroom that she'd taken a big chance in calling his bluff. Still, she wouldn't take back a thing she'd said or done.

She sat down at the writing desk and began to eat, and as she did, realized that, for the first time in weeks, she was beginning to feel like her old self. She scooped up a spoonful of the soup and chewed, absently thinking that it needed a bit more salt. But she wasn't about to go back downstairs. She'd said her piece. No need diluting the fit she'd had for a little extra seasoning.

By the time the soup was gone, and the bowl rinsed and waiting to be taken back down tomorrow, Amalie had come to a very important conclusion, and it was oddly connected to the names she'd found on the hidey-hole wall. She'd been right to come home. The Vatican had not endured for nothing. It had been a refuge for all who resided under its roof, and she was no different. It was an empowering thought.

She glanced up at the wall between the two narrow windows to a framed quotation that had been Laura Pope's favorite.

This, too, shall pass.

Amalie shivered. Hopefully she would live through this to prove Nonna right. Despite the intruders who'd taken her hostage, she was finding her true center and regaining her strength.

Night fell, and Amalie hadn't come down from her room.

Way and Lou had been gathering floor lamps and extension cords since shortly after supper. The plan was to work through the night, get the tree off the car, and by daylight, attack the issue of raising the roof.

Way was in Tug's room, feeding him some soup. Nick and Lou were in the living room, watching the local news in hopes of an update on what was happening in Bordelaise.

"Think they're still looking for us?" Lou asked, as the program went to commercial.

Nick shrugged. "Probably. But they're bound to move their air search to another area soon, although we don't know where they're still searching on foot."

"Shit," Lou muttered, then leaned forward on the sofa, resting his elbows on his knees.

Nick could tell the man was stewing about something

and figured whatever it was, it wouldn't be good. When Lou stood abruptly, Nick knew he'd been right.

"Damn it, Nick. I need a piece of tail."

Nick stood, too, well aware that he overwhelmed Lou in size and strength.

"Don't go there," he said softly.

Lou shoved a finger in Nick's chest.

"She doesn't mean anything to any of us."

Nick's fingers curled into fists.

"She's not going to be collateral damage. The sooner you get that through your fucking head, the better off you'll be."

A dark flush spread up Lou's neck and onto his face. His nostrils flared, and his lips went slack.

"You don't call all the shots…and you'd better watch your back."

"You want to get off…? Go fuck yourself," Nick snapped.

Before Lou could react, the program returned from commercial, and the newscaster's next story ended the fight.

"To continue our coverage on Bordelaise, the town hard-hit by last Sunday's tornado, we've just learned that searchers have been unsuccessful in locating any signs of the four missing prisoners. There have been no sightings, and while a ground search is still under way, we've been told the air searches will, most likely, end. While authorities aren't willing to come right out and say the prisoners were taken by the tornado when the jail was destroyed, rumor has it that they're leaning toward that theory."

Lou clapped his hands together in glee.

"Hot damn! They think we're dead."

Nick stifled a sigh of frustration. All this did was take the pressure off of them needing to get out of the area as soon as possible, which wasn't what he'd wanted to hear.

"What's all the fuss?" Way asked as he walked into the room.

Lou spun, his anger at Nick forgotten as he delivered the news.

"We just heard it on TV. They're discontinuing the air searches. They think we're dead!"

"They didn't say that for certain," Nick corrected.

"But that's what they meant," Lou argued. "So the pressure to get away is off."

"Only if you're willing to let Tug die," Nick said.

Wayman reeled as if he'd been punched.

"We don't slack off on anything. You hear? We get outside tonight and get that stuff off the car. We gotta get out of here as soon as possible."

"Yeah, right," Lou said. "I only meant—"

"Tug's asleep. I say we go outside now and get busy," Way said.

"Let me go check on the woman. Make sure she's asleep, and then I'll join you," Nick said.

Wayman nodded, then left the living room with Lou right behind him.

Nick took the stairs up to Amalie's room on the run,

then hesitated outside her door. He couldn't hear anything, and the lights were off. Still, he needed to make sure she was where she was supposed to be before he left the house.

He turned the knob quietly. The door swung inward on well-oiled hinges, revealing the darkened room and the woman asleep on the bed.

He stood for a moment, making sure she wasn't faking it, and watched the even rise and fall of her breathing before leaving to join the others.

Outside, the air was thick and muggy, causing sweat to quickly bead on the surface of Nick's skin. The lamps they'd confiscated had been lined up beside each other about six feet from the car and debris, giving them maneuvering room while still casting some light by which to work.

Wayman was trying to start the chain saw, while Lou was using the handsaw.

Way looked up as Nick approached.

"Damn thing won't start," he muttered.

"Let me try," Nick said.

Way handed it over, then stepped back, watching as Nick pulled the rope several times in rapid succession. Then he stopped, walked over to the lights, removed the gas cap, then tilted the opening toward the light.

"What?" Way asked.

"It's empty," Nick said. "That's why it won't start."

"Then we gotta refill it," Way said.

Lou paused. "There's not any more fuel."

"How do you know?" Way asked.

"'Cause when I found the saws, I also found the gas cans. They were all empty."

Wayman waved his hand toward the car. "We'll siphon off some gas from the tank."

"Won't work," Nick said.

"Why the hell not?" Wayman asked.

"Chain saws don't use straight gasoline. It's a mixture of gas and chain saw oil, and if the mixture's not right, it won't work."

Wayman kicked at the dirt, then threw his hands in the air.

"I don't get it! Why does everything bad keep happening to us?" Then he grabbed the chain saw out of Nick's hands and flung it halfway across the yard into the darkness. "To hell with the damn chainsaw! I'll drag that tree off with my bare hands."

He pivoted angrily and strode back to the car, encircled the base of the limb with his arms, and began pulling and twisting until his hands suddenly slipped and he fell backward with a shout of dismay. He was moaning loudly as he rolled over onto his knees, then staggered to his feet.

"Your arms! Look what you went and did to your arms!" Lou cried.

Wayman glanced down. In the dark, the blood oozing through his skin appeared black. The bark had shredded the skin on both arms all the way to his wrists.

"Fucking hell!" Wayman wailed, and doubled over in pain.

Nick felt like cursing right along with them. Not only

had Wayman injured himself, but his twisting and jerking had firmly wedged the upper half of the limb even deeper into the crease in the metal roof.

"The only way that limb comes off now is in pieces," Nick said. "Way, you need to go wash your arms good and make sure there aren't any splinters under the skin. Use some of that alcohol from the sack in Tug's room when you're done."

"Hell no! Alcohol will burn like fire," Wayman said.

"Better a little sting than both arms infected," Nick said.

Lou glared. "Well, great. Now that just leaves one saw and both of us to do all the work."

"So start sawing," Nick said. "Once you get a piece off, I'll do the next."

Wayman stumbled his way through the dark and back into the house, moaning as he went.

Cursing beneath his breath, Lou began to saw. Little by little, they made headway on the smaller branches. But the work was slow going. The tree was green and the sap sticky, causing the saw to drag and buckle frequently.

Time passed, and Nick was guessing it was close to midnight. He'd just sawed through a chunk and was helping Lou carry it away when all of a sudden, a sound carried through the night that made them stop in their tracks.

"What was that?" Lou asked, looking fearfully

beyond the weak halo of light. Then the sound came again.

"Dogs," Nick said.

"Like hounds? Bloodhounds?" Lou asked.

Nick tilted his head. "Hounds for sure. That baying sound is familiar. Probably just hunters."

Lou shook his head and dropped his end of the piece of wood.

"They're close. Real close. What if it's bloodhounds? What if it's the searchers?"

Nick frowned. "Not at night. I don't think they'd run at night."

Another long, mournful bay shattered what was left of Lou's nerves.

"Hell no! Those are bloodhounds. I can tell. They're looking for us, and I am not standing around here waiting to get my ass caught."

He made a run for the house, moving as fast as he could go.

"Lou! Get back here! We've got to get this off the car tonight!"

But Lou wouldn't slow down, and Nick couldn't stay out here and work alone, for fear of what the other man might do to Amalie.

"Damn it all to hell and back," Nick muttered, then let go of the wood and sprinted for the house.

Lou was standing at the window, peering through the curtains.

"The lamps. We left those damn lamps burning."

"So go outside and unplug something," Nick said.

Lou bolted back out the door. Moments later the yard went dark. Then he hit the back porch on the run, locking the kitchen door behind him as he entered.

"We gotta turn off the lights in the house, too."

"Knock yourself out," Nick muttered.

With work over for the night, there was nothing left to do but sleep. Wayman was on his pallet at the foot of the stairs, still bemoaning his misery.

"Did you get your arms doctored okay?" Nick asked.

Wayman nodded. "Yeah, but they sure do burn."

"Sorry, man," Nick said. "They'll be better by morning."

"I hope so," Wayman said. "See you then."

"Yeah…in the morning," Nick said.

His frustration was growing as he climbed the stairs. He was beginning to wonder if they would ever get away from here. As soon as he reached Amalie's door, he took off his shoes and shirt, pulled the mattress back in place, then lay down, positioning himself so that if anyone came up the stairs, he would see their approach. And after the tirade Lou had just indulged in, he didn't trust him not to try something.

But nothing happened, and he fell asleep within minutes.

Wednesday it rained again. The day came and went with little to no work being done. Tempers were short. The food supply was shorter. By the time night came, everyone was on edge.

Amalie went to bed fully dressed, certain that something bad was bound to happen.

She was dreaming she was in Jasper, and that it was hailing outside her home. In the dream, she was fretting about the dents that would likely be left in her car when something shifted in her subconscious and she woke up with a start. The rapid *thump, thump, thump* that she'd interpreted as hail while she was asleep was actually footsteps. Someone was coming up the stairs on the run.

Panic shifted as she threw back the covers and jumped out of bed, surprised to see that it was morning.

Though her shoulder was still sore, the shooting pains were gone. Nervous as to what must be happening, she ran a shaky hand through her hair and waited.

All of a sudden the door flew inward. It was Nick— out of breath and obviously frantic.

"I need you downstairs! Now! There's a man on an ATV coming down your driveway toward the house. Whatever you have to do to get rid of him, do it. Don't give him a reason to be suspicious. The last thing I need is another hostage situation on my hands."

Amalie was so startled that it didn't occur to her to wonder why Nick would be worrying about being responsible for hostages. And when he grabbed her by the hand and began dragging her out of the room, she resisted.

"Wait! My shoes."

Nick cursed beneath his breath and ran back to the

other side of the bed, grabbed her tennis shoes and then dumped them at her feet.

"Here. And hurry," he said.

Amalie could hear the sound of an approaching engine as she slid her feet into the shoes. The moment she tied the last lace, Nick grabbed her by the arm and started running. They made it down the stairs in record time. By the time Amalie got to the living room, she could see a green ATV pulling to a stop at the front of the house. Then she recognized the driver as her elderly neighbor, Louis Thibideaux, on his John Deere Gator.

Wayman and Lou had stationed themselves at different parts of the living room, and both were armed with butcher knives from the kitchen. The expressions on their faces said it all. They would do whatever they had to do to stay free. All of a sudden, she understood Nick's concern. They were only moments away from bloodshed. She ran toward the door, then turned to face them.

"Wait! Please! That's Mr. Thibideaux. He's almost eighty and was one of my grandmother's best friends. I'm sure he's just come to check on me. I'll get rid of him. Don't hurt him. Please, don't hurt him."

"If we had that four-wheeler, we could get away," Lou argued.

"There's no 'we' on a four-wheeler," Nick muttered. "And how far do you think you'd get? They're not legal on the highway. I say let Amalie get rid of him."

They looked at Wayman, waiting for him to add his two cents, with Tug still out of the loop.

"Well? What's it gonna be?" Lou snapped.

The doorbell rang, startling them all into silence.

"Get down," Nick whispered, motioning at Lou. "Easy does it. All of you. Amalie, this is on your shoulders. If you want your neighbor to leave here in one piece, don't give us away."

"I won't. I promise," she said.

She glanced back once, making sure everyone was out of sight, pasted a smile on her face and then opened the door.

"Mr. Thibideaux! How nice to see you." She stepped out onto the veranda without asking him in. She gestured toward a setting of wicker furniture a few feet away. "Please sit. It's been a long time since I've seen you."

Louis Thibideaux was a tall slender man with a quick wit, a neatly clipped beard and a full head of snowy-white hair. He'd been a widower for more than ten years and had made tending to Laura Pope part of his business. Now that she had passed, he wasn't going to abandon her granddaughter. Everyone in the area knew about the shooting at the school where Amalie taught. They'd all been horrified to learn that one of their own had suffered in such a way. To have Laura die while Amalie was still fighting for her life had been a tragedy. It wasn't until he'd been running his hounds with his grandson last night and had seen a light on inside the Vatican that he'd realized Amalie was home. Although he had not been invited, he felt it was only proper that he come to pay his respects.

Polite as always, he ignored her disheveled appearance and wrinkled clothing as he seated her first before choosing the chair beside her.

"It is a blessing that you are alive, *mon cher,* but a sadness that we have lost your Nonna."

"I know. Thank you for coming by. You look well."

"I am well. Well enough for a man who has outlived his usefulness, at least. You are healed?"

Unconsciously, Amalie brushed a hand across the place where she'd been shot.

"Almost." Then she realized what she must look like. "You must excuse my appearance. I fell asleep in my clothes last night and then woke to hear your engine coming down the driveway. I'm still in recovery mode, I'm afraid."

Louis frowned. "Is there anything I can do for you? Anything you need?"

Amalie thought of her dwindling food supply and the car beneath the storm debris, and shook her head.

"No, no, I'm fine. Really. My phone's not working yet. Is yours?"

"No. No phone service, although we were fortunate to be on a different electrical grid than the one serving Bordelaise. Parts of the area are still without utilities."

"Oh, my!" Amalie said.

As he frowned, his brow curled into deep, weathered furrows. "Yes, yes, what has happened in Bordelaise is, indeed, a tragedy. An entire family died in the tornado.

The Norths. You remember the Norths? Their daughter was a famous author…wrote mysteries."

"Oh, no!" Amalie said. She did remember them and was horrified that they'd died.

"Also, a child is missing and presumed dead. Katie Earle's little boy."

Amalie gasped. She'd gone to school with Katie Earle. She was reeling as Louis continued his litany of bad news.

"They're still looking for the child's body. And there is even more. Four prisoners who were in the local jail disappeared, as well. You have seen the search helicopters, no doubt?"

"Yes, I noticed the choppers, but I assumed they were just assessing storm damage."

"No. Chief Porter had search parties all over the bayou, although when I went into Bordelaise this morning, I heard that they had called everything off. Either the prisoners are long gone, or their bodies have yet to be found."

Amalie's heart sank. If they called off the search, what did that mean for her? The pressure on the men to avoid being recaptured would be lessened. God only knew what would happen.

Louis noticed she'd gone quiet—too quiet. This wasn't like the Amalie he knew, although she had been through a lot lately.

"*Cher,* I am sorry to remind you of your sadness, but my heart hurts for your loss. Is there anything I can do for you?"

His kindness touched Amalie, bringing tears to her eyes.

"No. Not a thing, but thank you for asking. I've moved home and will be announcing myself soon enough. However, for now, I'd still like some time on my own. I know you understand."

Louis took the information as a cue to leave and quickly stood.

"Of course, of course. You must take all the time you need."

Amalie nodded, willing herself to stay calm. She needed all her wits to get him off the property without giving anything away. Just to make her point, she added, "When you see me in church, you'll know that I'm receiving visitors."

"I will pass along the word so that you will not be disturbed until you are ready."

"Thank you, Louis. You were a dear friend to my Nonna. I hope you'll be as good a friend to me, as well."

He smiled, his dark eyes twinkling. "But of course. Take care of yourself, and remember the missing prisoners, although I personally believe that the tornado surely took them. The back of the jail was completely destroyed."

"You're probably right," Amalie said, then stood up and walked to the edge of the veranda as he got on his ATV.

Within moments he was on his way down the driveway, heading back to the road. Amalie watched and waved until he disappeared around the bend, then her shoulders slumped. It had been hell watching him leave when she'd wanted so badly to go with him.

Suddenly the door opened behind her. It was Nick.

"Good job," he said.

Amalie was relieved that her old friend was safely away, but even more concerned for her own safety now than ever. They must have heard the news about the search party being called off, and that the phones were all still out of order. She gave him a nervous glance, trying to read the expression on his face, but as usual, he was giving nothing away.

She walked inside, only to find herself in the middle of a fight. Lou was in Wayman's face, jamming a finger in his chest over and over.

"We just lost a damn good chance of getting out of here. One of us could have taken that ATV and gone to find a phone."

"And who would we choose?" Wayman asked. "I won't leave Tug, Nick won't leave the woman, and if you left you'd never come back. Besides, we all heard the old man. The news last night was right. They've called off the search. And since the old man doesn't have a phone, either, no telling how far you'd have to go to find one. Not that you'd be coming back to tell us anyway."

"That's a lie! I wouldn't abandon you and Tug...we're a team!" Lou yelled, and spun toward Nick, thinking he'd told what had passed between them. "You're the new guy. You're the one who's trying to cause trouble. You said something, didn't you?"

Wayman grabbed Lou's hand and bent it backward.

"Shut the fuck up! You're gonna upset Tug."

Lou's face turned a deep, angry red. "Shit! Let go! Let go! You're gonna break my hand!"

"Turn him loose," Nick said. "With your arms all skinned up, the two of us have to stay healthy to get that tree off the car."

Still furious at being the odd man out, Lou turned on Amalie.

"What are you looking at, bitch?"

She was so exhausted and stressed that she snapped before she thought.

"A bunch of idiots fighting among themselves, and I'm hoping you kill each other and save someone else the trouble," she said, then left the room without looking back.

Lou cursed and started after her.

Nick stepped in front of him.

"No," he said softly, and put a hand in the middle of Lou's chest.

Lou glared, but backed up. He still didn't have the guts to take Nick on face-to-face, but that didn't mean he wouldn't have a go at him if his back was turned.

Amalie was beyond caring who she'd pissed off. She hadn't eaten anything since noon yesterday, and her stomach was growling.

Although no one stopped her, she knew they were

keeping track of her. When she got to the kitchen, she paused in the doorway, eyeing the mess and the dirty dishes piled in the sink, then sighed.

Her spirits were already low, but then she opened the refrigerator they sank even more. It was almost empty.

"There's not much left," Nick said, as he walked up behind her.

"I wasn't planning on guests," she muttered, as she took out the butter and a couple of eggs, and set about scrambling them.

"You want toast with your eggs?" Nick asked.

She paused, then turned around. He was standing at the toaster with the dwindling loaf of bread in his hand. She hadn't expected him to help. Then she shrugged.

"I guess not. That wouldn't leave any for the three of you."

"To hell with that," he said shortly. "We obviously haven't been worrying about leaving anything for you."

Once again, his behavior was so out of character. Something about him was off, but she couldn't put her finger on what it was that kept bothering her.

"Toast would be fine," she said.

He slipped a slice of bread in the toaster and pushed down the lever.

Wayman and Lou came into the kitchen.

"That smells good," Wayman said.

"This is for Amalie. She hasn't eaten since noon yesterday, and you two ate all the soup that was left this morning. You've both been eating nonstop since we got here. And seriously…there's not much left."

Lou's eyes widened; then he looked away, aware that he'd been eating more than his fair share of everything. He walked out of the house before someone decided to jump him about that, too.

Wayman frowned. "What's Tug gonna eat?"

"You and Lou weren't worrying about Tug when you ate all the soup."

Wayman's frown deepened. Amalie could tell by the look on his face that he was thinking of how much more they would have if she wasn't alive to be eating. Then her toast popped up. She plated her eggs, buttered her toast and got a glass of water.

"I'll eat in my room," she said, and slipped out of the kitchen before Wayman could challenge her.

The moment she was gone, Wayman turned on Nick.

"If she wasn't here, that would be that much more for us."

"We don't touch her," Nick said.

"You're not in charge!" Wayman shouted.

"I don't care who the hell is in charge. I'm saying if you—or anyone—tries to hurt Amalie Pope, you'll have to go through me to do it."

"There's three of us against you," Wayman muttered.

"No. There's two of you. Tug isn't fighting anything but infection. And as for who comes after me first, you and Lou need to decide between you who it will be, because that's who's going to die first."

Wayman paled. "You would kill one of us for some bitch we don't even know?"

Nick laid a hand on the butcher knife on the cabinet without picking it up, making his point without any need to brandish it.

"I don't hurt women," he said softly.

Wayman grunted. He'd known a man like that once. His father. It hadn't stopped him from beating the hell out of him and Tug when they'd been growing up, but he'd never laid a hand on their mother. It was a philosophy he understood.

"I better go see about Tug," Wayman said, then made a point of examining his scraped arms as he walked away.

Nick listened to the sound of Wayman's fading footsteps, then glanced out the kitchen window. Lou had the handsaw and was hacking awkwardly at a limb. When the door slammed at the other end of the house, he knew where Wayman was, as well. That left Amalie upstairs on her own. He decided to give her some time to eat her meal in peace, and began loading the dirty dishes into the dishwasher before going outside to give Lou a hand.

Stewart Babcock was coming out of a meeting when his cell phone began vibrating. He dug it out of his pocket and then answered.

"Babcock."

"Sir, we have information on Agent Aroyo."

"Finally," Babcock said. "Talk to me."

"He was one of four men who were arrested in Bordelaise, Louisiana, last Friday night."

"Get me the name of the police chief and his phone number."

"Already got them, sir," the agent said, then added, "but you might have some trouble getting through. The town was hit by a tornado over the weekend."

"All right," Babcock said, as he took out a pen and notepad. "Just give me the information."

The agent complied, and Babcock disconnected.

Within moments he was calling the Bordelaise Police Department.

Hershel was talking to Lee Tullius about the missing boy when the phone rang—and thank God the phones were back, he thought—when Vera called for his attention. "Chief, phone call for you."

"Is it an emergency?" he asked.

She shrugged. "DEA?"

He sighed. "I'll take it in my office. Wait here," he told Lee, then headed down the hall. Once inside his office, he glared at the stack of paperwork waiting for him—he would get to it as soon as he got off the phone, he promised himself—and sat down, then picked up the receiver. "Chief Porter here."

"Chief. Stewart Babcock, DEA. I understand you have some prisoners in your jail. By any chance, was one of them a man named Nick Aroyo?"

Hershel frowned. "He was here, but he's not

anymore," he said. "Not him and not the drug ring he was running with."

"You turned them loose?"

"No, sir. Last Sunday our town was hit by a tornado. Among other things, it took out the back of the jail, and as far as we can tell, the prisoners went with it. We don't know if they were taken by the tornado or if they're on the run. I had search parties scouring the area for days, and they found nothing to lead me to believe they were still alive. We called off the search a couple of days ago."

"Damn it," Babcock said. "Look, I want to send a team down to help you search."

"You can send whoever you want, but they'll be on their own. I can't afford the manpower to go back out again, because we're working the case of a kidnapped child."

"Tough," Babcock said. "What's the ransom?"

"There never was a request for ransom. We're leaning toward the theory that it's either the father or a child molester."

There was a long moment of silence, and then Babcock cleared his throat. "That's a tough one," he said. "As for the missing prisoners, if you do find them, you need to let me know immediately. Nick Aroyo is one of us. He's been undercover with that drug ring for months."

"The hell you say!" Hershel said, thinking back to the dark-eyed man who'd been so quiet during booking.

"Yes," Babcock said. "So be on the lookout for my

men. I'll have them check in with you to get them started."

"Glad to help out," Hershel said, and they disconnected.

Hershel grabbed his hat and stomped out of the office, too pissed now to tackle the paperwork piling up on his desk.

Nine

A half dozen men were waiting in the outer office of the police department when Hershel got to work on Friday. Despite their matching haircuts and casual clothes, he would have recognized them by their serious expressions alone. When he noticed they were carrying, he knew he was right.

DEA.

Babcock's search team had arrived.

The tall, sandy-haired man nearest the door stood up first, as the others followed.

"Chief Porter?"

"That's me," Hershel said. "Gentlemen, would you join me in my office?"

Vera's eyes were big as saucers, but she knew enough to refrain from comment.

Still, Hershel could only imagine what she was thinking. Six armed men waiting for him to walk in. She'd probably freaked herself out a half dozen times before he'd gotten to work.

As he walked past her desk, it occurred to him to wonder what the agents had thought about her. Sometime between last night and this morning she'd gone from red and curly to long and blonde. He sighed. Vera sure was fond of her wigs.

"Hold my calls," he said shortly.

She nodded, watching curiously as the men followed her boss down the hall.

Hershel entered the office, stepped aside for the men to follow, then closed the door.

"Sorry, I don't have enough chairs for all of you."

"Chief Porter, pleasure to meet you, sir." The sandy-haired man offered his hand. "Agent Edwards, DEA." Then he went down the line, introducing the other men. "As you've probably guessed, Babcock sent us. We'll be helping you search for the missing prisoners. What exactly is the status of the search?"

"It was called off a couple of days ago. I ended up with four search teams going in four different directions for days. We were looking for prisoners, and also the body of a little boy who'd gone missing. However, we just learned last night that the child was not a victim of the storm but, we believe, of a child molester."

The men were visibly concerned about the news.

"That's a rough one. I take it you had no luck with the search for the prisoners, either?" Edwards asked.

"Not so much as a footprint or a shred of clothing. You understand that this is bayou country. That means swamps and gators in abundance. If those prisoners had the misfortune to go airborne, then land in the swamps, their bodies are long gone."

Edwards blanched. He was friends with Nick Aroyo, and the thought of his friend meeting such a fate was daunting.

"If you don't mind, we'd like to see the jail, then we'll begin our own search from there."

"Yeah, sure. They're about finished with repairs. Still have to shingle the roof, but the concrete block walls have been replaced. Follow me."

Nick and Lou had been working so intently on removing debris that they hadn't noticed the sky was clouding up, or that the sun was momentarily hidden by a swiftly building cloud bank. They did notice that the air had gone dead still. It was like working in a sauna.

Amalie's day had been unusually silent. She'd dug through the pantry and then through Nonna's deep freeze, where she'd found a frostbitten package of frozen weiners and a half package of frozen hamburger buns. That meant there were ten weiners and four buns for five hungry people. She'd also found a small can of soup but wasn't sure what to do with it. There wasn't enough to share.

Once the men went outside to work, she'd been relegated to a chair on the back veranda.

Nick and Lou spelled each other using the handsaw, and little by little managed to whittle down the debris until the car was finally freed.

Lou whooped and yelled, then did a little dance.

"By God, we did it! We did it!"

Nick shoved his hands in his pockets, quietly surveying the rest of the problem. There was a crack in the windshield, and the back half of the roof was caved in. There was a hole in a door on the passenger side where a limb had gone through the metal, and the back window had shattered into hundreds of popcorn shaped pieces.

Wayman frowned. "How we gonna drive this thing? There's no room for anyone to sit in the back."

"We're going to have to raise the roof."

"The window's busted out, too," Wayman said.

"That's the least of our troubles," Nick said, eyeing the crushed metal.

Then he heard the back door slam and looked up. Amalie had gone inside. He started to go after her, then decided that if she hadn't tried to run by now, she wasn't going to do it today, so he stayed. Getting these men out of here had to be his top priority.

Back in Bordelaise, Agent Edwards and the rest of the search team had tried a street-by-street sweep around the jail, questioning people about the missing prisoners, but no one had anything to relate. Everything happening on a Sunday morning was the worst kind of luck from their point of view. All the businesses except a couple of gas stations and a restaurant on the other side of town had been closed, and the people who weren't sleeping in had either been out of town or in church.

It was midmorning when they stumbled onto their first clue, and then it was by accident. The owner of a department store that had been hit hard by the tornado had just sold the damaged contents to a man who owned another store, and whose stock consisted of water and fire-damaged goods. The man who'd bought the contents was parked in the alley, loading up his purchases as the agents walked over.

Edwards first thought the guy was a looter; then he saw a half dozen other people inside the store and realized they were in the middle of some sort of cleanup.

"What's up?" Edwards asked.

"Not much," the man said, as he dumped the load he was carrying and went back for another. An employee passed him with another load of clothes.

Edwards read the sign on the side of the van—Good As New—and figured out the rest. Just as they were about to move on, he caught sight of a color in the armful of clothes that made him look twice. The only places he'd seen that particular shade of orange had been on hunting vests and prison-issue jumpsuits.

"Hey! Do you mind if I take a look at that load?" Edwards asked.

"Talk to the boss," the man said, as he dumped the load and went back inside.

"I will, when he comes back," Edwards muttered. "In the meantime, I feel like shopping."

Agent Lord grinned at Agent Smith, and then they both stared as Edwards actually climbed up in the van.

"Are you serious?" Lord asked.

Edwards grabbed the orange sleeve sticking out of the clothing pile and pulled.

"Bingo," he said softly, then held it up so the others could see. "Look what we have here."

Within the hour, Edwards, Lord and Smith had found three other jumpsuits just like the first. And that was when they knew they were looking for live men, not gator-ravaged bodies.

"You gonna tell Porter?" Smith asked.

Edwards frowned. "They had their shot at searching, and this is our clue to follow. If we find out anything definitive, I might rethink it."

The agents bagged the jumpsuits as evidence, then headed for their SUV's. Now they knew the escapees were wearing regular clothes, the next thing the men would have needed were wheels. The agents spent the rest of the morning and part of the afternoon running down reports of missing cars. Dozens upon dozens of cars had disappeared during the storm and were slowly turning up all over the area. They needed to cross-check the records to see if any were still unaccounted for.

By the time they stopped to eat some lunch, they'd managed to clear all the reported cars except for two.

They grabbed some sub sandwiches from Pinky's Get and Go, while Edwards gassed up their two vehicles. Assuming the escapees had found something to drive, it was time to branch out. They split up into threes, then began checking all the small gas stations and houses in the surrounding area, checking to see if anyone had seen strangers on foot, or driving one of the two cars that were still missing.

Everyone they talked to made a point of telling them that they'd already spoken to Chief Porter or one of his men, but the agents persevered.

It was after three-thirty when Agents Edwards, Lord and Smith came upon a bridge spanning a wide, deep creek. As they started to pass, Lord suddenly yelled, "Stop! Big white Lincoln down in that creek! Wasn't one of those unaccounted for cars a Lincoln?"

Edwards, who was driving, put the car into Reverse and backed up. It wasn't until they got out that they began to realize the car had not been dumped in the creek by a tornado. There was a hole in a four-wire fence, and some small bushes had been broken off at ground level in a direct line with the car's trajectory. Which meant that someone had driven it—or pushed it—into the creek.

"Five days is a long time in this heat. I hope to God no one's in it," Smith muttered, as Edwards climbed down the steep slope and waded into the water.

Moments later, Edwards called back, "It's empty. Run the plates."

Smith ran back to their SUV and grabbed the list they'd been working.

"It was reported missing from Bordelaise!" he yelled.

"It was probably dumped by the storm," Lord said.

But Edwards knew better. "It couldn't have been. The storm came through here first, then hit Bordelaise.

Tornadoes do not pick up debris in one place, then go backward fifteen miles to dump it."

"Good point," Lord said.

Edwards pointed to Smith. "Get a tow truck out here, stat. I want this car out of the creek. The water isn't over the dash. We might still be able to lift some prints. If we're lucky, we might find out who was driving this baby."

More calls were made, and within thirty minutes a local showed up with a tow truck, hooked onto the bumper of the car and pulled it out of the creek.

Edwards grabbed some gear out of the back of their SUV and began dusting every dry surface for prints. Every time he would find one, he photographed it and e-mailed it to Quantico. Aroyo's prints were on file, and he'd already contacted a tech, who was processing the info as it was received. With luck he would confirm Aroyo soon.

Nick slapped a mosquito that lit on his arm, then swatted at another one buzzing around his ear. Now he knew why Amalie had gone into the house earlier.

"Let's give it a rest," he said. "The mosquitoes are chewing me up alive."

"I'm hungry, anyway," Lou said.

"Me, too," Wayman said. "And I need to go check on Tug."

"Whatever we eat tonight, there will be no second helpings," Nick said, as he started toward the house.

"Why the hell not?" Lou asked, as he hurried to catch up.

"For the same reason we've been saying for days— we're running out of food."

Lou frowned but didn't comment. There was always tonight, after everyone else went to bed.

As they entered the kitchen, they saw thawing weiners and buns, sitting in a puddle on the counter, but Amalie was nowhere in sight.

"Where's the bitch?" Lou asked.

Nick glared. "Maybe she's in the bathroom. Wash up," he said. "I'll look for her."

"I'm gonna check on Tug," Wayman said, and left the kitchen.

Nick followed, thinking he was going to have to check upstairs, when he and Wayman both heard voices down the hall and realized Tug was awake—and talking to someone.

"What's going on?" Wayman said.

Then they heard the sound of breaking glass.

"What the hell?" Wayman said, and took off down the hall with Nick right behind him.

Tug had been drifting in and out of a feverish sleep in a state of pain and confusion. Part of the time he remembered what had happened to put him in the bed, but sometimes everything morphed into memories from his childhood, and the summer he'd been bitten by a poisonous spider and nearly died. In the dream, his mother had been talking to him, telling him how much she loved him, and how they would all go to the lake when he got well. He could feel the cool, wet compress she kept putting on his forehead in an effort to take down the fever, and the slight stirring of air from their small table fan blowing across his face.

Then the scent of something savory slipped into his consciousness, and he stirred and opened his eyes. For a moment he thought his mother was standing at the foot of his bed, but then she spoke and said something about soup, and he knew the voice was all wrong. He blinked a few times before it dawned on him that this wasn't his mother, it was the woman from the house.

She was a looker—no doubt about that—but a little skinny for his taste. The jeans she was wearing looked like she'd slept in them, as did her white T-shirt. Sweaty wisps of her short dark curls were stuck to her forehead, and there were shadows underneath her eyes. All he remembered was that this was her house they were hiding in. Then she moved toward the side of his bed.

"I found a can of soup. Do you think you could eat?"

Suddenly he felt anxious. She was too close, and he was too helpless.

"Where's my brother?" he mumbled. "Where's Wayman?"

"He was still outside with the others when I came in. Do you want the soup?"

Tug got another whiff of the aroma. His belly growled in protest.

"Yeah, yeah. Sounds good," he said, and started to

sit up, but then the room began to spin. He groaned, fell back on the pillow and closed his eyes.

His obvious pain and the ashen cast to his skin were all it took for Amalie's compassion to kick in. She put down the tray.

"Let me help you," she said, and gently scooted a couple of pillows behind his head and neck, elevating him enough so he would be able to swallow without choking.

"My head hurts like a son of a bitch," Tug said.

Amalie glanced at the bandages. The stains were old. Obviously Nick's attempt at stifling the blood flow had worked, but there was no telling what kind of injury had been done inside.

"You need a doctor," she said.

Tug eyed her expression. It was obvious she wanted them gone, but he didn't see a hint of retribution. He eyed the bowl of soup. The aroma was getting to him, but he knew he couldn't sit up and feed himself.

"I don't think I can eat that after all," he said.

Again, compassion for his condition overrode her desire for revenge.

"If I helped you, do you think you could swallow?"

Tug's eyes widened in surprise.

"Help me how?"

Amalie almost smiled. "I dip the soup. You open your mouth. I put it in. You swallow."

Tug chuckled, then groaned. "Oh. Shit. Don't make me laugh."

Amalie stifled a smile in return. She didn't want to like these people. They'd done bad things and broken the law. But just now, when Tug grinned, she saw the redhead, freckle-faced boy he must have been. Instead of leaving him to suffer on his own, she pulled a chair up to the side of the bed, grabbed a clean washcloth from the bathroom to use as a bib, and then sat down with the bowl of soup. She spooned up the first bite, then blew on it, cooling the broth.

Tug frowned. Once again, the line between this stranger and his mother blurred.

"My mother used to do that."

"Do what?" Amalie asked.

"Blow on my soup so it wouldn't burn my mouth."

Amalie sighed. Compassion for the child he'd been overrode her rejection of the man he'd become. She stuck the spoon near his mouth.

"Take a sip at first to make sure it's not too hot."

Tug stuck out his tongue. The thick, salty mix of flavors was the best thing he'd tasted in ages.

"It's good…and it's not too hot," he said, then accidentally knocked an empty glass off the bedside table. It shattered on the floor.

"Damn it," he muttered.

"It's all right. I'll clean it up in a few minutes. Let's finish this while it's warm."

"Okay," he said, and opened his mouth.

Amalie slipped more soup into his mouth. As she did, they heard the sound of running footsteps. The hair rose on the back of Amalie's neck. It didn't feel good to be sitting with her back to the door. She sat up straighter, clenching the spoon, as the door swung inward.

"We heard glass breaking! What are you doing to Tug?"

Amalie flinched, assaulted by Wayman's loud, angry accusation.

Tug swallowed, then frowned as his brother stomped toward him.

"She's not doing anything, and *I* knocked a glass off the table," he said, then opened his mouth for more soup.

Nick had come into the room on the run, thinking he was going to have to fast-talk his way out of yet another situation. But when he saw what was happening, his protective mode shifted to one of relief, then disbelief.

He'd seen Tug French pick up a man and nearly break him in half because he hadn't liked the way he'd looked at him. To see him quietly having soup spooned into his mouth by a woman half his size was hard to absorb.

But what was even more amazing to him was Amalie Pope. They'd invaded her home, frightened her, threatened her, and she still had the grace to offer sustenance to an enemy. Once again, he was humbled by her spirit and courage.

But Nick wasn't the only one surprised. Wayman was at a loss. He was the one who took care of Tug. He was the only one Tug trusted. That was the way it had always been. To see Amalie Pope sitting in his place at Tug's bedside in a position of trust and acceptance was unsettling.

"So, uh…Tug, what do you want us to do?" he asked.

Tug frowned. His head was pounding, and the room was starting to spin again. He couldn't think. He waved off Amalie's next bite.

"I had enough. Thanks," he said.

Amalie set the bowl aside, took the washcloth off Tug's chest and casually wiped a drip of soup from his chin.

"You two might want to move those extra pillows so he can lie down again," she said.

Nick moved to the side of the bed and grabbed hold of the pillows as Wayman lifted his head.

Movement exacerbated Tug's misery, causing him to moan, then curse beneath his breath.

"Are you all right, bro?" Wayman asked.

Tug shivered. "Hell, no, I'm not all right. I'm sick, Way…I'm real sick."

That scared Wayman. Tug never admitted to weakness. Without knowing how to commiserate, Wayman filled him in on what they'd been doing.

"We got the tree off the car, Tug. Soon as we pop that roof back up, we'll be outa here. Right now I'm gonna clean up that broken glass. Wouldn't want you to cut your feet or anything when you get up."

Amalie didn't want to feel sorry for the injured man, but she did. When she picked up the soup bowl and started out the door, Nick fell into step beside her.

"You continue to surprise me, Amalie Pope," he said softly.

The words washed over her like a gentle caress. She sighed. God help her, but she was losing her objectivity where he was concerned.

"Really? Because I fed another human being? There's nothing surprising about that."

Nick slipped his hand beneath her elbow, pulling her even closer to him as they walked.

"Deny it all you want, but you know exactly what I mean."

She was so weary of the drama and tension in this house that it was all she could do to keep moving.

"Whatever," she muttered, pulling away from his grasp. She couldn't let herself weaken by believing she could rely on any of them.

Nick read the stress on her face. Again the urge to confess his duplicity was strong, if for no other reason than to reassure and comfort her.

He had yet to admit there was another reason he didn't want Amalie Pope thinking badly of him. She was proving to be the kind of woman a man dreamed of having in his life. Then he shook off the fantasy and hurried to catch up with her. Losing his edge was the fastest way to get them both killed.

Amalie entered the kitchen and caught Lou wrapping a boiled weiner in half of a bun. It was obvious from the opened package that this wasn't his first helping.

When Lou looked up and saw them, his rage took her by surprise.

"I know what you're thinking, and I'm warning you now—just keep your fuckin' mouth shut!"

Amalie froze, shocked by the outburst and afraid to go closer. Then suddenly Nick was at her side.

"I've got it," he said softly, as he took the bowl from her hands and carried it to the sink.

Lou continued to glare, watching every step Nick took.

"Something you want to say?"

Nick ignored him as he took a couple of clean plates from the cabinet.

"Move it," he said softly.

Lou's face flushed a dark, angry red. "You son of a bitch."

Nick stared back without answering the taunt.

Finally Lou looked away and returned to the table, cursing beneath his breath with every step. Rage continued to build as he ate. He'd had it with Aroyo. He wasn't the boss, and he damn sure wasn't in charge of that bitch. Just thinking about her made him hard. It had been a long damn time since he'd had a piece of tail, and she was here and ripe for the taking. To hell with Aroyo, and to hell with her. He'd show them.

Amalie didn't know what this was about, and she didn't care, as long as they left her alone. When Nick handed her a bun-wrapped weiner, she took it outside to eat.

It felt good just to be out of the house. The tension between the men was palpable, and when she was around, it only escalated. She settled into a wicker chair, and then leaned back with a slow, exhausted sigh and took a small bite. The late evening air was sultry, but it felt good to be out—away from all the tension.

As she looked up at the sky, a large gray crane flew past her line of sight. She imagined herself flying with it—away from this place and these men. But reality returned as it disappeared. She looked down at her food, then shivered. She needed to eat, but her stomach was in knots.

Her solitude ended when Nick emerged from the house and took a seat in the other wicker chair. She felt his stare but purposefully ignored it. She was already losing her sense of self when he was around.

Nick caught the dejection in her demeanor and said the first thing that came to mind.

"This tastes good."

Amalie blinked, then took another bite.

"Yeah, it's an old family recipe," she muttered, and then ate without tasting, knowing she needed the sustenance to keep up her strength.

Nick grinned, but when she didn't look up, gave up the pretense. So she didn't want to talk. He got that. He just didn't have to like it.

He finished eating, then leaned back in the chair to gaze at the car, running scenarios through his head as to how they might raise the roof enough to get Tug and Wayman inside.

"The windshield is in good shape except for a crack," he said.

"The crack was already there when I drove up," Amalie said.

"Really? How did it happen?" Nick asked.

"A hawk flew into the windshield on the way here."

Nick's eyes widened. "Wow, talk about a freak accident."

"Yeah, I seem to be getting a lot of that these days."

Nick sighed. There was nothing else to say.

Shadows were spreading across the yard. It would be dark within a couple of hours. Just for a moment, he let himself play with the notion that all was well with the world and they were an ordinary couple, spending a quiet evening together out on the porch. It set off a longing he wasn't prepared to face.

Amalie was lost in memories of her own, remembering the times when she and Nonna had sat out here together and regreting the loss of her grandmother's company.

All of a sudden the sultry air shifted, lifting the hair from her forehead. She glanced up.

"The wind is rising. It will storm tonight."

Nick frowned. Another delay. He glanced up at the sky, surprised by the swift gathering of dark clouds.

Amalie stood abruptly and walked off the porch, curious as to the amount of damage to her car. The closer she got, the more her hopes fell. The dent in the back of the roof was deep. She circled the car, eyeing the other dents and scratches, and the broken glass.

"What do you think?" Nick asked, as he walked up beside her.

"That my Chevrolet is shot and the world has gone to hell."

He wanted to hug her. Instead he answered in a matter-of-fact tone.

"We'll be gone soon."

Amalie spun, fixing him with a hard, steely glare.

"And what about me? I can't see your friends being the kind to leave witnesses behind."

Despite the angry tone of her voice, he knew her words were driven by fear.

"I won't let them hurt you," he said.

"Why not? You're just as culpable as they are. You'll go back to jail, too, if you're caught."

Before he could answer, the back door slammed. He frowned when he saw it was Lou, then turned back to Amalie.

Lou walked to the top of the steps. His belly was full, but his rage had not been sated. From day one, when Aroyo had first appeared on the scene, they hadn't bonded, but it hadn't mattered as long as Tug was in charge.

Now things had changed. Tug was out of the loop and he didn't like Aroyo running the show. His gaze slid to the dark-haired woman. He could tell by the way Aroyo was looking at her that he wanted her—had probably already had her. The thought made him furious.

Lou's hands clenched into fists as he watched her walking around the car, thrusting her breasts and twitching her butt in Aroyo's face. She was asking for it, and Lou was in the mood.

He came down off the steps and started across the yard, oblivious to everything but taking her down.

Amalie's back was to the house, her arms crossed beneath her breasts as she watched the growing cloud bank.

Nick was trying to open the driver's side door when he heard approaching footsteps.

"Hey, Lou, there's a crowbar beside the front wheel. Hand it to me, will you?"

Lou picked up the tool, hefting the weight of it in his hands. But instead of handing it to Nick, he drew back and swung.

Nick looked up just in time to catch a glimpse of Lou's reflection in the window. He threw up his hand as he spun, deflecting part of the blow, which would have cracked the back of his head like a melon, otherwise. The force of the blow knocked him backward against the car. He felt a sharp burst of pain, and then everything went black.

Lou grinned. "Not so damn tough now, are you?"

He dropped the crowbar beside Nick's motionless body and looked up just as Amalie screamed.

She had seen it all.

When Nick went down and didn't get up, she knew she was in trouble.

Then Lou started toward her, his fists doubled and a look on his face that stopped her heart.

That was when she began backing up.

"You're not calling the shots anymore," Lou said softly.

"Just leave me alone!" she screamed.

"I'll leave you bleeding and begging for mercy!" he yelled back.

"God help me," she whispered, then bolted, knowing her only hope lay in outrunning him and losing him in the swamp.

"Bitch!" Lou yelled, and started after her.

Amalie cleared the yard in less than a minute, panic lending speed to her feet. She dashed past the old barn, then beyond, past where the slave cabins once stood.

The brush was thicker here, which made it harder to run, but she knew it wasn't far to the edge of the swamp. She could hear the sound of Lou's footsteps coming up behind her but didn't dare look back. There was no time to gauge her lead. She just kept running.

Hershel hadn't been in his office long when his phone rang. He glanced at the caller ID. When it read Number Blocked, he frowned.

"Hello?"

"Chief, Agent Edwards here. We have info regarding your missing prisoners."

Hershel stood up, vaguely registering that cell service must have been restored. If this was true, it didn't look good for him or his office. The DEA search team had been here less than a day and found something his men hadn't?

"I'm listening."

"We discovered an older model Lincoln in a creek several miles outside Bordelaise. It was one of the cars reported missing right after the tornado. There appears to be blood on the seats, both in back and in front. We lifted prints from the dash and steering wheel, and faxed them to Quantico. Just got verification that the driver of the car was our missing agent, Aroyo."

Hershel was speechless for a long moment, then he asked, "Prints and blood types aside, you're sure it wasn't dumped in the creek by the tornado?"

"Not unless tornadoes are in the habit of going backward and forward at the same time."

"What?"

"We're at Bonaventure Bridge, and according to our information, the storm that spawned your tornado came through here first. So it couldn't have gone into Bordelaise, picked up this car, then backtracked nearly fifteen miles to dump it in a creek. It got here because someone was driving it. Nick Aroyo's prints are on the dash, the steering wheel and the door panel. Also, we found four bloody jail-issue jumpsuits among some storm-damaged goods at the local department store. We're guessing they crawled in through the broken windows, took fresh clothing off the racks and dumped their prison garb in among the damaged clothing on their way out of town."

Hershel was dumbfounded.

"Shit."

"It's not bad news from where we're standing," Edwards said. "This means our man is still alive."

"I'm glad to know Aroyo is alive, but at the same time, this almost certainly means I have three very bad men on the loose in my parish," Hershel snapped, then immediately shifted mental gears. "Sorry. Didn't mean to go off on you. Thank you for the information. Give me your location. I'll send my deputies out with a tow truck to bring it in. You understand we'll have to collect our own evidence."

"No problem, Chief. Just wanted to keep you up-to-date. We've already got a tow out here—I'll just tell him to bring the car to you. And just so you know, we intend to continue our search until we locate our agent. If your missing prisoners are still with him, we would be happy to assist you in returning them to your custody."

Hershel sighed. "When we arrested them for possession of meth, they were awaiting arraignment and then transportation to New Orleans on outstanding warrants. If you find them, don't bring them back to me."

"Understood," Edwards said.

Hershel disconnected, then opened his drawer and pulled out a bottle of aspirin.

Wayman was swallowing his last bite of hot dog when he heard Amalie scream. He ran to the window just in time to see Lou swinging a crowbar at the back of Nick's head. When he saw Nick fall, Amalie run and Lou give chase, he panicked. His first instinct was to tell Tug. He went running down the hall and into his room.

"Tug! Lou just hit Nick in the back of the head with a crowbar and took off after the woman."

"Stupid damn bastard," Tug said, and rolled over onto his side in an attempt to get up. But the moment his head came off the pillow, the room started spinning. "Damn it! I can't handle this, Way. You've gotta do it."

Wayman nodded. "You just tell me what you want and it's done."

"Make sure Nick's okay. Then go get Lou and bring him back. If we didn't need him to get away from here, I'd say let the gators get him. But the woman doesn't deserve this. She's been good to me when she didn't have to be. I don't want anything happening to her. You hear me?"

"I hear you," Wayman said. "I'll be back. Don't you worry, Tug. I'll do what you say."

He raced out of the house to where Nick had fallen. Wayman dropped to his knees and quickly rolled the other man onto his back, then slapped his cheek and shook his shoulders in an effort to wake him up.

"Nick! Nick! Are you—"

All of a sudden Nick's eyes flew open, and he made a grab for Wayman's wrist, thinking he was Lou; then his gaze focused.

Wayman rocked back on his heels.

"Man…I thought you were a goner."

Nick groaned. As he sat up, he carefully fingered the back of his head. There was a cut in his scalp and blood on his hand. When he saw the crowbar near his leg, he remembered what had happened.

Then it hit him. Amalie had been out here, too. Where was she?

He bolted to his feet, his thoughts in a panic.

"Where is she? Where's Amalie?" he asked.

"When you went down, she started running. Lou took off after her."

"Shit," Nick whispered. "Which way did they go?"

Wayman pointed. "Toward the swamp."

Nick felt sick. He'd promised he would keep her safe.

He turned toward Wayman, poking a finger hard against his chest.

"Just so you know...if he hurts her before I find them, I'll kill him."

Then he started to run.

"No!" Way yelled. "Tug says bring Lou back. You can't hurt him." But his words fell on deaf ears.

Wayman cursed, then began to follow. He wasn't sure where they'd gone, but Tug had said to bring them back, and that was what he was going to do.

Amalie felt like she'd been running forever. Her shoes were soaked, and her clothes were wet all the way up to her waist. Her breath was coming in short, painful gasps, and her lungs felt ready to burst. Even worse, last time she'd looked, Lou was still there behind her, pursuing her with dogged determination.

The wind continued to rise as the sky grew darker. Within an hour, the sun would set, and she was about to run out of even semi-solid ground. Everywhere she looked, there was water and nowhere to go but through it.

She said a quick prayer and waded in again, holding

her breath to see how deep it went, then breathed a sigh of relief when it didn't go past her knees. She strode through it as fast as she could, desperate to get out and back onto dry ground.

Suddenly something splashed in the water behind her. She gasped and spun, expecting to see the gnarled snout of a gator coming at her, but instead she saw a turtle slipping off a partially submerged log into the dark, murky slough. Somewhere to her right she heard a louder splash and tried not to think of what had caused it as she made a dash for shore.

Just get out. Get out. I've got to get out.

Finally she was climbing out onto a narrow spongy mudbank. She paused to look behind her, sweeping the area with a frantic gaze, but Lou was nowhere in sight. Had she finally outrun him? Even better, had a gator pulled him under?

All of a sudden the muscles in her legs began to cramp. She shouldn't have stopped. She took a few steps forward, but it was no use. Her muscles knotted as she dropped to her knees.

Exhausted and afraid, she couldn't think what to do next. Then, out of nowhere, the secret room and the names on the wall flashed through her mind. Those same people had most likely run through this very swamp from something far worse than the man who was chasing her. It was the thought of their courage and bravery that got her up and on her feet.

No sooner had she straightened than she heard a crashing in the trees behind her. She turned just in time to watch Lou push his way into a clearing. With only fifty yards between them, she felt cornered.

But like Amalie's, Lou's clothes were drenched in sweat, and his steps, too, were beginning to lag. He was questioning his sanity when suddenly he saw her. The sight renewed his purpose as he laughed aloud.

"Run, bitch! Run while you got the chance!"

The laugh made her skin crawl. Despite the impending thunderstorm and the growing hour, Amalie wasn't about to give up.

She spun on her heel and once more started running, heading deeper into the swamp. She heard Lou jump into the span of water she'd just crossed and couldn't help but think, where was a hungry gator when you needed one?

Nick had no trouble following where they'd gone. The trail was obvious, from the deep footsteps left in the mud that were slowly filling up with water, to the crushed grass and broken vines and bushes.

The cut on his head was throbbing. The blood seeping from the wound was running down the back of his neck and soaking into his shirt. But pain was secondary to his fear for Amalie. He kept an eye to the trail as he ran, desperate to catch Lou before he got to her.

Then, suddenly, he heard Lou yell. He didn't understand the words, but it was reassuring to know that he was close enough to him now to hear his voice. So he kept on moving, thinking only of keeping a promise, aware that night and another thunderstorm were fast approaching.

Within moments he heard Lou shout again, and this time the sound was loud, proof that he was gaining. Nick's hopes rose as something else dawned. The fact that Lou was still moving and taunting her meant he had yet to catch her.

Ignoring the pain in his side, Nick increased his speed and within a couple of minutes caught a brief glimpse of white through the trees. He recognized it as the back of Lou's dirty T-shirt. He couldn't see Amalie, and at that moment, he didn't care. He hadn't thought past his intent to stop Lou. But as he began to draw closer, he began to worry that after the threat was gone, she might keep on running. God knows he wouldn't blame her. But he didn't want to lose her in the Louisiana bayous in the dark.

Ten

Knowing he was only yards away from catching up with Lou gave Nick a fresh burst of energy. With his gaze fixed on the spot where he'd last seen the shirt, he vaulted over the knee of a partially submerged cypress stump, landing in ankle-deep water. Something hissed in the trees above his head, then jumped across his line of vision in a caramel-colored blur.

Panther!

His shock at seeing the animal was only slightly less than the panther's disapproval of Nick's appearance as it leaped into the branches of another tree. The cat went one way and Nick the other as he waded the small arm of water and kept on moving.

Lou paused to catch his breath. He felt good. This chase was just what he'd needed to feel alive again, and even better, the prize at the end of the run would be the woman. He was gaining on her, and the thought of nailing her was all the incentive he needed to keep moving. He was pushing through a shallow slough when he began to feel something crawling up his leg. Immediately he stopped and yanked up the hem of his sodden jeans.

"Son of a bitch!" he yelped, and peeled off a leech that was about to attach, then flung it against the side of a cypress. Still shuddering, he gazed around at the morass of trees, moss and water.

"Damn creepy-ass place," he muttered.

Just as he was about to move, he began to hear the sounds of something splashing in the water behind him.

"What the hell?"

He looked for Amalie. She'd already disappeared. Unwilling to lose her, he started off in the direction she'd been moving, then once again heard the sounds and stopped to listen. They were getting closer and louder. Whatever it was, it was gaining on him. He wanted to go after the woman, but he was beginning to worry about what might be coming at him from behind.

When he heard a grunt, his heart skipped a beat. Was it some kind of animal? Panicked, he began looking for something to use as a weapon but saw nothing. Accepting that he was down to his fists, he climbed out onto a knob of solid ground and braced himself for the worst.

He was beyond stunned to see a man come running into view. That it was Nick Aroyo nearly stopped his heart. He thought he'd left him dead, or at the least nursing a busted head. He'd certainly swung at him hard enough.

Panic shifted up a notch. Without a weapon, he already knew he was at a disadvantage. Aroyo was a foot taller and in far better shape. Lou's only defenses were his fists and a bad attitude, so he began to yell as Nick waded into the dark water between them.

"I told you, Aroyo, but you couldn't mind your own fucking business! You're not the boss! You don't tell me what to do!"

Nick's rage at what this man had done was beyond words. He didn't answer. He just kept moving until he was on solid ground.

Lou did a little sidestep, then jumped forward, right into Nick's fist. The smaller man staggered beneath the blow, then gathered the momentum to swing back. Nick blocked one blow, but took another on the chin.

Lou crowed, thinking he might have a chance after all, but his cocky assurance didn't last long as they began fighting face-to-face. Nick's reach was longer, his body stronger, and no amount of ducking and feinting, or swinging and cursing, protected Lou from Nick's blows.

Lou continued to curse as much as he swung, sometimes connecting a body blow, but more often than not swinging at air while Nick's blows continued to connect—to Lou's face, to his chest, to his belly. Over and over—blow after blow—until Lou's face was bathed in blood and his eyes were nearly swollen shut.

The wind picked up sharply, sending the silver-gray

tendrils of Spanish moss and dangling kudzu vines into a frenzy. The scent of rain was in the air, but no one cared about the storm. Nick kept swinging, delivering one blow after the other, with no thought of stopping until Lou Drake was dead.

Wayman French came out of nowhere, screaming Nick's name and telling him to stop. But Nick didn't respond. Wayman shoved in between the two men, using the mass of his body to block the blows. He was gasping for breath, his thoughts in a panic. He'd finally caught up, but from the shape Lou was in, he might have arrived too late. In a panic, he lurched forward, screaming at the top of his voice as he pushed Nick in one direction and Lou in another.

"Damn it to hell, Aroyo! I said, stop it!"

Nick staggered backward against a tree trunk, then stood with his chest heaving and his hands still fisted.

"Is he dead yet?"

Wayman's jaw dropped as he stared at Nick with newfound respect. The man had been serious. He'd said he would kill Lou if he tried to hurt the woman, and he'd nearly done it.

"No, he's not dead," Way said. "And you're not hitting him anymore. Tug said."

Nick shuddered where he stood, oblivious to the pain in his head and body, numb to the throbbing pulse of blood in his swelling hands and fingers. He was soaking wet, dripping blood, and still riding an adrenaline high.

Lou swayed on his feet, gave a deep, shuddering groan and went to his knees.

"I can't see," he moaned. "I can't fuckin' see."

Nick flinched. "If you're still breathing, you scummy bastard, it's more than you deserve."

Wayman turned, pointing at Nick. "No more! You made your point, now get back to the house."

Nick fired back. "You do what you want with the son of a bitch, but you don't tell me what to do! If you want him alive, keep him out of my sight."

Wayman frowned. "But Tug wants—"

Nick glared at Wayman then pushed past him.

"Hey!" Wayman said. "The house is the other way."

Nick turned, his voice thick with rage.

"I'm not going to the house. I'm going after the woman, and you both better hope to hell nothing happens to her before I find her."

Amalie had been running for so long she no longer knew where she was. The upside to being lost was that Lou Drake was no longer behind her. She stopped at a narrow finger of water and bent over to catch her breath, bracing her hands against her knees.

As she did, she caught a brief glimpse of her own reflection, and even though it was an indistinct image, accepted that she looked like hell.

She caught movement from the corner of her eye and straightened abruptly, only to find it was the wind blowing the trees. Thankful it was nothing related to man, she took a deep breath and waded into the water again, wincing as it filled her shoes and soaked into her jeans. Blocking out the thought of snakes and alligators, she began moving toward the opposite bank.

About halfway across, she stepped off into a hole, and before she knew it, the water was over the top of her head. Before she could find footing, something bumped against her belly, sending her into a panic. She immediately shot upward, gasping for air and flailing wildly in an effort to get out of the water.

By the time she crawled out onto the bank on her hands and knees, her heart was pounding, her body shaking with exhaustion. Even more disturbing, the storm front was even closer, and it would be dark within the hour. The need for shelter was becoming a necessity.

Seconds after she pushed herself upright, something slithered out from beneath a layer of leaves and headed toward the bank.

"Cottonmouth…cottonmouth," she shrieked, running sideways as a big gray water moccasin slid silently past her and into the swamp.

It was, for Amalie, the last straw. She tried to take a step, but her legs felt like rubber. She staggered a few yards more, and then the earth suddenly tilted beneath her feet. Once again she was on her knees, her chest heaving, her heartbeat thundering in her ears. The urge to lie down, close her eyes and never get up was overwhelming. It would be so easy to just quit. She was tired of fighting. It shouldn't be this hard to stay alive.

Then she heard the sound of splashing water and someone shouting her name, and a new wave of panic washed over her.

Oh, my God! He found me.

She made herself get up, but when she tried to run, she staggered again, then grabbed onto the trunk of a tree.

"Amalie! Amalie!"

She gasped! That wasn't Lou's voice. It was Nick's!

She'd thought Lou had killed him.

Thank God, oh, thank you, God…he's alive.

She started to answer, then stopped. Did she want to be found? Could she face going back, knowing who and what would be waiting for her? A sob slipped up her throat. She didn't know what to do. What she did know was that she was almost as afraid of the bayou at night as she was of Lou.

"Amalie! Amalie! Where are you?"

She sighed, but there was a purpose in her manner when she finally turned around.

"Here! I'm here!"

Still struggling with the knowledge that she might have just sealed her fate, she watched Nick come crashing into view.

The moment he saw her, he slid to a stop. His relief in finding her alive had him near tears.

"Amalie," he said softly.

Then his relief quickly changed to concern as he saw

the hesitation on her face. His heart sank. She was trying to decide if she trusted him enough to stop running.

Amalie sighed. She could no longer deny what was in her heart. Despite the fact that he was an escaped felon, all the panic, all the fear, all the uncertainty she had been struggling with, was gone. She took a step toward him, her decision already made.

Nick was motionless until she took that first step. After that, the joy he felt was like coming home.

"Come here, baby," he said softly, and opened his arms.

Amalie's breath caught on a sob, and then she started to move, stumbling toward him in small steps, then faster, as he came to meet her.

Nick caught her on the run, pulling her off her feet and into his arms as she burst into deep, gut-wrenching sobs. It tore at his conscience, ripping away the last shreds of reticence about getting involved. God help him, where she was concerned, he was already in over his head.

When Amalie buried her face against his shoulder and wrapped her arms around his neck, he pulled her closer.

"I'm sorry, baby, I'm so sorry. I never meant for this to happen."

Amalie couldn't stop crying. When she felt the blood on the back of his neck, she cried harder.

"I thought you were dead."

Something crashed in the woods behind them. Amalie gasped as she twisted out of his grasp, thinking

Lou had found her again. But it was only the wind sending a dead limb crashing to the ground. The storm was finally upon them.

Amalie grabbed Nick's arms.

"Lou! Where is he?"

"Probably on his way back to your house with Wayman."

Amalie shivered. "What am I going to do?"

Nick frowned. "What do you mean, what are you going to do?"

Her grip tightened as her voice rose in panic.

"He won't stop until he gets me. I can't go back. I escaped once, but I don't have enough strength to do it again."

Nick felt sick at the terror she'd been through. Enough was enough. She deserved the truth.

"Amalie...sweetheart...stop." He cupped her face in the palms of his hands. "He's in no shape to bother anyone. If Wayman hadn't pulled me off him, he would be dead. He won't hurt you or anyone else for a very long time."

Amalie pulled his hands from her face to stare at his raw and swollen knuckles, then shuddered.

"Seriously?"

"Seriously. And there's something else you need to know. Something I should have told you from the start."

She hesitated, bracing herself for more bad news.

"My name is Nick Aroyo, but I'm not a drug dealer, and I'm not in trouble. I'm not on the run.

I'm an undercover agent with the Drug Enforcement Agency."

Amalie felt like she'd just been sucker punched. For a few telling moments, she simply stared until he reached for her.

Desperate, she grabbed his hand, then pulled it against her heart.

"You're not just telling me this?"

"No, God, no. I promise." His touch was as tender as the tone of his voice. "I would have told you before, but I thought we'd be gone. I kept thinking the less you knew about the whole situation, the safer you would ultimately be. I didn't count on everything that kept happening. And I wasn't sure that I could trust you not to let it slip without thinking. This investigation I've been on isn't just about me. I've been gathering info for months. I have enough to take down the entire cartel and was just about to turn it all in when we got arrested. I weighed the risk to you against my duty and waited... almost too long."

"You're really a federal agent?"

He nodded again, then wrapped his arms around her.

"Thank God."

She slid her arms around his waist and laid her face against his chest, taking comfort in the hard, steady rhythm of his heartbeat against her ear.

Nick was thankful the lie was no longer between them. But his concerns still grew as the wind began to whip through the swamp.

"We don't have much time left before this hits us. I think we need to try to find shelter. Are you strong enough to walk?"

"I will walk as far as I have to."

Her bravery continued to amaze him. Despite the fact that they needed to move, he hated to let her go. Then the wind began to whine, bringing with it the first drops of rain, and the decision was taken from them.

"Damn it. We're going to get soaked."

"I can't get any wetter," she said.

Nick touched her cheek, then held out his hand.

This time there was no hesitation. She threaded her fingers through his, and, together, they began backtracking as fast as they could move—through ankle-deep bogs, wading murky, waist-deep inlets, past groves of ancient cypress draped in long, clinging veils of moss— ever on the lookout for snakes and alligators while the rapidly moving storm front pushed at their backs. But apparently everything in sight, except for the two of them, had already taken cover.

The storm caught up with them just before the sun went below the horizon.

"We have to find cover now!" Nick yelled, then flinched as lightning was followed by a loud clap of thunder rolling over their heads.

Amalie squinted through the curtain of rain, trying to figure out where they were. They were losing light so fast and the rain was so hard, her homing sense was off-kilter.

"This way...I think," she said.

"Works for me," he said.

Within minutes the light was gone and they were stumbling through the dark, taking advantage of the brief, blinding flashes of lightning by which to navigate.

All of a sudden Amalie grabbed Nick by the arm, her face close to his ear.

"Nick! I know where we are! Just across the water... we need to get across the water!"

His gut knotted. The water was steadily rising. What if it was already over their heads?

When lightning flashed again, he saw the expression on Amalie's face. She did know where they were. In that moment, the tables had turned. Now it was his time to trust her.

"Show me," he said.

She grabbed his hand, and they stepped off solid ground and into the treacherous depths. Within seconds the swirl of runoff from the storm was strong against their legs.

Nick tightened his grip.

"Whatever you do, don't let go!"

They started forward, wading slowly in the dark, taking care with each step that they didn't lose their footing.

Lightning flashed again.

"Look out!" Nick yelled, and pulled her against him just as a partially submerged log went floating past.

The farther they walked, the higher the water rose.

By the time they reached the middle, the level was up to Amalie's chest.

All of a sudden she slipped. One minute she was standing beside Nick, and the next she was gone. Panicked, he pulled as hard as he could on her hand, and she popped back up, gasping and coughing.

"Jesus!" Nick cried, and yanked her up against him. "Wrap your arms around my neck and your legs around my waist."

"But you'll—"

"Don't argue! I'm a foot taller than you."

When he lifted her up, she did as she'd been told, taking comfort in the strength of his arms wrapped around her body.

If the added weight slowed Nick down, it was difficult to tell. Slowly but surely, they finally reached the other side.

"Let go," he said, and as she turned loose of him, he lifted her up and onto the sloping bank, then climbed out of the water beside her.

Another flash of lightning streaked across the sky before forking into three separate fingers of fire. Thunder rumbled. Nick stood, then pulled Amalie to her feet.

"Where do we go from here?"

She pointed through the rain. "The ground slopes up. There's an abandoned barn about fifty yards that way."

He grabbed her hand.

The going was easier on solid ground, even if they

were moving upward. The silhouette of the barn loomed as they reached the crest of the slope. Amalie tugged on Nick's hand, and they began to run.

In the dark, the barn door yawned like the open mouth of a giant, waiting to swallow them whole. Once they reached it, they darted inside. They were still cold and soaking wet, but the barn was welcome shelter.

Amalie fell against Nick, shivering where she stood, then wrapped her arms around his waist.

"I'm so cold I can't quit shaking."

Nick held her close as he peered into the shadows, wishing for a flashlight. He'd already crossed paths with a panther once today and didn't want to think about what might be using this barn for a shelter.

"Is there a house that goes with this barn?"

"No. It burned about ten years ago. The VanAnsels, the family who lived here, moved away soon after."

Lightning flashed, striking close—too close—but it also lit up the inside enough that Nick got a momentary glimpse of the floor plan.

"There's a loft," he said, pointing.

She nodded. "I know. I used to play in this barn with the kids who lived here. If the floor is still good, it would be a great place to wait out the storm."

Nick moved toward the ladder that went up to the loft. When Amalie started to climb, he stopped her.

"Wait," he said. "Let me go up first and check out the floor to make sure it's still intact."

She nodded, but continued to shiver.

When Nick started climbing, she leaned against the

wall and watched his ascent. The higher he climbed, the more he blended into the shadows until she could no longer see him.

"Nick?"

"Yeah?"

"Is it okay?"

"I'm waiting for another flash of lightning."

"Oh."

She looked out the doorway into the darkness, and even though she was waiting for it, she still jumped when the flash came.

"All clear!" Nick called. "Hang on. I'm coming back down."

Amalie was shivering so hard her teeth were starting to chatter as she paced beneath the ladder. When Nick's feet hit the ground, she turned toward the sound and walked into his arms.

He frowned. She was shaking so hard it felt like every muscle in her body was in spasm. He wished he had a hot bath and some food waiting for her up above—or, at the least, something soft to rest on. But from what he'd seen in that brief flash of light, the loft was bare.

"Honey, are you sure you can make it up that ladder?"

She hesitated, then realized her answer needed to be the truth. "I'm not sure of anything anymore."

"Then to hell with climbing," he growled. "Hang tight a minute while I check out some of these stalls."

"No…no…I can do it," Amalie said, grabbing his arm. Then she grabbed the first rung and lifted her foot.

"I'm right behind you," he said, and as she began to climb, he was only a rung below, using his body as a safety net, should she slip.

After what seemed like an eternity, she emerged through the opening, then crawled onto the loft floor.

Nick quickly followed.

"Over here," he said, as he helped her stand, then led her into a corner.

Amalie dropped to her knees. The adrenaline rush that had kept her moving was coming to a crashing halt. Now that they were out of the swamp and out of the storm, she felt herself coming undone.

"Amalie…?"

She heard him, but she couldn't focus enough to answer.

Another flash of lightning cast a brief but telling light. He reached for her, then gasped when he felt the chill on her skin. He needed to get her warm, but without fire or covering, he was at a loss. As he pulled her into his arms once more, he was struck by the sodden weight of her clothing.

Suddenly he rocked back on his heels and reached for the edge of her shirt.

Amalie reeled. "What are you doing?"

"You're freezing. I've got to get these wet clothes off you or you'll never get warm."

"So cold…" she mumbled, as he yanked the shirt over her head, then unhooked her bra.

"I know, baby…I know. But you'll be warmer soon, I promise." He pulled off her shoes and socks, then reached for the waistband of her jeans. "Help me. We need to get the jeans off, too."

Amalie groaned. The more time that passed, the more lethargic she felt. She fumbled with the snaps and then started to cry.

"I can't. My fingers won't work."

His touch was gentle, his voice rough with concern. "It's okay…it's okay. For God's sake, don't cry or you'll have me crying, too. I'll do it for you. Just don't cry."

But once she'd started, she couldn't stop.

Nick stripped her bare, and then himself. "This is not how I imagined this moment," he muttered, as he lay down beside her, then wrapped her in his arms.

Her skin was like ice, but the gentle swell of her breasts was soft against his chest. As he tucked her head beneath his chin, offering his arm as a pillow, he felt a momentary resistance.

"Easy, baby…easy. Nothing is going to happen to you except that we're going to get you warm. I promise— and you know I keep my promises."

Amalie shuddered on a sob, but soon realized he was right. Slowly, slowly, the heat from his body began to seep into her being, making her aware of every aspect of his shape—from the rough thatch of hair on his chest to the powerful jut of his erection. The last thing she remembered as he spooned her close was that he was so tall she couldn't feel his feet.

And then they slept.

* * *

Nick woke at first light. Sunrise was still a few minutes away as he opened his eyes to the woman in his arms. Sometime during the night Amalie had turned to face him, and now she was sleeping with her head pillowed on his arm.

It was a relief to hear the soft, steady sound of her breathing, which meant the crisis of her chill had passed with no ill effects. However, he had a new set of worries. Between the swell of her breasts and the silky-soft mound of her pubic hair pressing against his belly, she was making him hard.

He wanted her.

In every way possible.

Now.

But she'd been through holy hell for days, and he didn't want to come off like a bad imitation of Lou Drake. So he gritted his teeth and closed his eyes, willing himself to another place, trying to think of anything that would take his mind off what it would feel like to bury himself within her depths.

"Are you awake?"

He started, surprised by the sound of her voice.

"Yeah, baby…I'm awake. Are you all right?"

"I think so," she said, then stretched, and as she did, the movement pressed her belly even closer against him.

Nick stifled a groan and rose up on one elbow. To his surprise, Amalie rolled over onto her back. Now they were eye to eye. His gaze slid to the scar on her shoulder where she'd been shot, and he thought, if she had died, he would never have known what a brave, amazing woman she was. Unable to resist, he leaned down and kissed her.

Once.

Testing the waters, so to speak.

When she didn't object, he did it again—centering his lips, feeling the silky soft give of her mouth as she wrapped her arms around his neck and kissed him back.

Somewhere between the second kiss and the catch of their breaths, the sun had come up, casting light into the hayloft where once there had only been darkness.

The thought went through Amalie's mind that since she was naked as a jaybird with a very sexy, equally naked man, she should probably be just a little bit embarrassed—or at the least pretend to be. Trouble was, she wasn't embarrassed, but she was darn sure intrigued.

"Nick…"

"Hmm?"

"Since we got naked together, and we've kissed each other good morning…twice… I thought I should at least know a little bit more about you."

He grinned.

"Jonathan Nicholas Aroyo…the second, at your service. My dad is John. My mother refused to let anyone call me Junior, so I was Nick."

Amalie was listening but kept losing track of what he was saying for watching his changing expressions.

"You have a very sensuous mouth, and your eyes are almost as black as your hair," she said, and traced the curve of his eyebrow with her fingertip.

He growled deep in his throat. Damn. She was flirting. And naked. He didn't have to be hit over the head—again—to know where this was going.

Amalie's heartbeat fluttered. It was going to happen. They were going to make love. Lust rose in her belly, growing and coiling into a hot, urgent need. She wasn't blind. He wanted her. And God help her, she wanted him back. Now.

"Nick…"

There was a question in her voice. Please, he thought, don't let this be about changing her mind.

"Yeah?"

"I realize foreplay is usually a prerequisite for sex, but I also believe that there are times when it is highly overrated."

"I could not agree more," he said, and parted her legs with his knee as he rolled over on top of her. "We're about to do this without protection."

"I've never felt as protected as I do right now," she said softly.

Nick took her there, burying the ache she'd given him into her tight, hot depths, then shuddered as he struggled to control his emotions.

At that point Amalie wrapped her legs around his back, pulling him even deeper.

He slid his hands beneath her backside, hoping

to protect her tender skin from the harshness of the weathered flooring, then started to rock.

Amalie sighed. He was everything she'd imagined—and more. The sad and painful journey life had been dragging her through had just taken a turn for the better, and all she could think was, It's about damn time.

Dust motes danced in the bright yellow rays of sunshine coming through the cracks in the walls. It was the last thing Amalie saw before she closed her eyes, giving herself up to the ride.

Nick was lost. From the moment he sank into her heat, he'd seen his fate. For better or worse, this was the woman he'd been waiting for all his life. After that, time became his enemy—knowing there was going to come a moment he could not hold back.

And still he followed the heat, taking them both farther and faster, higher and harder, minute by minute, thrust by steady thrust.

Suddenly she moaned. The sound came from deep in her throat. Her fingernails dug into the back of his neck, her legs tightening around his waist.

"Oooohhh...Nick...oh, God."

And then she screamed.

It was the signal he'd been waiting for as he finally let go.

Eleven

It was difficult for Nick and Amalie to go from making love to the reality of their situation, but they had no choice. Even worse was having to put back on the stained, filthy clothes from the day before. Their jeans were dry, but stiff and caked with everything they'd waded through. Their shirts had long since lost their original color and were both a muddy-brown. Amalie didn't know until she started to put on her bra that one strap had been ripped loose.

She sighed as she picked it up, dangling it between her thumb and forefinger, as if it were roadkill.

"This looks a lot like me this morning."

Nick was fastening the last button on his jeans and looked up to see what she meant. The breath caught in the back of his throat. She was nude from the waist up, and kneeling in a wide swatch of sunlight and dust motes. From where he was standing, there was an aura of light emanating from her silhouette—like an earth-bound angel, unabashed by her seminude state.

Then he saw the bra she was holding and tried to figure out what she could possibly have in common with it.

"I don't get it."

"We're both past redemption," she drawled, and then tilted her head back and laughed.

The dust motes shifted in the sunlight, changing their appearance to gold dust. It seemed fitting—an angel kneeling in a cloud of gold. God. He didn't know whether to bow at her feet or strip her naked and let lust have its way. He'd never been turned on by a woman's laugh before.

"You're something else," he said softly.

When he held out his hands, she tossed the torn bra aside and grabbed hold. He pulled her up, then into his arms, kissing her over and over until she seemed to melt into him. Finally he pulled away with a muffled groan.

"Either we stop now, or you need to take those jeans back off."

Amalie stepped out of his arms, then reached for the zipper.

His eyes widened. When she stepped out of the jeans, his heart slammed against his rib cage with a thud.

"What are you waiting for?" she asked.

He put a hand on his chest, right above his heart.

"Just making sure it didn't quit beating."

Amalie sighed. She loved to look at him—at the hard, sinewy muscles and the long, lean body. He triggered every lustful thought she'd ever had—a pretend-to-be-bad man wrapped up in one seriously sexy package.

His jeans hit the floor, and he took her down with them.

This time, when they began to dress, they did so without words. The reality of what they had to do now was sobering. But the passing of time had also given Nick time to think, and with that had come a revelation.

No one knew he'd found her, so he wasn't taking her back. He just needed to figure out how to get her to safety and still get back to the house without wasting anymore time. He would have preferred to walk away with her, but for the time being, he needed to maintain his less than proper identity.

He watched as she pulled her T-shirt over her head, sans the misbegotten bra.

"What do you think?" she asked. "Think I'll make the best-dressed list in this?"

He shook his head and took her in his arms, then, remembering what had happened last time, stopped and held her close to him instead—as if memorizing the way she fit against his body.

"We need to talk."

Amalie frowned. "Is this the place where you say we shouldn't have just done what we did?"

He frowned. "Hell, no! This is the place where I get your pretty ass to safety."

"What do you mean? I thought I had to go back with—"

"I was dodging too many lightning bolts last night to be thinking clearly, but this morning I realized they don't know that I found you. For all they know, you got away, and I got lost and had to wait until light to find my way back. I'm also going to be on the defensive and angry at all of them. Partly for the fact that Lou tried to kill me, and also for fear that you could be dead. So if you went walking from here, how far is the nearest house?"

Amalie was beginning to shake. The thought of not having to go back to face Lou Drake was nothing short of heaven, but parting company with Nick was anything but.

"Remember the man who came to the house on the John Deere Gator? Louis Thibideaux? His house is about five miles that way." She pointed.

"Hopefully not as the crow flies, because neither one of us is going back through that swamp."

"No, no…there's a road."

Nick took her by the shoulders. "Then here's what I want you to do. You get to Louis's house. And if the phone's still not working, you get him to take you into Bordelaise. Tell the police chief everything."

"Okay, but what about you?"

"In a minute," he said. "There's one more thing. How good is your memory?"

"Good enough to remember the names of about three hundred students."

He grinned. "That'll do. When you get to a phone, I need for you to call my boss. His name is Stewart

Babcock. He's the deputy director of the DEA in D.C."
Nick rattled off the number, then made her repeat it back
to him twice. "Tell him what's happened, and that the
info he needs is in a private mailbox in a Box and Post
in New Orleans just off Rampart Street. It's box 125.
Got all that?"

Amalie repeated the phone number, and the number
and address of his private mailbox.

"If that's what I'll be doing, then what about you?"
she asked.

"I'm going back to your house. If we can, we'll leave
in your car. If we're still there when the authorities show
up, then that's where we get caught."

"But why—"

"For now, I think it's best that I maintain my cover.
Let myself get arrested again with the others. My boss
will get me out when he's ready."

"What if you're not there?"

"Then tell them to look for us to show up at a hospital in New Orleans, because if Tug's still alive, that's
where we'll be headed."

"All right." Then she threw her arms around Nick's
neck. "Don't go and get yourself killed. I might like to
see you again."

He groaned. "You'll see me again. Count on it." Then
he kissed her—hard and long—as if branding the shape
and taste of her into his soul.

When they finally pulled away from each other,
Amalie was crying and Nick was shaking.

"Damn it, don't cry."

Amalie swiped at the tears on her face.

"And you don't get yourself killed."

He nodded, then held out his hand.

"Deal."

Amalie gripped it, telling herself this had to work out.

"Deal."

"Go!" Nick said. "And be careful."

"You, too," Amalie cautioned.

Nick darted away, anxious to get back to her house and see where things stood. It had already occurred to him that, if they got the car in drivable condition before he got back, they would leave him behind. He didn't want that to happen. Now that Amalie was safe, he had a score to settle with Lou Drake.

Amalie stood for a few moments, watching Nick go. The farther he went, the faster he moved. Picking up on his anxiety, she turned and started walking. By the time she got to the main road that would take her to Louis's house, she was running.

Wayman was in a panic. Tug was out of his head, and Lou's eyes were swollen completely shut. Besides which, after the beating Nick had given him, the man was so sore he could barely move.

But what was worrying Wayman more than Tug's and Lou's conditions was that Nick hadn't come back. Once the storm had passed, he'd kept expecting him to show up. When he didn't, every bad thing he could think of went through his mind—from Nick drowning to him being eaten by a gator. Finally, to keep his mind off his troubles, he'd gone to work on the car as soon as it began to get light.

His massive size was against him as he tried to maneuver within the crushed interior. Finally he'd gotten the idea to take out the bucket seat on the passenger side. After that, he had some room to move. Then, using the jack and adding wood blocks as needed, he literally jacked up the roof.

When he'd first begun, it had creaked and popped, but he kept adding blocks. Every time he raised it another few inches, broken glass would fall out of the windows, much of it inside the car. When the ceiling finally popped up, glass flew in all directions.

But Wayman was ecstatic. Although there were still obvious dents in the metal and the only solid window was the windshield, there was finally enough headroom for them to fit, and that was all that mattered.

Excited, he'd run back inside to tell Tug, but Tug was burning up with fever and totally out of it. He found Lou asleep on the sofa and woke him up to tell him they would be leaving soon. But all Lou could do was talk about the pain he was in and how hungry he was with nothing to eat.

Disgusted, Wayman went back outside to replace the seat. Once he had it reinstalled, he began cleaning out the glass. One of the back doors wouldn't open, and the other was ajar and wouldn't shut. But Wayman had a plan. As soon as they got in the car, he would just wire the door shut and off they'd go. If no one looked very close, they would just look like they were driving with the windows down.

His biggest concern now had to do with how to get back to a main highway without going back through Bordelaise. What if he got turned around and drove right back into town? Then all of this would have been for nothing.

It was ten minutes after eleven when he backed out of the front seat. The car was devoid of glass. There was more than half a tank of gas, and he'd found a package of peanut butter crackers in the console and was downing them without conscience. Lou didn't deserve them, and Tug couldn't eat them, so by rights, they were his.

Satisfied with the job he'd done, he shook the headrest on the bucket seat, making sure the seat was secure. Now all he had to do was get Lou in the front seat, then go back and get Tug. Wayman was counting on Tug being able to walk some, or he would never get him into the car on his own.

He tossed the wrench he'd been using back into the box of tools that he'd found and was dusting his hands off on his pants when he happened to turn around.

When he saw Nick coming across the grounds toward the house, all he could think was, *Thank God*.

It took him a few seconds to realize Nick had come back alone. That was when his elation turned to concern. What was it Nick had said? If anything happened to the woman…

He swallowed nervously.

* * *

The first thing Nick had seen was that the car roof was up. So Wayman had finally done it. That meant they could leave. Now all he had to do was to let the rest of his plan play out. By the time he reached the house, he had his game face on.

"Where's the woman?" Wayman asked.

Nick shook his head, his voice low and angry. "I couldn't find her. Where's Lou?"

"Now, Nick…he's laid up real bad. Just leave him alone, okay? I got the car fixed. At least we can leave now. Whatever happened to the woman is her fault. She's the one who ran."

Nick doubled up his fist and swung before he thought.

Wayman reeled from the blow. The urge to hit back was strong, but he was pretty sure he was going to need Nick's help to get Tug into the car. Besides, he wasn't so sure that, in a fair fight, he could beat Nick Aroyo. Especially when he was mad.

Nick was shaking with rage.

"Her fault? She ran for fear of her life, you stupid son of a bitch. And after she went out of her way to help your brother, that's all you have to say? She probably died in that godforsaken swamp last night. How freakin' ironic is that? Survive being shot by some asshole kid you spend your life teaching, only to come home and die like that? Damn it, Way! I thought better of you! Damn it all to hell!"

Wayman was almost in tears.

"I didn't mean it like that. I just—"

"Fuck you. Fuck all of you," Nick said softly. "As for the car, looks like you were going to leave without me. So consider yourself on notice. I'm leaving here in fifteen minutes, with or without the rest of you."

"No, no, we're ready. I was just about to go get Tug."

Then Way flushed. He'd just all but admitted he was going to leave without waiting to see if Nick came back.

Nick let it slide. Just the fact that Wayman was already worried and on the defensive was all the edge he needed.

"I'll help you get Tug into the car," he said.

"We can't leave Lou behind," Wayman said.

"I can," Nick muttered.

"He can't see. His eyes are swollen shut. I'll get him. I'll do it myself."

Nick didn't argue. He just headed for the house with Wayman right behind him. He strode through the kitchen, then into the hall, and saw Lou sitting in the living room. The television was on, but it was obvious the man could only listen. His eyes were swollen shut, and his nose appeared broken and was leaning at an odd angle to the rest of his very battered face.

A muscle twitched in Nick's jaw as he took satisfaction in the fact that the beating he'd given Lou would leave a permanent mark.

Then, as if sensing he was no longer alone, Lou tilted his head toward the doorway.

"Way…is that you? I need to take a piss."

"No. It's not Way. It's me, you sorry son of a bitch."

Lou grunted, then struggled to his feet. Even though he couldn't see, he thrust his arms out in front of him and began backing up.

"I can't see! I can't see! You can't hit me now. I can't see!"

"Yeah, well I didn't see you, either, when you came up behind me with that crowbar."

Lou started to whine.

"I'm sorry, man. I'm sorry. I was just jonesing for a piece of tail so bad…. You know how it is…when you want it, you want it. Tell the woman I'm sorry. I won't bother her again."

"I can't," Nick said.

"Why not?" Lou asked.

"Because I couldn't find her. She either got away clean, which means our safety here is over, or she's dead. Either way, your ass is mine. Once we get Tug to a hospital, I just might finish what I started."

Lou whimpered like a dog that had just been kicked.

Wayman came up and grabbed Nick by the arm.

"Leave him be. I'll tend to him after we get Tug in the car."

Nick shrugged him off and headed for Tug's room.

"Do the phones work yet?" he asked.

"No," Way said.

Nick frowned as he strode into the bedroom.

"Tug! Hey, Tug…we're ready to leave."

But Tug wasn't talking.

Nick put a hand on the man's forehead.

"He's burning up with fever."

He pulled back the covers, then frowned.

"He's also not dressed."

Wayman was already grabbing Tug's clothes.

"Yeah…I know, I know. Just help me get his pants on him."

Nearly fifteen minutes elapsed before they managed to get Tug's clothes on him. He kept going in and out of consciousness, muttering words that made no sense. By the time they finished, Wayman was in tears.

"Is he gonna die? Is my brother gonna die?"

"I'd say the only chance he has left is if we get him to a hospital in time."

"But Tug said—"

Nick grabbed Wayman's arm. "Way! Listen to me, damn it! We are going to New Orleans. We are going to take Tug to a hospital. You can either stay with him, or you can drop him off and we'll make another run for it together. But either way, Tug's running days are over. If he doesn't get medical help, hell, yes, he's going to die."

Wayman swiped away snot and tears, slid an arm beneath his brother's shoulders and sat him up on the side of the bed.

"Tug. Tug! You gotta help me now," he said. "We're gonna walk to the car, and then we're heading to New Orleans."

Tug mumbled, then tried to stand.

Nick got on the opposite side to steady him.

"Move your feet, Tug. We're walking," he said, and somehow Tug French found the will to move.

By the time they got him out of the house and into the backseat of the car, he was nearly unconscious again.

"I'll get Lou," Wayman said.

Nick didn't comment. He wanted all of them to stay uncertain. He needed the upper hand to get through the rest of this day.

A couple of minutes later Wayman emerged from the house, leading Lou. Nick watched as he paused long enough to shut the door, then guided the other man down the steps and toward the car.

Nick's nerves were on edge. He couldn't quit thinking about Amalie. Had she gotten to Louis Thibideaux's house all right? Had the old man been home? Had she been able to call the police chief, or did they have to drive into Bordelaise? Everything that would happen to the four of them within the next few hours hinged on her timing.

"Lou can sit in the back beside Tug," Wayman said, as they reached the car.

"Hell, no," Nick said softly. "He sits in the front beside me."

Lou flinched. "No. No. I don't want to."

"You lost your choice in the matter yesterday," Nick said. "I want you right where I can see you, not behind me. Not ever behind me again."

Lou argued all the while Wayman was putting him in the passenger seat, but it did no good.

When Lou was finally seated, Nick crawled in beside him. "Stop talking," he said softly.

Lou took a deep breath and then dropped his head.

Wayman crawled into the backseat, then pulled a piece of wire from his pocket and wired the door shut.

"We're ready," he said.

Nick started the car, put it in gear and drove away from the house without looking back.

Twelve

Amalie had started running once she made it to the road, but after her race through the swamp the night before, it didn't take long for her energy to run out. Then one of her shoes began rubbing a blister on her heel, and she stopped long enough to take them off. She tied them together and slung them over her shoulder, then tested the blacktop with her bare feet.

The day was already hot. She was guessing in the high nineties, but nothing she couldn't handle. All she had to do was put one foot in front of the other for the next few miles, so she started walking.

One mile came and went, and when she started on the second, she couldn't remember ever being so hungry or thirsty. She kept reminding herself that, thanks to Nick, she was still alive to be miserable. A little misery was a good reminder.

When she passed the intersection marking the beginning of the third mile, she began wondering if Nick had made it back to the Vatican. She increased her stride, aware that if they'd left without him, it would be even more important than ever for her to get word to the police. She wouldn't rest easy until she knew for a fact that Lou Drake was back behind bars.

As she walked, a shadow passed across the ground in front of her, and she glanced up, watching as a small patch of white fluffy clouds moved between the earth and the sun.

"Not complaining here, Lord...but we could have used this clear weather last night."

Every so often she repeated the phone number Nick had given her, well aware of what was riding on the safe delivery of his message. Then her thoughts would slide to Nick himself. She wouldn't let herself think beyond the immediacy of the moment. Yes, they'd made love. And no, she didn't want to lose the first man she'd been attracted to in years. But she wasn't sure he was really hers to lose. Had they come together simply out of relief and a need to reaffirm their lives when they'd come so close to losing them? Or had they made love because there was really something between them that they could build on?

She wanted a forever kind of love, like her parents had enjoyed—like her Nonna and Pappa had known. But did sharing a few days in hell with a man who was good to her constitute the beginning of a relationship? She didn't know, and she couldn't worry about it—not yet. Not until everyone was safe.

So she kept on walking with her head down and her bare feet slapping the steamy blacktop. The only hint she had of what time it might be was the gnawing hunger in her belly.

By the time she reached the driveway that led to Louis's house, the soles of her feet were sore and burning. Stepping off the blacktop onto dirt was a huge relief. But as she began the quarter-mile trek to his house, the relief soon gave way to more misery. Walking barefoot in dirt consisting mostly of gravel and drying ruts was, if possible, an even worse trial.

When the old man's house finally came into sight, Amalie was on the verge of tears. She hadn't thought of what she would do if he wasn't home.

The single-story low-country house wasn't nearly as fine as the Vatican, or half as old, but to Amalie, it looked like heaven.

The light gray siding and black shutters were as neat and trim as Louis Thibideaux's beard. Just knowing she was within walking distance of comfort and safety made the last one hundred yards far easier to walk.

As she neared the fence surrounding his yard, a dog began to bay. It was Rounder, Louis's redbone hound. When he came bounding out to greet her with long ears flapping and his tongue hanging, she couldn't have been more touched. At last. Something kind and familiar after a week of hell.

And then the front door opened and Louis emerged. She lifted her hand in greeting, but tears quickly blurred her vision as she saw the look of shock come and go on his face.

"Amalie! *Cher!* What has happened?" he cried, as

he came flying down the steps far faster than she would have imagined he could move. "Where is your car? Were you in an accident? Your clothes! Your hair! *Mon Dieu*...your feet! Your poor little feet!"

Amalie started to explain, but instead of words, a harsh, ugly sob ripped up her throat. When he put his arms around her, she buried her face against his chest and wept.

Finally Louis led her to the porch, then into his house, even as she was trying to protest her sorry state and muddy feet, insisting that she would ruin his furniture and floors.

Louis quickly shushed her concerns, seated her in his most comfortable chair, then pulled up a cane-back chair beside her and took her by the hand.

"Talk to me."

"Could I have a drink of water first?"

He bolted from the room and came back carrying a tray with a pitcher of water and a crystal drinking glass. He filled the glass with water, ice clinking against the sides as he handed it to her.

Amalie drank thirstily, not stopping until the glass was empty.

Louis was horrified. He could not imagine what had befallen her, but now that he had time to look closer, it was obvious it had not just occurred. Whatever she'd gone through had been happening over a period of time. Her clothes were filthy and stained, but the stains were dried into the fabric. Her face, which should have been flushed from the heat, was pale. There were shadows beneath her eyes that he didn't like, and from the condition of her feet, she appeared to have come a long way on foot.

When she handed him the glass, he filled it again, then set it beside her on the table.

"Does your phone work?" Amalie asked.

"No. Still no phones…but I know that they are working in Bordelaise, so maybe soon. Why, *cher?* What do you need? You have only to ask and I will give it to you this moment!"

Once again, Amalie caught herself struggling with tears.

"I need to ask you to take me into Bordelaise."

"Of course. But you must answer some questions for me, as well." He leaned forward and covered her hand with his. "What has happened to you, my child? Where is your car?"

"A tree fell on my car last Sunday…the day of the storm."

His eyes widened. "But you said nothing to me of this when I visited you."

"I know. Remember the prisoners that escaped from the jail?"

His expression stilled. Fear gripped him so tightly that he was afraid he would not be able to catch his next breath.

"Yes. Please tell me they did not do this to you," he whispered.

Instantly Amalie realized what he must be thinking, that she had been the victim of some kind of assault.

"Not in the way you mean," she said quickly. "But they were at my home. In fact, they were there the day you came. It's why I didn't invite you inside."

Louis bolted up from his chair. His face instantly flushed with shock and anger.

"No! I cannot believe this! You should have said something to me then. I would have…"

"…never left my house alive," she said.

Her words silenced him. Still shaking in disbelief, he grabbed her hand.

"Where are they now? Are they after you? How did you get away? Do not worry, *cher*…I have a gun."

"No. No. Nothing like that," Amalie said. "It's a long, convoluted story, but they didn't, although one tried… a man named Lou Drake. But another man—a good man—stopped him. I look like this because when Lou finally came after me, I ran. I lost him in the swamp, then spent the night in the VanAnsels' old barn. When I woke up, I headed for your house."

"But the storm. You were in the swamp last night during the storm?"

She nodded.

"*Mon Dieu!* I cannot believe this horrible tale. I am horrified that you had to endure this on your own."

Immediately she thought of Nick, but this wasn't her story to tell. Until she got word to the proper people, she felt obligated to keep his identity to herself—just in case.

"I will get the car keys," he announced. "You must tell Chief Porter of these facts."

Amalie stood, then winced as she tested her weight on the soles of her feet again.

"May I ask two more favors of you?" she asked.

"Anything," Louis promised.

"To use your bathroom, and for something to eat. We ran out of food at the house about a day and a half ago. Except for a bite here and there, I haven't eaten in—"

Louis threw his arms around her. This time he was the one who wept. Amalie cried along with him again, but this time it was tears of relief. This nightmare in which she'd been caught was about to come to an end.

Then, just as quickly as Louis had started crying, it was over. Once again he was all business—albeit a little teary-eyed.

"You remember my house. You know where the facilities are located. Go. Go. Whatever you need, help yourself. I will make you some food. You will eat on the way into town."

"Thank you very much, Louis."

His voice was almost angry as he answered.

"You do not thank family for such things—and whether you recognize it or not, this is what we are, Amalie Pope. We are family...you and I. You make yourself fresh. I will get food."

It occurred to Amalie as he strode out of the room that she'd never seen him in such a light. It was as if in hearing her story, he'd shed his age. She could almost see what a magnificent man he must have been in his prime. Then, as she headed for the bathroom, she amended her thought. He was still a magnificent man.

And as he'd reminded her, she was no longer alone. Whether Nick became a part of her life or not was an unknown, something for the future. For right now, she was very thankful for this man from her past.

The ride into town was oddly silent. Louis refrained from questions until she'd had time to finish eating. Amalie wolfed down the two sandwiches he'd made for her out of leftover biscuits and sausage. She was a drink away from the end of a cold bottle of Dr. Pepper when Louis broke his silence.

"I have to ask this for my own sake," he said. "You said they did not…that you were not…"

"No. They didn't rape me."

He sighed. "Thank God. You have endured so much. I could not bear to think that you survived being shot to come home to that."

Amalie laid a hand on Louis's arm as he drove.

"You don't know how many times that same thought went through my mind. I kept wondering why this was all happening to me, then had a small revelation in the middle of the crisis."

"And what was that?" he asked.

"On one of the days when I'd taken refuge in Nonna's bedroom, I found something in the back of her closet. Something I might never have found had I not been in such dire straits."

He frowned. "What was that?"

"There is a secret room on the other side of the inner closet wall."

Louis's eyebrows arched. "And you knew nothing of this before?"

"I remembered finding the door when I was small. But it was dark inside, and I was little and thought I'd broken the wall. I soon forgot. Did Nonna ever speak of it to you?"

"No, never," he said. "What was in it?"

"It's not what was in it. It's what I think it was used for that makes it so amazing. Oh, Louis, there are names written all over one wall. Some scratched into the wood, others written in pencil. One even appears to have been written in blood!"

"Names of your Pope ancestors?" he asked.

"I don't think so. These people only wrote their first names. Few were spelled properly, and many were only an X."

He frowned. "I don't understand."

"In the history of the South, who only had a first name?"

"Why, I suppose that would be the slaves, but—" Then he gasped. "Surely you aren't supposing that slaves were hidden in that room? Your ancestors owned slaves, as did mine. A despicable practice, but it happened."

"I know they did once. But I don't know all the history of my ancestors. It's very possible that one of them, in later years, became an abolitionist. If the Vatican was once a stop on the Underground Railroad, I want the historical society to know this. It has to be verified, of course, but it was an amazing thing to discover, even when I was so frightened. I found myself empathizing with them as I, too, escaped and then ran for my life."

Louis nodded. "I know someone in the Louisiana Historical Society. I'll help you get started on the verification process, though, you do know you might lose some of your privacy should this come to light, don't you?"

Amalie shrugged. "It would be an honor for me to learn I'm right about this."

Louis maneuvered past a rather large pothole in the middle of the old blacktop.

"It is a remarkable discovery, for sure. But back to the immediate issue. When we have finished talking to the police, you will come home with me. I won't have you in that house alone until we know that those men have been arrested again."

Amalie didn't argue. She had a feeling that, once she delivered her messages, it wouldn't take long for the escapees to find themselves back in custody. As for staying alone in the Vatican again, she knew she wouldn't be afraid. She was just one in a long line of enduring people. Like the words that had been scratched into the window ledge in Nonna's room: *We're still here.* Amalie had lived through her own kind of war, and she, too, was still here.

Then she took a deep breath and closed her eyes. The next thing she knew, Louis was patting her knee and telling her to wake up, that they were driving into Bordelaise.

Amalie woke immediately, sat up in the seat and ran her fingers through her hair, then wondered why she bothered. Her hair couldn't look any worse than her clothes. Within minutes they were pulling up to the curb in front of the police department.

Louis killed the engine.

"Remember, *cher,* you're no longer alone."

"Thank you, Louis."

Before Louis could get out, she was heading for the door of the building. Her belly was full, and her thirst had been quenched. She might look as if she'd been dragged through hell backward, but that, too, would pass. Right now, she had some information for Chief Porter, and a phone call to make to one Stewart Babcock of the DEA.

Amalie walked in with Louis right behind her, then beside her.

"Vera, we need to see the chief. It is a matter of extreme emergency," Louis announced.

Vera knew she was staring.

"Amalie Pope…is that you?"

Amalie nodded.

"Yes, it's me."

"Have a seat," Vera said, then added, "We were all so sorry about what happened to your grandmother, but it's good to see you up and around. Lots of prayers went up for you after we heard that you'd been shot."

"Thank you, but I really need to talk to Chief Porter now," Amalie said.

Vera picked up the phone and buzzed Hershel's office. When he didn't answer, she frowned.

"He must have gone out the back door. Hang on and I'll get him on the radio."

At that moment the door opened behind Vera's desk and the chief walked out.

"I was on the way down the hall when I heard you buzz my office," he said. "What's up?"

Vera pointed at Amalie and Louis as she stood up.

"They want to talk to you. Said it was an emergency."

Hershel's mouth gaped.

"Amalie Pope…is that you?"

Amalie sighed. Damn. She must look worse than she thought.

"Yes, it's me. And I do need to talk to you."

"Then come back to my office," he said, and opened the door for her. When Louis followed, his frown deepened.

As soon as they were settled, he took a seat behind his desk.

"You seem to have recovered from your injury, but at the risk of being rude, what the hell happened to you? I didn't even know you were back. Last I heard, you were still in Texas."

"I arrived last Sunday, only a couple of hours ahead of the storm."

"Good timing," Hershel said; then his eyes widened as what she'd said suddenly sank in. "You've been out at the house all week?"

"Yes, and I understand you're missing some prisoners."

His heart dropped. Shit. "Yes, ma'am. I'm sure hoping you're not going to tell me that they had anything to do with your condition."

Louis couldn't stay quiet any longer.

"They've been holding her hostage since Sunday!"

Hershel jumped up from the desk. "The hell you say. Excuse my French! Where are they now? Did they—"

Amalie held up her hand. "I'm not sure where they are. I escaped late yesterday evening. Spent the night in the old VanAnsel barn."

Hershel's eyes widened. "In that storm?"

She nodded.

"Holy Mary, Mother of God," Hershel whispered. "Are you all right?" He looked at Louis. "Have you taken her to the E.R. yet? I can call—"

Again Amalie stopped him. "Please! It's really important that you hear me out. One of the men who's with them…he's not…he didn't—"

This time it was the chief who interrupted.

"Are you talking about Nick Aroyo?"

She nodded.

"I already know."

Amalie exhaled slowly. "I need to call his boss." She rattled off the number, watching as Hershel grabbed the phone and punched the buttons for her, then handed her the receiver without hesitation.

"Thank you," Amalie said, listening as the phone began to ring.

Then a man's voice sounded in her ear. She felt the urgency in his tone before she got out a word.

"Chief! Tell me you have good news."

Amalie blinked. Caller ID had deceived him.

"Is this Stewart Babcock?" she asked.

There was a long moment of silence, then the urgency changed to distance.

"To whom am I speaking?" he asked.

"My name is Amalie Pope, and I have a message for you from Nick Aroyo."

Stewart Babcock exhaled slowly as relief seeped through his body. This had to mean Aroyo was alive.

"I'm listening."

"He wants you to know he's okay…that he's still with the men. He says that in case something happens to him, he wants you to go to a place in New Orleans off Rampart Street called the Box and Post. He said to tell you that all the information you need is in mailbox 125."

Stewart was making notes as they talked.

"Where is Nick now?" he asked.

"I'm not sure, but he and the men he was with took me hostage and have been hiding out at my house since last Sunday."

"Good Lord! Why didn't they just leave?"

"A tree fell on my car during the tornado, so they had nothing to drive. Also, one of the men, Tug French, was badly injured. He was unable to walk, so they've been trying to clear off my car and fix it enough to drive ever since their arrival."

"You said they were holding you hostage?"

"Yes."

"Then how did you get away?"

"There was an, uh…an incident yesterday afternoon. One of the men tried to kill Nick, then came after me. That man's name is Lou Drake. Nick chased him down in the swamp. Later Nick found me, and we took shelter in an abandoned barn. When it got to be daylight, he headed back to my home. Said he couldn't break his cover, but he was going to tell them that he couldn't find me. I walked to a neighbor's house for help. I don't know if they're still at my house, or if they finally fixed my car enough that they could drive it. It's a blue, late model Chevrolet Impala. All the windows are broken out except the windshield, and there are a whole lot of dents in the body. I'm thinking it would be difficult to miss."

"Your home…give me your address," he snapped. "I have men in the area. They can check it out."

"There aren't signs or markers to find the place. It's sort of complicated," Amalie said. "I'm going to let Chief Porter give you directions. Oh…and one other thing…"

"Yes?"

"If they're no longer at my house, Nick said to tell you that they'd be heading to New Orleans to take Tug to a hospital, but I don't know which one."

"Thank you, Miss Pope. This is the best news I've had in days."

"You're welcome. But it's Nick you need to thank,

because he not only saved my life, he helped me get away." Then she handed the phone to the chief.

"He needs to know how to get to my house. I'm not very good at giving directions."

Hershel took the phone.

Amalie sat down, then leaned back in the chair and closed her eyes. The chief's voice rose and fell as he spoke, but she tuned out the words. Louis patted her shoulder, reminding her that he was still here.

She wanted to cry, which was silly. There wasn't anything to cry about. She was safe. She'd been fed, and she'd delivered Nick's messages. But her heart was still out there somewhere with him.

Was he safe? Were they still at her house, or were they gone?

Suddenly she realized someone was talking to her.

"Hmm? What?"

"The chief wants to get you checked out at the E.R.," Louis said.

"I don't need a doctor. I need a bath, clean clothes, some groceries and a car."

Hershel stifled a grin. "I can call Rent-a-Car for you. Where do you want it delivered?"

"She will be spending the night at my house," Louis said. "I won't have her at home alone until I know those terrible men are back in custody."

"Fine," Amalie said. "I can come back into Borde-laise and shop for groceries after the car is delivered."

"And I will make sure you do not go hungry again," Louis said.

Hershel frowned. "What's this about being hungry?"

"They...ate all my food," Amalie said. "Basically, we ran out about a day and a half ago."

"Good Lord," Hershel muttered. "I'm so sorry that this happened. We didn't know until yesterday, when the DEA search team found their car, that there was even a possibility that the men were still alive."

Then he stood. "Louis, good to know you'll be looking after Amalie's needs."

"Amalie will be looking after her own needs, with Louis's help," she said.

Both men grinned.

"Yes, ma'am," Hershel said. "Now I'm going to round up some help and head on out to your place. You don't go back there until you hear from us, okay?"

"The phones are still out of order," Louis said.

"So I'll come to Louis's house and tell you myself, then," Hershel replied.

"Thank you," Amalie said, then turned to Louis. "I'm ready when you are."

Louis nodded, then offered his arm. "Then it is time to take you to my home. You can have your bath, clean clothes, good food and a safe place to sleep."

Amalie sighed. It all sounded like heaven. But as they drove out of Bordelaise, she couldn't help but wonder if she would ever see Nick Aroyo again.

Thirteen

The team Babcock sent to Amalie's house consisted of Agents Edwards, Lord and Smith. They came down the driveway leading to the Vatican just ahead of a Bordelaise police cruiser, both circling the house to check for the car as they'd been instructed. When they saw it was missing, they all knew they were too late. Still, they had orders to check out the house.

Edwards was the first man out of the car.

Chief Porter and his deputy, Lee Tullius, were in the cruiser that pulled up beside them.

Edwards nodded at the pair.

"Looks like we're too late."

"Still gonna check it out, though, right?" Hershel asked.

"Absolutely," Edwards said. "Chief, if you and your deputy will take the front of the house, we'll cover the back."

Hershel nodded and headed around the house on foot,

with Lee right behind him. Both of them had already unholstered their weapons, ready for any surprises.

Edwards motioned to Lord and Smith, who armed themselves and headed for the back door.

Their footsteps echoed loudly on the wooden floor of the veranda as they came up the steps. Edwards frowned and motioned for Lord to walk easy.

Lord frowned. "It's not like we were invisible as we came down the driveway," he muttered, but eased his steps.

They proceeded to the back door, taking care not to silhouette themselves in front of any windows. The old screen door squeaked as they opened it, but when Edwards tried the back doorknob it turned easily, unlocked.

Although the screen had squeaked, the wooden door opened on well-oiled hinges as they slipped inside. Ignoring the jumble of dirty dishes and an overflowing trash can, they quickly moved through the kitchen toward the front of the house.

Edwards pointed to the front door. "Let them in," he said, nodding toward the Bordelaise officers coming up the front steps.

Together the five men made a sweep through the house, checking all the rooms on all three floors before they were confident the house was empty.

They found Amalie's bedroom, taking note of the mattress on the floor outside her door. The hair stood up on the back of Hershel's neck as he thought about what Amalie Pope had endured. Thank God Aroyo had been one of the good guys, or she might not have come out of this episode alive.

Downstairs, they found the bed Tug French had been using. Given the bloody stains on the sheets and pillowcase, it wasn't difficult to ascertain.

"I'll call it in," Edwards said, while Hershel and his deputy secured the house, locking doors behind them as they finally exited the premises.

Hershel found a key to the back door hanging on a hook inside the kitchen and took it with him as he left. They needed to lock up the house, but he didn't want to lock Amalie out.

"I'll notify the State Highway Patrol," he said. "According to Amalie, Aroyo said they'd be heading to New Orleans. You have the make and model of the car, right?"

Edwards nodded.

"We'll be in touch," Hershel said, then headed for the cruiser. He had made a promise to Amalie Pope, and he wasn't going back to Bordelaise until she knew her home was safe again.

Edwards punched in the direct number to Babcock's office, then waited for an answer. It wasn't long in coming.

"Babcock."

"Sir. It's Edwards. We're at the house. The car's gone, and the house is empty."

"I figured as much," Babcock said. "I've already alerted New Orleans PD. They have men stationed at every hospital in the city. Wherever they show up, we'll be waiting."

"Chief Porter was going to contact the Louisiana Highway Patrol."

"Already done," Babcock said. "They've been advised to be on the lookout for Amalie Pope's car."

"I have to say, sir…if it's as badly damaged as she claimed, it would be difficult to miss."

"Agreed. They won't take the main roads until they have to, but we'll get them."

"What about us? Do you want us in New Orleans?"

"No. I already have men moving into place. Report back to headquarters."

"Yes, sir," Edwards said, and disconnected.

"What next?" Lord asked, as Edwards climbed into their car.

"This gig is over for us. We report back to headquarters."

"None too soon for me," Smith said, swatting at a mosquito. "I've already seen too damn many snakes and alligators." He slapped his neck, then made a face at the dead mosquito splattered on the palm of his hand. "As for the bugs…just roll up the windows and drive."

They drove away laughing, glad their buddy was still alive and that their part in this mess was officially over.

Nick had been driving for more than two hours, taking the back roads and lesser-traveled highways to get as close to New Orleans as possible before finally getting onto Interstate 10. His evasive driving had been a screen, maintaining the appearance of trying to elude the police. If the others knew how badly he wanted to be found, they would have killed him on the spot.

Lou was hunkered down on his side of the front seat and had wisely stayed mute.

Wayman was as close to losing it as he'd been since the first day of their escape. Tug was incoherent and moaning constantly, which upped his panic even more. Wayman grabbed the back of the driver's seat and then yelled in Nick's ear, shouting to be heard above the whistle of the wind whipping through the car's missing windows.

"Do we have enough gas? Don't want to run out of gas!"

Nick glanced at the gauge. It was still over half full from their last stop, and they were less than thirty minutes from the outskirts of New Orleans.

"We're good," Nick said. "How's Tug?"

Wayman scooted to the edge of the seat. "Not good. Not good at all."

A semi sped past them, stirring up even more wind and leaving behind a thick cloud of diesel smoke, which was sucked straight into the car.

"Son of a bitch!" Wayman said. "That stinks."

Lou silently agreed, but after the warning Aroyo had given him, he hadn't opened his mouth.

He'd bounced uncomfortably over parish back roads with dust blowing in the windows and the hot wind whipping through the car. He was still in pain from the beating Nick had given him and didn't like this feeling of helplessness—of not being able to see or defend himself. But when he realized Wayman was close at hand, he got up the courage to voice an opinion.

"I need a drink. I'm thirsty. Can't we stop to get something to eat and drink?"

"No money," Wayman reminded him. "Used what we had for gas."

Lou dropped his head and began fidgeting with his seat belt, trying to unlock it.

Nick glanced over at the man, and when he saw the seat belt come off and then Lou reach in his pocket, he swerved out of the lane of traffic onto the side of the road and slammed on the brakes.

"What the hell?" Lou screamed, as Nick grabbed him by the throat.

The silence within the car after the roar and whistle of the wind was as shocking as Nick's behavior.

"Keep your hands where I can see them," Nick said softly.

"Money...I was just getting out some money," Lou cried, and slapped a wad of money into Nick's lap. "See! See! Money!"

Nick picked it up, frowning as he counted over a hundred dollars in cash.

"Where did you get this?" he asked.

"Out of the bitch's purse days ago, damn it."

"You were holding out on us," Wayman growled,

and slapped Lou on the back of the head. "What else did you take that you're not talking about?"

"Nothing!" Lou screamed. "I swear...and don't fuckin' hit me again."

Nick picked up the money and handed it to Wayman. The simple act seemed to calm the situation. Wayman pocketed the money, then leaned back in the seat and nodded at Nick.

"First convenience store you come to, I guess we can stop."

"Too risky," Nick said. "We need to keep moving. We can stop after we get Tug to a hospital."

Wayman glanced at his brother, then let out a gasp.

"He's bleeding again! Look, there's fresh blood on his bandage!"

Nick glanced up in the rearview mirror, then frowned. Way was right. A new patch of bright red blood was seeping through. "This isn't good. Whatever caused this probably happened when we moved him."

Now it was crucial that they get to New Orleans as soon as possible. He put the car in gear and pulled back onto I-10.

The wind picked up as they picked up speed, whistling through the interior, irritating Lou's swollen eyes, and once more whipping at their clothes and hair.

Lou ducked his head, afraid to open his mouth again.

Wayman was near tears, afraid his brother was going to die before they could get to New Orleans.

But Nick's worries went deeper. He kept thinking

about Amalie. What if something had happened to her? He shouldn't have left her like that. He couldn't bear to think that he'd put his job ahead of her well-being again, but it was beginning to appear that was what he'd done. If she'd gotten to her friend's house and alerted the authorities, they should have caught up with them by now. Granted, he'd taken a lot of back roads to get to the main highway, but they'd been on I-10 long enough and had yet to see a highway patrol car.

He wanted to be found. He wanted to turn in his evidence and get this fiasco over with, and he wanted to get back to Amalie Pope. They'd started something that he wanted to pursue.

She'd become more to him than just a pretty woman days ago. Making love to her had solidified those feelings. She was strong and amazing, and he'd already faced the fact that he was falling in love. He didn't want to lose that—or her.

More minutes passed while his thoughts bordered on panic. No cops—no choppers—no police of any kind in sight. It had to mean something had happened to her.

Just as he was about to give up hope, he caught a glimpse of a helicopter flying parallel to the highway and moving in their same direction. Within seconds it went up and out of his line of sight. His heart skipped a beat. Was that them? He wanted to look again but didn't dare. The last thing he needed was to start a situation inside the car. There was no way Lou could see it, and luckily Wayman was too concerned with what was happening to his brother to be bothered by anything else.

A couple of minutes passed before Nick ventured another look. It was still there—tracking right along with them. Then he saw the insignia of the Louisiana Highway Patrol and stifled a grin.

She'd done it! By God, Amalie had done it!

Now all he had to do was keep on driving and wait for them to make the first move.

Stewart Babcock was pacing the floor of his office, following the chase with his phone set on speaker. The chopper pilot had just radioed in that they'd spotted the blue Chevrolet Impala in question and been patched through to Stewart's office.

"Can you tell how many men are inside the car?" Stewart asked.

"Counted four heads," the pilot responded. "Driver is a dark-haired male. Appears to be a big guy."

Aroyo. Babcock's mood was getting better by the minute.

"Remember, we do not want to try and stop them on the interstate. The last thing we need is a high-speed chase that could endanger innocent citizens. We do not believe they're armed, so we'll take them down once they reach the hospital. Just maintain a visual and keep us informed."

"Ten-four," the pilot said, and signed off.

Babcock sat down behind his desk with a plop. He was anxious to bring in Aroyo. This was the closest thing to a disaster they'd had in a long time, and he didn't want it getting any worse.

He'd already sent a team to the New Orleans Box and Post with a warrant to retrieve the info inside mailbox 125, and as soon as Aroyo was arrested and booked, he would be taken into federal custody on an old, trumped-up warrant.

All they had to do now was wait.

"We did it!" Wayman shouted, and slapped Nick on the back as they passed the New Orleans city-limit sign. "How far to the nearest hospital?"

Nick was heading for the exit to Ponchartrain Expressway.

"I don't know about nearest, but I know where the old University Hospital is. It reopened after Hurricane Katrina under the name Interim Public, or something like that. It has an E.R., but it's small. We won't draw as much attention."

Wayman nodded. That sounded like a good idea. Staying under the radar was what they needed.

"What do we say happened to Tug?" he asked.

"The truth. That he got injured during one of the storms that's been hitting the coast since the hurricane passed."

"Yeah, yeah, that's good," Wayman said.

"Are you planning to stay with Tug?" Lou asked.

Tug groaned, then reached out and tried to shove Wayman away.

Wayman frowned. Tug was out of his head again.

"We're all gonna stay until we know for sure he'll be okay."

Lou freaked. "I'm not gonna sit there and wait for the cops to show."

"You need some doctoring, too," Way muttered. "You can't see shit."

"The swelling is going down," Lou argued. "All I need is some ice."

"What do you say, Nick?" Wayman asked. "We stay with Tug, right?"

Nick wasn't going to commit himself one way or the other. "Let's just get there and see what the doctors have to say about him, okay?"

Way's defenses shifted to the logic of the answer. "Yeah. Yeah. We'll wait and see."

Lou muttered something about being a sitting duck but didn't argue further.

Tug moaned again, then slumped across the seat.

"We're almost there, Tug," Wayman said. "Just hang in a little longer."

Nick turned onto the expressway, heading south. It wouldn't be far now. He ventured one last look up, saw the chopper and breathed a sigh of relief. Just a few minutes more and this would be over.

The chopper pilot was still on target. When the car left the interstate, he relayed the info.

"They're southbound on the Ponchartrain Expressway. It appears they're heading for Interim Hospital on Perdido Street."

The NOPD team on standby at Interim heard the broadcast and relayed the info to their men.

"Be ready. Possible sighting heading our way."

The police cruisers were out of sight and the policemen in position. Suddenly one of them pointed up.

"Chopper inbound."

"Is it medical?"

"No. Highway patrol."

An officer stationed near the entrance to the parking lot radioed in.

"Late model blue Chevrolet sighted…severely damaged…four men inside. Taking the E.R. entrance."

The chopper pilot was next.

"Target is in the parking lot. They're all yours, boys."

"We're here," Nick said, as he pulled up to the Emergency Room entrance.

"Just give me a minute," Wayman said, and grabbed at the wire he'd used to hold the door shut.

"I gotta piss," Lou said, and opened his door.

"Wait, Way…I'll help you," Nick said, as he jumped out and circled the car.

Suddenly they were surrounded by more than a dozen uniformed officers, all shouting at once.

"You're under arrest! Get down on the ground! *Get down on the ground!*"

Nick dropped gratefully, belly down, with his arms and legs spread out. The last thing he intended to do was resist.

Lou was cursing and screaming as the officers forced him to the ground.

"I can't see! Don't push! Don't push! I can't fuckin' see!"

Wayman was crying as they pulled him out of the car and forced him down to the ground.

"My brother! You gotta help my brother!"

They handcuffed the three of them, then pulled them to their feet.

"Your brother is getting help. They've already taken him into the E.R.," one officer said.

"I need a doctor, too," Lou insisted. "Look at me. Just look at me."

When Nick saw a couple of familiar faces in the crowd of police officers, he realized the DEA was also on the scene; then he quickly looked away as they put him in the back of a police car.

Relief. That was what he felt. A huge sense of relief. Babcock had his information, and Amalie was safe.

Then the back door of the cop car opened, and once again Nick found himself looking at the man who'd tried to kill him.

Lou could see just enough to know there was already someone inside the cruiser. And when he recognized the length and shape of the man, he began to yell.

"Don't put me in here with him! Don't fucking put me in here with him! He already tried to kill me once."

The officer paused and looked straight at Nick.

"Are you responsible for this man's injuries?"

Nick didn't hesitate.

"Yes."

The officer grinned. "Out of curiosity…what does

it take for two drug dealers to get on the wrong side of each other?"

"I don't rape women," Nick said shortly.

The officer's eyes widened as he looked from Lou to Nick and back again, then tightened his grip on Lou's arm.

"Watch your head," he said shortly, and pushed Lou forward into the car. Just before he shut the door, he leaned in with one last word of advice. "You two play nice in there."

Lou was still shrieking when the door slammed shut, but the moment he realized they were alone in the car, he went quiet.

Nick wasn't about to start anything, but it felt good to let Lou think he might.

As the silence lengthened between them, Lou began to relax. After all, they were both handcuffed, and the cops were just outside.

And then, once his panic about Nick receded, Lou began to concentrate on the fact that the cops had been waiting for them.

"That bitch got away, didn't she?" he said. "How else would the cops be able to find us so quick?"

"Who knows?" Nick muttered. "That car we were driving had 'look at me' written all over it. Big dents... all the windows broken out."

"Yeah, but then they would have just stopped us and given us a ticket. Not tracked us to a hospital."

Nick didn't like the way Lou's thoughts were heading. The man already had it in for Amalie.

"Whatever," he said. "Ultimately, this was bound to happen. It's like I said before. If we'd just bonded out of jail and then paid a fine, this would already have been over. But when the jail came apart, we ran. Then we stole stuff, and took a woman hostage. We made a mountain out of what would have been a molehill. It's our own damn fault."

"She's probably laughing at us right now," Lou muttered. "If I could, I'd wipe that smile right off her face. Permanently."

Suddenly the door beside Nick came open and the same New Orleans police officer who'd put him in the car was pulling on his arm to take him back out.

"Nick Aroyo?"

Nick slipped back into his undercover persona.

"Yeah...so what?"

"Looks like you're going to bypass our fine city. There's a federal agent here with an outstanding warrant for your arrest."

"Shit," Nick muttered.

Lou wasn't happy about going to jail, but he was happy that he wouldn't be riding with Nick.

He laughed. "What did you do to piss off Uncle Sam?" When Nick didn't answer, he raised his voice and asked, "Hey, Officer. What did he do?"

The arresting agent glanced at Nick, who was poker-faced and unresisting as the transfer was being made.

"They've been looking for you for a long time, Aroyo," he said, ignoring Lou.

"So now they found me," Nick said, then let himself be led away.

The policeman came back and looked in to check his other prisoner before he shut the door.

Lou fired a string of questions at him.

"Hey! Where are they taking him? What did they have on him? Is it the DEA?"

The policeman shook his head.

"FBI had an outstanding warrant for his arrest. I don't know where they're taking him. Now sit back and be quiet. You've got enough of your own problems to worry about."

But Lou couldn't let it go.

"What did they have on him? What was the warrant for?"

"Murder."

A sudden chill ran down Lou's back.

"Murder?"

The cop stood up. "Yeah. They said he beat a man to death with his fists."

Lou gasped, then swallowed nervously as the door shut in his face.

The cop grinned to himself as he walked away. He had no idea what the warrant was for, but it did him good to give the little bastard something to think about.

Lou leaned back and closed his eyes. What a fuck-up! What a royal fuck-up! From the night they'd been arrested at that bar in Bordelaise to this. All that misery, and for what? They'd gained nothing by hiding. Nothing by waiting. Nothing by finally getting away. He was right back where he'd started—no, worse.

And he never had gotten himself a piece of tail.

Amalie Pope's face flashed through his mind, and his rage increased.

It was all that bitch's fault. He should have nailed her, then killed her, when he had the chance.

"You just wait, woman. Payback is a bitch."

Fourteeen

It was nearly suppertime before Louis and Amalie got back to his home. Immediately upon entering the house, he escorted her to the guest room with its own private bath, laid out fresh towels, and pointed to all the toiletry items she might want to use.

Grateful to be in a cool, safe place, she shut herself in the bathroom and stripped, then turned to look at herself in the full-length mirror on the back of the door.

The sight was daunting, to say the least.

She had scratches and bruises everywhere, and was sore in so many places that the newly healed place where she'd been shot was no longer the focus of her pain.

Her gaze slid from the weight of her breasts to the curve of her hips. To her critical eye, she was bordering on being too thin. She turned, angling for a better view of her back, and frowned at the large purple bruise on her shoulder. With no memory of how she'd gotten it, she decided it was probably just as well. But when she saw identical scrapes on her butt cheeks, she had no question as to how they'd come to be: making love on the floor of a barn loft was hard on tender skin.

The sight of those two small scrapes brought back other memories—memories of Nick. The knuckles on his hands horribly cut and swollen from fighting with Lou. The faint growth of black whiskers on his face. The glint of sunlight against the single earring in his ear. The way his eyes had darkened as he'd taken her in his arms, and the feel of his lips against her skin. The way he'd looked at her—as if she was a most desirable, most beautiful woman. They'd made magic together when they'd made love. She wanted that magic back.

But the decision was out of her hands. Frowning, she turned away from the mirror and stepped into the shower. Reaching for the shampoo, she moved beneath the spray and lifted her face to the warm jets of water.

Fifteen minutes later her hair was clean and drying in short wispy curls, her skin glowing from the scrubbing she'd given it. But when she looked down at the pile of filthy clothes she'd taken off, she wrapped herself in a bath towel instead and opened the door. The first things she saw were a long white nightgown and a matching cotton robe lying on the bed. Obviously Louis had come back while she was in the shower.

She remembered Nonna telling her that after Louis's wife, Charity, had died, he'd refused to pack away her belongings, stating he didn't intend to change anything in their room, including her clothes hanging with his in the closet.

Amalie fingered the fabric of the gown, guessing

these were some of her things. Louis had no control over losing his wife, but he'd taken control afterward by refusing to give up anything else—especially anything that had belonged to her. She was touched that he was willing to share some of Charity's clothes, and at the same time sad that his joy in living was all linked to the past.

She wondered if, when she died, someone would grieve for her in such a way, then thought of Nick. She was way past infatuation and sexual attraction with the man. He'd become her knight in shining armor when he'd followed Lou into the swamp and saved her life. But protectiveness had changed to passion by the time they'd taken shelter in the barn. She wanted to see him again, to fall asleep in his arms and wake up the same way as in the loft: making slow, sweet love as first light washed away the dark. Just thinking about it made her ache. God. She loved hearing him laugh, and watching the way his long, lean body moved as he walked across the floor. But since she had no way to contact him, all she could do was wait and hope he felt the same way.

The nightgown was soft against her skin as she pulled it over her head. It smelled faintly of lavender. The down-filled comforter on the bed looked inviting, and she was tired—so tired. Thinking she would rest for just a minute, she lay down on top of the comforter, covering herself with a knitted afghan from the foot of the bed, and drifted off to sleep. When she woke, she could smell something cooking and glanced at the clock. She'd been asleep almost an hour.

She rolled over onto her back and thought of home, wondering if Nick and the others had still been there when the police arrived. And if they were gone, wondering where they were and what was happening to him.

Then she sighed.

Wondering was all she could do until she heard the facts, and the smell of food was calling her. But when she swung her feet off the bed and stood up, pain shot up her legs. The long walk in her bare feet had left her footsore—a small but brutal reminder of her ordeal.

Suddenly there was a knock on her door.

"Come in."

Louis opened the door, holding a pair of backless slippers. "Ah, good, you are awake. You need to get up. I have a pair of house shoes that should fit you. They are soft and should not pain your feet."

"Thank you, but why do I need to get up?"

"Chief Porter is here to see you."

Amalie's heart leaped. "Tell him I'll be right there… and, Louis?"

"Yes?"

"Thank you for loaning me the clothes."

He smiled. "You are most welcome. We are in the living room. Come when you are ready."

Slipping her feet into the shoes, she grabbed the robe from the foot of the bed, stepped into the bathroom long enough to give her hair a quick brushing, frowned at the circles beneath her eyes, then hurried from the room.

Hershel had not been in Louis's house since the day Charity Thibideaux dropped dead ten years earlier. As he sat waiting for Amalie to show up, he couldn't help but notice that very little, if anything, had changed. It was spotlessly clean, as it had been in her day, and there was an enticing aroma of gumbo wafting through the rooms. It was as if she'd just stepped out and would be returning any moment with a welcoming smile.

The only difference here was Louis. He had aged drastically after her death. His hair and beard had gone completely white within a year, and his stride, over the years, had slowed considerably. Hershel had been unaware of Louis Thibideaux and Laura Pope's friendship, so he was somewhat surprised by the proprietary manner in which Louis had stepped in on Amalie's behalf.

Then he heard footsteps coming down the hall and took off his hat and stood up, thinking it would be Amalie. But it was Louis.

"I didn't have to wake her after all. She will be here shortly. I have coffee, or would you prefer something cold to drink?"

"Neither, but thank you," Hershel said. "It's been a long day. I'm heading home as soon as I leave here."

Then Amalie walked into the room, a far cry from the dirty, disheveled woman who'd shown up at his office earlier. She was wearing a long white nightgown and robe, and the stark color against her pale skin was practically ethereal.

"Chief! You have news?" Amalie asked, as she seated herself.

"Yes," he said, as he sat down near her. "Your house was empty when we arrived, and the car was gone."

Amalie frowned. She didn't know how to react.

"Has anyone had news of the men since?"

Hershel nodded. "Got a call on my way out here that they'd all been arrested without incident at a hospital in New Orleans. The New Orleans PD impounded your car. I have all the information you'll need to claim it."

"There's not much left to claim. I'm hoping the insurance company will just total it out and let me get a new one."

Hershel handed her a note and two sets of keys.

"This is the info regarding your car. The name and number of the impound lot...the whole mess. When we left the Vatican, I locked it up. This is your house key, and the key on the black and white ring is to your rental car, which is parked out front."

Amalie was pleasantly surprised.

"How on earth did you manage that so quickly? Usually you have to show an insurance verification card, a driver's license...all kinds of stuff."

Hershel grinned. "I'm the law, remember? People trust me. Besides, the man who owns the rental agency was a friend of your grandmother's. He said to tell you that he's real sorry to hear about what happened, and that the next time you come into Bordelaise, you can bring your driver's license and insurance verification, and sign the necessary papers."

Amalie smiled. "That's wonderful. Thank you so much, Chief."

Hershel stood up and then jammed his hat on his head. "You're very welcome. If you need anything, just give us a call."

"If the phones ever get fixed," she said.

"This entire area is still without phone service."

"I'll see what I can do about passing that message on to the proper authorities."

Louis beamed. "That would be wonderful. Are you sure I can't offer you something to drink to take with you?"

"No. I'm good." Hershel turned to Amalie. "Again, I'm real sorry about everything."

"It's not your fault, so you have nothing to apologize for. And if it hadn't been for Nick Aroyo, things would have turned out far worse for me," she said.

Hershel nodded. "Who knew...right? Undercover DEA. Don't often get that kind of firepower around here."

"I'll see you out," Louis said, and walked outside with the chief, leaving Amalie alone to consider the little bit Chief Porter had disclosed.

So the men were back in custody. Nick's message had reached the proper ears. The news was welcome but nowhere near as much as she wanted to know, but at the same time, she was anxious to get home. Hopefully, the second week of her homecoming would be far calmer than her first.

Nick scraped off the last bit of shaving cream and whiskers from his jaw, then rinsed the razor under the stream of running water.

He leaned toward the light, checking to make sure he hadn't missed any spots, then washed and dried his face. He'd been whisked from beneath the noses of the men he'd been running with under the pretense of an outstanding warrant and, as far as they knew, was on his way back to face charges in Virginia. In reality, he'd been flown straight to D.C. and secreted in a hotel near DEA headquarters. Tomorrow he would spend the day with Babcock, going over all the intel he'd gathered, making sure the ensuing arrest warrants for all concerned would hold up in court.

He stepped back from the mirror, casually eyeing the bruises and cuts all over his body, then tenderly tested the healing cut on the back of his head. There was no doubt in his mind that Lou Drake had tried to kill him. Good thing he had a hard head.

He ran a finger along the cut on his lower lip and realized he'd made love to Amalie without knowing the lip was even split. He sighed. The only pain he'd felt when making love to her was that it had eventually come to an end.

He'd already tried to call her, only to discover the phones still weren't working. As soon as he could, he was heading back to Bordelaise. He needed to see a woman about the rest of her life.

Amalie woke to the sound of birds chirping in a tree outside her bedroom window and the sunshine warming the covers over her feet. According to the clock beside her bed, it was 8:12 a.m. She glanced out the window and saw sunshine. Not only did it look like the beginning to a good day, but it felt like one, as well.

Louis was a dear, but she was ready to go home and get a change of clothes, then drive into Bordelaise. It was past time to let the world know she was back. If she hadn't been so set on slipping in without notice, maybe those days in hell would never have happened.

She threw back the covers and padded barefoot into the adjoining bathroom. A few minutes later she was on her way down the hall, following the scent of freshly brewed coffee.

Louis was coming in the back door as she entered the kitchen. His eyes lit up as he saw her.

"Good morning, *cher.* You are awake. Did you rest well?"

"Very well, thanks to you," Amalie said. "I was about to help myself to some coffee."

"Of course," he said, as he waved toward the kitchen cabinets. "Cups are behind the first door to the left of the sink."

Amalie filled a cup, stirred in a little sugar, and carried it to the window.

"It's a beautiful day," Louis said. "You sit. I will make you some eggs. How do you like them?"

"Scrambled?"

He smiled. "Coming up. I have bacon and biscuits already made."

Amalie grinned. "You could easily spoil a woman."

Louis's smile slipped. "It has been a long time since

I've been offered the opportunity. Do not begrudge me the chance."

The poignancy of the moment was not lost on Amalie.

"Then I await your most gracious meal," she said, and sat down at the table with her coffee.

Soon a plate of steaming, hot food was place in front of her.

"It smells and looks wonderful," she said, as she picked up a fork and took her first bite. "Mmm, and it tastes good, too."

Louis beamed.

"Then I will leave you to eat in peace. Just so you know, I washed and dried the clothes you were wearing. Some of the stains would not come out, but at least they are clean."

"Oh, Louis! That's wonderful."

"It is nothing. I'm happy to be of service. Eat while your food is hot. I have something I need to give you."

With that, he left the kitchen, his stride long and sure.

Amalie wondered idly what it might be, then turned her attention to her meal. She was just finishing up her last bite of biscuit when Louis returned. She didn't notice what he was carrying until he plopped it on the table in front of her.

"Can you shoot a gun?"

Amalie blinked—surprised by both the question and the rifle he was carrying.

"Yes, actually, I can. Why?"

Louis laid a box of shells beside the rifle.

"I know you're determined to go home. And I know the escaped criminals have been arrested. But that is a very big house, and you are but one woman. I will sleep a lot better knowing you are at least armed and able to protect yourself."

Amalie stood up, then kissed him on the cheek.

"You know, it's strange, but all my life I've been against people owning weapons. And being shot even enforced what I'd believed. I kept thinking that if the boy hadn't had such easy access, maybe it would never have happened. Maybe no one would have died. Then I came home and was taken hostage. I have to admit, I would have given anything to have been able to protect myself. If one of those men had not been an undercover cop, I don't think I'd be alive today. So, yes, I gratefully accept the loan of your rifle."

"No. You don't understand. I am giving it to you," he said. "I have others."

"Then thank you again," Amalie said. "I hate to eat and run, but as soon as I've dressed, I want to get home."

"I understand," Louis said. "Just know that I will check on you daily, at least until the phones are fixed."

She grinned and hugged his neck.

"You are a lifesaver."

He smiled, then gently cupped her cheek.

"It is my pleasure."

A short while later Amalie was dressed in her own clothes and waving goodbye as she drove away. The rental car was a godsend. As soon as she got home and changed into some decent clothes, she was going into Bordelaise. She needed to go by the car rental and sign papers, use the phone to call her insurance company, check in with the family lawyer, open an account at the bank and buy groceries. Most especially buy groceries.

After that, she had a house to tackle. No matter how long it took, she intended to remove every trace of the intruders, even if she had to burn the sheets they'd slept in to do it.

After spending over two hours in Bordelaise, Amalie was almost home. When she turned off the blacktop and started up the driveway, she had a momentary sensation of déjà vu. She had done this very same thing only a few days ago. She'd driven onto Pope property with hopes of rebuilding her life, a suitcase full of clothes and a couple of sacks of groceries.

Today she was going home with three sacks of groceries and the hope that they would last longer than the first ones she'd brought.

When she came around the curve and saw the house once again, she was filled with a sense of well-being. The danger around her had been removed, and the storm front associated with the hurricane was gone. She glanced at the clock on the dashboard of the car. It was after one, which explained why her stomach was growling. As soon as she unloaded the car, she was going to dig into the jambalaya and rice she'd purchased from Mama Lou's Crab Shack in town, and then finish off her meal with the piece of pecan pie she'd bought for her dessert.

She eyed the scattered debris as she drove around behind the house and made a mental note to ask Louis to recommend a handyman. There were some minor repairs that needed doing, as well as some landscaping and mowing.

But all in good time, she reminded herself, as she parked and got out.

A short while later she had the groceries put away and was carrying her dirty dishes to the sink. Her belly was full, and for the first time in days she could breathe without panic. It felt good to have purpose, and today her purpose was to give the Vatican back its pride.

Soon she was striding down the hall to the room where Tug French had slept, a garbage bag in one hand, and some cleaning rags and a bottle of Lysol in the other. She entered the room with a glint in her eye and intent in her step; the bloodstained sheets and pillowcases were a gruesome reminder of her uninvited guests.

"Sorry, Nonna," she muttered, as she stripped the bed all the way down to the mattress and began stuffing everything into the garbage bag to burn later.

When she was done, she set the bag out into the hall, then grabbed the rags and disinfectant, and began wiping down everything in sight. When she was finished with the bedroom, she headed for the adjoining bathroom and did the same thing in there.

She came out with an armful of dirty towels and washcloths that the men had used, and stuffed them into the garbage bag along with the sheets, then carried the bag to the back porch and set it by the steps to deal with later on.

Back inside, she grabbed a fresh set of rags and began cleaning the entire first floor. By the time she was through, sweat was running from her hair and down the middle of her back. The clean jeans and T-shirt that she'd worn into Bordelaise earlier were sweaty and dusty. She wanted a bath, but there was one more place that had to be put back to rights.

The lemon scent of the furniture polish she'd used followed her as she moved from room to room. Sunlight came through the windowpanes, gleaming on the clean cypress floors. It was as if Amalie had given the house a new dress, and it was preening in pride.

She paused at the foot of the stairs and looked up, half expecting to see Nick Aroyo looking down. Then she sighed. Today it was enough to be safe and alive. No need wishing for something she might never get.

"Get over it," she told herself, as she headed upstairs.

She paused at the door to her room. There was no ignoring the mattress where he'd slept. Just the sight of it was enough to weaken her resolve. She might get past what had happened between them, but she wasn't going to get over Nick. Not if the sight of a stupid mattress he'd slept on was all it took to make her ache. Not that easily. And certainly not that soon.

By the time she had the mattress back on its frame and the spare bedroom back in order, her steps were dragging. She paused in the doorway, giving the room the once-over, then closed the door and crossed the hall into her own room.

She began stripping off her clothes as she went and stepped into the shower, turned on the water without waiting for it to warm, and then gasped when the cold hit her face and belly.

Her hands were shaking as she reached for the soap; then she stopped and let them fall. There was a knot in her stomach and a ball of unshed tears at the back of her throat.

Emotion was finally taking over.

"Too much," she said, and leaned against the wall as the water slowly turned from cold to warm and cascaded down her body.

"Too much," she whispered, as she slid downward into the tub. She lowered her head to her knees, then wrapped her arms around her legs and curled her body into a ball.

"Too much," she moaned, and then choked on a sob.

Relief was the final crack in the mental wall she'd built and hidden behind. Before she knew it, she was crying—one gut-wrenching sob after another—her body washed clean by the water as well as her tears.

Tug French died in surgery.

Wayman received the news behind bars, and he, too, wept like a baby. Hours later, he was still inconsolable. He'd lost his anchor to the world and didn't know where to turn. He knew that after the kidnaping charges that had been added to his list of offenses, it was going to be years before he would see freedom again.

Lou Drake's situation wasn't much better. His only consolation was that the swelling in his eyes was beginning to subside and he could finally see.

He heard about Tug, but he knew the man's death did not lessen the law's vision of his own culpability in what they'd done. Along with kidnapping charges being added, he had also been charged with assault and attempted rape. He was going down for a long, long time, and he blamed Amalie Pope for all of it. If she hadn't gotten away, none of this would have happened.

His days and nights were full of rage at the injustice of it all, and his thoughts were of revenge.

Finally his day in court arrived. He'd been told his court-appointed lawyer was waiting for him at the courthouse as he was being loaded into a van for transport. Handcuffed and shackled, he stumbled as he stepped up into the van and had to suffer the humiliation of being laughed at by another prisoner, who was also being arraigned.

Pissed, he settled on the bench inside the van and stared down at the floor as they drove away.

The guards up front were talking and laughing. He didn't pay any attention to what they were saying until he caught a word here and there, and realized they were talking about Amalie Pope. His indignation grew as they kept remarking on how tough she must have been to have escaped her captors, then spent the night in the swamp before walking barefoot for miles to get help. They were calling her a heroine.

Lou fumed. Heroine? Hell! She was a bitch—a cold-hearted bitch.

All of a sudden there was a squeal of brakes, and then the van began sliding sideways. He heard one guard curse as another shouted, "Look out!"

Seconds later there was a bone-jarring crash, and then the van went airborne. It hit the pavement with a second bone-jarring blow, then began rolling.

Lou never lost consciousness. He went from the top of the van to the bottom and then the top again, as if the interior had suddenly lost gravity.

When the van stopped rolling, it was on its side and the back door was ajar. The prisoner who'd laughed at Lou was dead. Lou could tell by the angle of the man's neck and his wide, sightless stare.

Served him right for laughing.

Then Lou rolled onto his hands and knees. His head was pounding, and there were a dozen places on his body that were beginning to ache, but he could see freedom only a few feet away. The only problem was that he was still handcuffed and shackled. All of a sudden, he realized smoke was pouring out from under the hood and began to panic.

"God...oh, God...don't let me burn," he muttered, and began to crawl toward the door.

Then he realized people were outside, shouting.

"Help!" he yelled. "Help me!"

He could smell gas, and the smoke was getting thicker. He screamed again, afraid that the van was about to explode.

Suddenly he saw daylight, then felt someone grab him by the arm and drag him bodily out of the van. He fell to his knees, then crawled over to the side of the curb and lay flat on his back, staring up at the sky through the smoke, too rattled to think.

Moments later, they laid the dead body of the other prisoner beside him. He shuddered and scooted over. He'd seen dead people before but didn't want to lie beside one.

Then two men appeared through the smoke, carrying one of the guards, and set him carefully on the grass beside Lou.

Lou eyed the guard cautiously. This man was alive, but unconscious and bleeding from a deep gash in his forehead. The rescuers disappeared again into the smoke as they went back for the driver.

All of a sudden there was another loud crash, and then a third and a fourth, as cars began rear-ending each other, blinded by the smoke and confusion.

At that point the scene turned into a panorama of

chaos. People came running from everywhere. New victims were appearing, some staggering out of the smoke, others being carried to safety.

In the distance, Lou began to hear the sound of sirens. The police and rescue units were on the way. When he realized no one was paying any attention to the fact that he was in handcuffs and chains, he saw his chance and took it.

He crawled over to the unconscious guard and began going through his pockets. When he found the key to his cuffs and shackles, his heart skipped a beat. Hot damn, he'd done it! Within moments, he was free.

He stood abruptly, then realized his ankle had been injured. It hurt to put weight on it, and it felt like it was swelling by the minute. But it wasn't going to slow down his run for freedom.

He spied the nearest alley and started toward it, hobbling at first, and then ignoring the pain and turning it into an all-out dash as the sirens got louder. He ran through the alley, across another street and into a second alley. When he saw a produce van parked outside the delivery entrance to an Italian restaurant, he ducked inside it and squatted behind some stacked boxes of lettuce only seconds ahead of the driver, who exited the restaurant, then slammed the door shut as he got into the cab.

Within moments, Lou heard the van shift into gear and felt the motion as they drove away. At that point he grinned.

Freedom was a sweet bitch indeed.

Now all he needed was to find a ride and get the hell out of the state. It was time for a change of occupation and a change of residence, but before he left, he had to see a woman about a little dish of revenge.

Fifteen

Nick had an itch that only Amalie Pope could scratch. He needed to see her. To touch her. To put a smile on her face that a lifetime of years couldn't wipe off. He'd had no idea when he'd insinuated himself into Tug French's drug operation that he would meet a woman who'd steal his heart.

It was a miracle in itself, after what they'd put her through, that she'd been able to disassociate him enough from the others not to hate him. Even though he knew she'd suffered no real physical injuries from what had happened, he was concerned about her emotional well-being. Being a gunshot victim was traumatic enough for one lifetime, let alone being terrorized and held hostage in her own home only a few weeks later.

He glanced at his watch. It was just after 1:00 p.m. He tried to imagine what Amalie might be doing and realized how little he really knew about her normal habits. Then he smiled. He knew all he needed to know. He didn't give a damn about any quirks she might have.

God knew he had a few of his own. What he did know was that she was one of the most amazing women it had ever been his privilege to know. Tough. Resourceful. Beautiful. What else could a man want—except having his feelings reciprocated? But he wouldn't know if that was possible until he saw her reaction to his arrival.

He was topping a hill when his cell phone rang. He glanced at the caller ID, then frowned. Babcock! Whatever it was he wanted, the answer was going to be no, and when he answered, Nick made sure the tone of his voice reflected the fact.

"Hello."

"This is Babcock. Where are you?"

Nick's frown deepened. This sounded like the beginning of one of "those" calls.

"In Louisiana."

"What the hell are you doing back there? How are you going to explain yourself if someone recognizes you? You're supposed to be in prison, remember?"

"I lost the earring, shaved off the stubble, got a haircut and packed away the jeans and leather."

"Still, I don't want—"

Nick interrupted. "What's up, boss?"

He heard Babcock sigh. "Drake escaped."

Nick's heart dropped. "Son of a bitch! No! How?"

"The prison van wrecked as Drake was on the way to arraignment, resulting in a ten-car pileup. Concerned citizens took the situation in hand and began pulling people out of burning vehicles before the police and rescue units ever arrived. One guard dead at the wheel.

A prisoner dead inside the van. The other guard severely injured. Drake took the keys out of the injured guard's pocket, removed his handcuffs and shackles, and disappeared during all the confusion."

"Shit. When did this happen?"

"Today."

"Any leads?"

"Yeah, a delivery van and its driver have gone missing. His last known stop was two blocks from the scene of the accident. It's a little too coincidental to ignore."

"Was Drake injured?" Nick asked.

"Best we can tell, he was the only one in the police van who was able to walk away."

Nick cursed. "What's up with that? He lives through a tornado unscathed. Survives a massive pileup. I don't get it."

"Yeah, well...shit happens," Babcock said.

Nick felt sick, but given this news, there was something he knew that Babcock needed to know, too.

"If you want to catch him, send a team back to Amalie Pope's house. Drake will come back here."

Surprise colored Babcock's voice.

"Why?

"He's got a hard-on for her that won't go away, and now a grudge to boot. He blames her for our capture."

"Well, he's right. She *is* responsible," Babcock snapped.

"Thing is, Lou Drake doesn't care that any normal person would have tried to escape and call the police. In his mind, if he'd gotten to her the way he wanted to, she wouldn't have lived, which means we would have escaped. You savvy?"

"Hell, yes, I'm savvy," Babcock muttered. "Damn it. I hate stupid perps."

"All I'm saying is, if you want him back in custody, get someone down here fast. Hide him out so no one knows he's around, and have him wait for the little bastard to show up."

"What if he doesn't?" Babcock asked.

"If he's able, he *will* come back here."

"The Louisiana State Police will be interested. I'll pass your message on to them. In the meantime, I know you're on R and R, but since you're already in Louisiana, if I send a couple of men down there, I don't suppose I could talk you into heading this up from our end? We were the ones who filed charges. We were going to prosecute. I want the bastard back behind bars."

"Since I'm less than fifteen minutes from Amalie Pope's house, I'd be happy to help out," Nick drawled, then heard a soft snort.

"Don't tell me you two had something going during all this?" Babcock asked.

"I'm not going to tell you anything except that I'll head up the security detail."

"Well, hell, could this get any more convoluted?"

"I'll let you know," Nick said, and disconnected.

His excitement at seeing Amalie again had just been dashed. He didn't know how she was going to react to being told she was back in danger, but he did know that this time he wasn't leaving her side. No more trying to hide his identity or maintain cover. He'd been thinking about getting out of undercover work anyway. This just might be the universe's way of telling him it was time.

He started to try her number, then decided against it. This wasn't the kind of news to give anyone over the phone. Instead he dropped the cell phone into a cup holder in the console and stomped on the gas.

Amalie felt aimless. She'd put her house in order. The loose ends of her life were in the act of being tied up. All the papers regarding her inheritance had been signed. Everything connected to this property was now in her name. The insurance agent had written her car off as a total loss, and as soon as she got the urge to look, she was cleared to shop for a new one.

Just before noon, her telephone rang. She was so startled at the sound that she jumped. Then she wondered who would be calling—hopefully Nick—and ran to answer.

It was Louis.

"The phones are working, *cher.* I just wanted to check in. Is there anything you need?"

"This is good news," Amalie said, pretending an elation she didn't feel. "I don't need a thing, but if I do, I won't hesitate to call, okay?"

"Okay," Louis said. "Talk to you later."

The dial tone in her ear matched her mood. Flat. Monotone. How many ways were there to describe longing?

She hung up the phone, then turned away and gave the room a studied glance. Nothing was out of place. Everything was clean and shining. Her shoulders slumped as the grandfather clock in the upstairs hall began to chime.

Twelve o'clock.

She'd completely forgotten about lunch. There was something she could do. Make herself something to eat. Something complicated. Something that would take a while to concoct. That would help pass the time.

She wound up making a ham sandwich and pouring herself a glass of sweet iced tea, and carrying everything out to the front veranda. She chose a seat that gave her a clear view of the grounds, and then sat cross-legged in the old wicker chair and leaned back. After a couple of bites and a sip of iced tea, she began to relax.

The sun was bright. The sky cloudless. A far cry from last week's weather. She took another bite as she thought about what needed to be done to the place, both inside and out.

The most urgent thing, she supposed, was clearing away the undergrowth that was threatening to overtake the immediate grounds, getting rid of some kudzu, trimming some trees and cutting the grass. When she was little, she could remember, an old gazebo had sat in a place of prominence off to the right of the house. She hadn't thought of it in years and wondered what had happened to it. Maybe she would have another one built. It had been a wonderful place to play.

Then she sighed. A gazebo was a place for lovers and

children. She had neither, and the prospect of either one was slim to none.

She'd sent a letter to the State Historical Society about the secret room and was curious to see what, if anything, would happen. It seemed like such a marvelous find, she couldn't imagine it being ignored, not if her suspicions were correct and the Vatican had once been a stop on the Underground Railroad.

She finished her sandwich and tea, and carried the dirty dishes back into the house, dug through the kitchen for something sweet to eat, then changed her mind and settled for a second glass of tea, instead. She was about to get some more ice when she heard the crunching of wheels on the gravel driveway.

Her first thought was that Louis hadn't taken her at her word and was coming to see for himself how she was doing. She'd sensed his loneliness while she'd been with him, and realized he must have checked in on Nonna as he was now checking in on her.

She wiped the dampness from her hands, smoothed down the front of her pink T-shirt and finger-combed the curls away from her face as she headed for the front door.

A car door slammed as she reached for the knob. Then she paused. The last time she'd opened the door to strangers, her house had been invaded. She stopped, backed up and peered through the curtains.

Oh, my God!

Her heart leaped. Nick! It was Nick!

She ran for the door and swung it wide, bolted out of

the house and down the steps with her arms open and a smile on her face.

Nick caught her in midleap as she skipped the last step and jumped into his arms. He knew he was grinning like a love-struck teenager, but he couldn't help himself. God. He'd waited a lifetime to be greeted like this.

His heart swelled as Amalie wrapped her arms around his neck and her legs around his waist.

"Hey, baby," he growled softly, and planted a hard, hungry kiss on her lips.

"Return of the conquering hero," Amalie said, and kissed him back, without caution or invitation.

Nick groaned as their kiss deepened, revealing more than words could say. All the days of worry and frustration were gone just like that. This hadn't been a passing fling, brought on by the tension of the situation. She was clearly as glad to see him as he was to see her.

"I tried to call," he finally said, as he carried her up the steps, her legs still wrapped around his waist.

She slid out of his embrace long enough to stand on her own two feet, then took him by the hand and led him into the house.

"The phones only started working about an hour ago," she said. "Are you okay? What happened? Did you have any trouble—"

Nick put a finger to her lips.

"I'm fine. Lots happened, all of which I will share, if I could talk you out of something to eat while I do it."

Amalie grinned. "We've been down this road before, haven't we?"

"I promise not to eat you out of house and home this time."

"You can have anything you want in this house," Amalie said, and led the way into the kitchen as Nick followed.

"Anything?" he asked, as she began making him a sandwich.

"Anything you want...it's yours," she said.

"I want you."

Amalie froze. The mayonnaise-covered knife slipped out of her hand onto the counter as she turned around to face him.

Nick's heart was pounding so hard he couldn't hear himself think. Had he spoken too soon? What if...

Amalie clutched her hands against her belly. "As in sexually, or as in—"

"That and more," Nick said.

She took a deep breath. "How much more?"

Nick frowned. "I'm not sure I want to answer that question. I don't want to spill my guts just to make a fool out of myself."

Amalie's hands were beginning to shake.

"Spill your guts. Play the fool," she whispered.

Seconds later she was in his arms, the food forgotten. Nick kept kissing her over and over, in quiet desperation.

"Somewhere between walking through your front door and chasing you through a swamp, I fell in love with you, Amalie Pope. I know this sounds crazy. We've known each other barely a week, but I lived a lifetime with you. I saw your heart. I saw your courage. I saw a woman beautiful both inside and out, and I got greedy. Leaving you was the hardest thing I've ever done, and if you'll give me a chance to make it up to you—give us a chance to do this right—I'll never turn my back on you again. I swear."

"Oh, Nick," Amalie said, and cupped his face. "Ever since you left I've had this unsettled, restless feeling… like I didn't know what to do next. And then you drove up, and it was gone. I'll give you all the time you…we… need to do this right, but just so you know, I fell in love with you, too."

Nick shuddered. "I've waited a lifetime to hear those words."

"Are we going to make love now, or are you going to eat this sandwich?"

Nick grinned. "I vote for making love." Then his smile slid sideways. "But I have something I need to tell you first."

Amalie frowned.

Nick sighed. He hated to put that look on her face, but he couldn't bring himself to take her to bed, make crazy love to her, and only after it was over drop the bombshell that the nut job who'd tried to rape her had escaped.

"So sit," Amalie said. "I'll finish making the damn sandwich. Then you'll eat and talk, and I'll listen."

"I'll be right back," Nick said.

"Where are you going?" Amalie asked.

"Don't worry. I'm not leaving again. I'm just going out to the car to get my suitcase. I'm on R and R, and you're stuck with me for a while."

Amalie smiled at the news, then watched with longing as he walked away. Heaven help her, but he had the sexiest walk of any man she'd ever seen. Whatever he had to tell her couldn't possibly be all that bad. God wouldn't do that to her again.

She made the sandwich in short order and poured him a glass of sweet iced tea. She was carrying it to the table when he reentered the kitchen.

He took the food out of her hands. "Thank you, baby," he said softly, as he set it down, then kissed her again, just because he could.

Amalie's heart lifted. No matter what he had to say, she felt the love.

"Aren't you having anything?" he asked as he slid into a chair.

"I already ate. But I didn't have dessert. I'll get some cookies," she said, and grabbed a bag she'd bought from the grocery deli, refilled the tea she'd been fixing when he drove up and then joined him at the table.

"So. What's up?" she asked, as she took a bite of cookie.

"Lou Drake escaped custody this morning."

The cookie turned to powder in her mouth. She tried to chew, but it wouldn't go down. Finally she took a drink and swallowed it like a dose of bad medicine.

Nick watched the color fade from her face and saw

her struggling to regain her composure. But the news had done exactly what he feared it would do. Amalie Pope was afraid again.

"Is that why you're here?" she asked.

"Hell, no!" he said, and reached for her hand. "I was less than fifteen minutes from here when I got the call. I would be here regardless."

She nodded. Tears were pooling, and there was a knot in the back of her throat. Damn it! She wasn't a quitter. Reacting like this was frustrating, but she couldn't seem to get a grip on her emotions.

Nick saw her eyes glaze over, saw her struggling to regain some control. He slammed the sandwich down on the plate and stood.

"I changed my mind," he said.

Amalie blinked. Her mind was going in a dozen different directions. He'd changed his mind? About what? About *her?*

"I don't want to eat. I want to make love to you. In a house…in your bed. It's time to put bad news on the back burner and think of us for a change."

Amalie stood up, then walked into his arms.

Nick pulled her close against his chest, cradling her cheek against his heartbeat.

"It's all right, baby. I promise it's going to be all right. I'm here, and I'm not leaving until either Drake is recaptured or you run me off. Period. Promise."

Amalie sighed, then looked up. "I have clean sheets on the bed."

He grinned. "Then let's go mess them up."

Amalie laughed, then shivered, surprised that she could still laugh in the face of what she'd been told.

"Did you lock the door when you came in?" she asked.

"Yes."

"Do you have a gun?"

His eyes widened. "Yes, actually, I do. Why? Do you need one?"

"No. I have one of my own now."

"Damn," Nick said, and picked her up in his arms as if she weighed nothing. "I'm sorry, baby. For everything you've been through. For everything you have yet to face."

Amalie wrapped her arms around his neck.

"But once again, I'm not having to face it alone, thanks to you. Now, would you please take me to bed? I don't think I want to wait, either."

Nick carried her through the house, kissing her every few seconds just because he could, then paused at the foot of the stairs.

"I'll be too heavy. I can walk," Amalie said.

"I know that," Nick drawled. "But ever since I saw this staircase, I've had an image of Rhett Butler and Scarlett O'Hara going through my head. Allow me the fantasy, okay? Besides, you're anything but heavy."

Amalie grinned.

"Then do your worst, Rhett."

"Only the best for you, Miz Scarlett," Nick said.

The trip up the stairs was surreal. Amalie knew a lot of the dramas and tragedies that had happened beneath this roof, but she couldn't help wondering how many times in the Vatican's past strong, handsome men had carried their women up these same steps for this very same reason.

Then they were in her room and Nick was carrying her toward the bed.

Amalie's heart began to beat faster. When he set her on her feet, her hands were shaking, but when she began to undress, Nick stopped her.

"Let me," he said

She sighed, then stood quietly as Nick pulled the pink T-shirt over her head and tossed it on a nearby chair. When he stopped long enough to kiss the hollow at the base of her neck, breath caught in the back of her throat. She closed her eyes, reveling in the tenderness of his touch.

When his hands moved to the waistband of her jeans, she shivered. Suddenly her jeans were around her ankles, then her bra and panties followed them to the floor. By the time Nick picked her up again and laid her on the bed, she was shaking all over.

The seduction of Amalie Pope had begun.

Nick stripped in seconds, then crawled onto the bed beside her.

Amalie hadn't missed a moment of his reveal, from his hard, flat belly to the lean, muscled length of his body. His shoulders were wide, his hips slim and narrow. But it was the look on his face that melted her heart. He was looking at her as if she were the most precious thing in his life, and when he began to touch her, she felt it, as well. But it wasn't until he began to kiss every healing wound and bruise on her body that she knew she was lost.

Nick Aroyo loved her.

She was no longer alone.

Sixteen

Amalie was Nick's dream come true. She came alive in his arms, yielding to his caresses—his kisses—willingly giving back everything she received and more.

When her fingers curled around him, he shuddered, fighting the need to bury himself deep inside her.

Not yet.

She sighed, then arched beneath his touch, wanting more of what he was doing, wanting him—inside her—now.

"Nick…"

Not yet.

"Easy, baby…just close your eyes and let yourself feel," he whispered.

Amalie shivered, then lay still.

He slid a finger into the velvet folds between her legs, searching in a circular motion until he felt a tiny nub, then rubbed until it was hard and pulsing. He watched her gasp as her body began to tense, but he was waiting for more.

Nick was one solid ache, but he needed to give before he would take. Her climax came suddenly, and it was everything he'd been waiting for.

Now.

Still reeling from waves of pleasure, Amalie was unaware Nick had moved until suddenly he was inside her, filling her—completing her.

She locked her arms around his neck.

Feeling the ripples of her climax was a sensuous caress that nearly made Nick lose it. But he was greedy. He wanted more. He slid his hands beneath her hips, tilting them just enough to rock her world one more time. When she bit the lobe of his ear, he groaned.

Then she laughed and pulled him deeper, and Nick was gone.

He rocked against her—the rhythm instinctive and without thought—lost in her heat and honey, caught in the magic of Amalie Pope.

Thrust after thrust.

Minute after minute.

Until they were bonded by the sweat of their bodies and the passion building between them.

The second climax caught Amalie unaware. One moment it had been all about giving him pleasure, and the next thing she knew she was flying.

Nick heard her cry out, and then the tremors of her climax were pulling at him, urging him to follow. He gave up and gave in, rolling with an explosion of sensations that gutted his energy and left him spent, his heart hammering against his rib cage in a wild, erratic beat.

"Ah…Amalie…have mercy…have mercy," he whispered, then rolled onto his back, taking her with him.

She sighed, stretching the lean, curvy length of herself on top of his body, and buried her nose in the curve of his neck.

"Am I still breathing?" Nick muttered.

Amalie shifted, putting her hand in the middle of his chest.

"If it helps…your heart's still beating."

"Thank you, Lord…because I can't feel a thing."

Amalie smiled, a slow, secretive smile of satisfaction. Nothing like a little power trip on your way to a climax to give a woman's ego a boost.

"You are an amazing lover," she said.

Nick's arms tightened their hold as he rested his chin against her head.

"It's easy to make love when you're in love with your partner."

"I love you, too," Amalie whispered.

"And that's the second miracle between us."

"What's the first?" Amalie asked.

"That you didn't end up hating my guts for not telling you who I was from the first."

Amalie rose up on one elbow and put her finger across his lips, silencing him.

"You saved my life. I owe you."

Nick grinned.

"You owe me?"

She nodded.

"And how do you propose to pay me back?" he asked.

"I'm not sure, but when the time comes, I'll know it."

"Good enough," he said, and kissed her soundly.

"Are you still hungry for that sandwich?" she asked.

"I'm definitely hungry. Just not sure I can walk that far."

Amalie arched an eyebrow.

"If you want to eat it, you're gonna have to come get it. I'm not starting this relationship off by feeding you in bed."

Nick's grin turned into a chuckle.

"God, but you're going to be fun to grow old with."

Amalie's heart skipped a beat.

"That sounds like more than a declaration of devotion," she said.

"Hell, yes," Nick said. "And if what we just did wasn't assurance enough that I'm not planning on giving you up, then I guess I'll have to try harder next time."

"Is that a promise?" she asked.

Nick's smile slipped. "It's more than a promise. It's a vow. Understand this, woman. I am going to love you like no man has ever loved a woman for the rest of my life. I'll ruin you for ever loving another man."

Suddenly Nick's face was a blur. This was what she'd always dreamed of. A happy-ever-after, forever-kind-of-love, with a forever-kind-of-man.

"Oh, Nick."

Suddenly there was a note of panic in his voice.

"Are you crying?"

"Well, yes," she snapped. "What did you expect me to do after you said something so damned romantic?"

"I'm a man. I see tears, I panic."

"Well, I'm a woman. We cry. Get over it."

Nick grabbed her in a bear hug as a gut-deep laugh bubbled up his throat.

"Let's get up and go eat before we get into a fight. I don't have the energy left to make up."

Amalie grinned.

Getting out of bed was easy. Getting dressed and keeping their hands off each other wasn't. It took longer than expected before they finally made it down the stairs and into the kitchen.

The ham was still out on the cabinet, as were the jar of mayonnaise and the loaf of bread. The cookies she'd been planning to eat were still where she'd abandoned them on the table.

"I think we can do better than this," Nick said. "Do you have eggs?"

She nodded.

"Omelet," he said. "I'm cooking. You can sit back and admire my prowess."

"I already did that once today," she said. "You sit. I'll cook. I don't want you to get a big head."

"How about we do this together?" Nick suggested.

Amalie sighed. He was almost too good to be true. Surely he had warts somewhere, although she'd pretty much seen all there was to see of him more than once today.

"That sounds like a plan," she said softly.

Nick was just sliding the omelet out of the pan when his cell phone rang. He glanced at the caller ID, then frowned.

"I need to take this. It's your security guards."

"My security guards?"

He nodded as he answered.

"Hello."

"Nick?"

"Yeah."

"Agent Edwards here. Smith and Lord are with me. Babcock called. Said we have a possible situation brewing with the guy who tried to take you out, and that you're the lead on this."

"Yes. Where are you?"

"About an hour away. We'll be there long before dark to set up a perimeter."

"He's not the subtle kind," Nick said. "He has one thing on his mind, and it's getting to Amalie Pope. I think he'll come, and I think it will be after dark. He won't wait around for days to do this. He knows he needs to put a lot of distance between himself and Louisiana, but he won't leave without getting revenge. It's all he talked about. He won't be expecting anyone to be here but her, so if you see him, let him come all the way to the house. Make sure he gets out of the car. We don't want to take a chance on him getting away again."

"Will do," Edwards said. "The State Police are looking for him on the highways. We're covering Amalie's home. When we get there and get set up, I'll let you know."

"Right," Nick said, and looked up at Amalie as he disconnected.

Her eyes were wide, her lips slightly parted, as she waited for him to explain.

Nick hated that she was worried again.

"That was one of the agents that Babcock is sending here to stake out your property."

"You're sure Lou will try to come back here?"

"I'd bet on it," Nick said. "But I'll be in the house, and there will be three really big mean DEA agents outside the house. We'll protect you."

"Are they really big and mean?"

Nick grinned. "No. But they're really good at their jobs. Does that count?"

She sighed. "Yes. So… I'm fine. Stop looking at me like that. Your eggs are getting cold."

"Sit with me," he said.

Amalie took her cold drink and a couple of cookies, and sat down across the table from him. She watched him as they ate, realizing that this was only the first of a lifetime of meals they were going to share, and could almost imagine Nonna smiling. She would have liked this man.

Lou had still been hiding in the back of the delivery van when it came to a stop. He'd peered out from behind the boxes of lettuce, but his view of the street was limited, and all he could tell was they were parked in another alley.

Once the driver came back here to get his next delivery, Lou knew he would be found. But he was ready, armed with a box cutter and a claw hammer. He had no qualms about killing. But he didn't want to get blood on the man's clothes. He needed them, so he was going for a knockout punch first.

Still squatting down between the stacks of food, Lou waited, his muscles tensing as he heard the outer door open, then footsteps as the driver started toward the back of the van to fill his next order.

All of a sudden Lou sprang up.

"What the hell?" the driver shouted.

Lou swung, coldcocking the man with the claw hammer before he could run. The man went limp as he hit the floor. Lou hit him again, splitting his forehead. Flesh popped. Blood oozed. It never occurred to Lou to care that he'd just killed a man. He was just happy he hadn't had to cut him and ruin the clothes he intended to take. But he couldn't take the time to undress the dead man here. After a quick glance to make sure he was unobserved, he jumped out and then into the cab, and drove away. It took him a few minutes to get his bearings, but as soon as he realized he was nearing an on-ramp to the Ponchartrain Expressway, he moved over into the right lane.

He drove onto the expressway, taking care not to bring attention to himself. Within minutes he crossed the Mississippi River and took the first exit, then drove around near the riverfront until he found a place to park unobserved. He got out and went back into the van.

A quick check of the driver's pulse assured him the man was indeed dead. This was definitely going to up the ante on his hide once the man was found. He needed to get out of New Orleans as soon as possible, so he quickly began stripping the man of his clothes and wallet. After a quick check of the contents, he found himself one hundred and ten dollars to the good.

The clothes weren't a perfect fit. The pant legs were too long, and he could barely button the waistband, but he would manage. He took the T-shirt the man was wearing under his uniform, but discarded the jacket, stuffed the wallet in his pocket, grabbed an apple from one of the boxes, then abandoned the van and took off along Franklin Avenue.

The sun was hot on the bald spot in the middle of his head, and his ankle was sore and aching, but he could walk. He stopped at a gas station, bought a cold drink from a self-serve dispenser outside, and then kept on moving, constantly on the lookout for a car he could snatch.

Finally he found a dark, late model car with a window partially down and a back door unlocked. After a quick glance around, he opened the door, unlocked the front, slid into the seat and hot-wired the car. Less than two minutes later he was driving away.

He drove until he found an on-ramp, then got back onto the Ponchartrain Expressway, drove back across the Mississippi into New Orleans proper, and kept on driving until he hit the I-10 westbound.

He knew he should be thinking about his escape plan, and he *would* do that—just as soon as he delivered a dose of revenge. Once he got his fill of Amalie Pope, he was going to take a lot of satisfaction in watching her die.

By the time Lou left New Orleans behind, he was riding a high. He'd done it! The gas gauge was registering less than a quarter of a tank. He pulled off the interstate at the first gas station he came to and filled up, then bought himself a couple of candy bars and a cold six-pack. He popped the top on the first beer, took a long swig of the sharp, yeasty brew, and then put it in the cup holder on the console as he pulled out onto the highway again. About a mile down the road he tore into the first candy bar and ate it in four bites, chased it with the rest of the beer and turned on the radio.

He drove with the air conditioner racked up to High, music blaring, and a growing hard-on. It would be worth everything he'd gone through to hear Amalie Pope beg before he tore her apart.

It was after three o'clock when he topped a hill and saw Bordelaise.

"Easy does it," he told himself, and tapped on the brakes, making sure he stayed well below the speed limit as he cruised through town.

A short while later he passed the bar they'd been in when they first got arrested. He blew it a kiss and then

Sharon Sala

laughed as he stomped on the gas while he watched Bordelaise disappear in his rearview mirror.

He drove over the bridge where they'd dumped the car after the tornado, then began watching for the turn that would take him back to the bitch's house. They'd walked up on the house from the swamp that first day, and the day they'd left, they'd gone in the other direction.

Finally, as he drove past a rusty trailer sitting out in a pasture, he realized he must have overshot his mark.

Muttering to himself, he reached for another beer as he began looking for a place to turn around. He'd just taken his first swig when he met a Jeep coming around a curve. He glanced at the driver, noted absently that he was wearing camo, then realized the other two men in the Jeep were dressed the same.

The driver, who was talking on the phone and pointing at something off to his right, sped right past Lou without notice.

Out of habit, Lou glanced at his sideview mirror. All of a sudden, his heart skipped a beat. The license tag! That was a government car! Cops? Feds? DEA?

Or were those guys soldiers? Maybe they were recruiters? Then he dumped that notion. He didn't think recruiters traveled in triplicate.

As soon as he could, he turned around, then sped up, hoping to catch a glimpse of the Jeep just to see where it was going.

A couple of minutes passed, and when he didn't see it, he decided he was making a big deal out of nothing and began watching for the his turnoff. He grinned when he saw it and took another swig of beer to celebrate. Just a little pick-me-up before the party got started.

He tapped on the brakes as he slowed down to take the turn, and was off the highway and on his way up the dirt road when he saw the back end of that damned Jeep disappearing around a bend up ahead.

The hair stood up on the back of his neck as he hit the brakes.

Three government men were on their way to her house. He wasn't sure what that meant, but if they didn't come back out soon, he was going to assume she was now under guard.

"Son of a bitch!"

This put a whole new spin on his plan of action. For a few moments he thought about letting it go. She was just a bitch who'd thrown a kink in his plans. But the longer he sat there, the madder he got. Once again, she was going to defeat him. The question was, was he willing to let her get away with it again?

It was the knot in his gut that gave him his answer.

Hell, no!

He drove a few yards farther up, then pulled off the road and drove into the woods, parking behind a wall of kudzu. The damned vines were a nuisance and grew faster than fleas on a dog's back, but in this instance, the overgrowth was welcome.

He got out of the car, felt in his pocket for the box blade, then popped the trunk and began poking around. Within minutes he was grinning.

Jackpot!

He'd heisted a car from a modern-day Davy Crockett. He found a fillet knife, a hatchet and a flashlight, along with a sleeping bag and assorted camping gear.

He put the flashlight in his pocket, grabbed the fillet knife and the hatchet and then started through the woods to reconnoiter. If the men in the Jeep drove away later, so much the better. And if they thought they were going to lay a trap for him, they had another think coming.

The DEA team arrived around 4:00 p.m.

Nick went out to meet them, and within minutes was helping them put their plan into effect.

Amalie watched from inside the house as the three men dressed in camouflage got back in a Jeep, circled the house and then drove out beyond the sheds to hide their vehicle behind the old barn.

Nick's stride was long and purposeful as he came back inside.

"That was Edwards and his team. They're going to hide the Jeep behind the barn and spread out around the perimeter. Whatever Drake's driving, he'll come straight up the driveway."

"How do you know?" Amalie asked.

"Because he can. And because he's egotistical enough to believe he can overpower you."

"Maybe, but he can't outrun me," Amalie muttered.

Nick brushed the side of her cheek. "That's for damn

sure, baby. But don't worry. You're not gonna have to run again."

She wasn't really worried, she just wanted this over.

As Nick turned away, she saw the handgun stuck in the waistband of his jeans. She shuddered. Lord. Would this nightmare ever end?

"What do you want me to do?" Amalie said.

"Nothing different," Nick said. "When it gets dark, turn on whatever lights you usually have on. Don't change your habits. Turn on the television…pull the shades you would normally pull."

"And what if he gets past the men? What are we going to do then?"

"I want him to drive past them. I want him at the house and out of his car before we take him down. That way there's less chance of him getting away again."

Amalie nodded. "I can live with that."

Nick took her in his arms and hugged her.

"Hang tough, baby."

"Okay…but what if he doesn't come tonight? What if he leaves the state?"

"Oh…he'll be planning on leaving, all right, but not until he gets to you. You really ticked him off. You outran him, and then you got away and turned us in. You didn't hear him ranting about it like I did. He'll come back. Drake isn't all that bright, but he's focused. And right now he's focused on getting to you."

Amalie shuddered. There were hours to pass before dark, but what to do? She needed to do something to kill time beside stare out the windows. Nick seemed certain that if Lou came, he wouldn't show up until after dark. That made sense, but that also meant she had more time to worry.

The rest of her belongings, which she was having shipped here from Texas, weren't due to arrive until later in the week. She would have given anything for her computer or some of her art supplies—anything to take her mind off the fact that Lou Drake was once again a threat to her existence.

She took a book from the library and tried to read, but she couldn't concentrate. She could hear Nick talking from the other room as he continued to coordinate the setup outside. Although she couldn't hear the words, the deep timbre of his voice and just knowing he was in the same house were reassuring. She turned on the television and began flipping through channels aimlessly, trying to find something to hold her attention.

She didn't realize Nick was back in the room until he slid onto the seat beside her and laid his handgun on the table.

She hit Mute on the remote.

"What?"

"They found the missing delivery van and driver."

It was the expression on his face that told her there was more, and that it wasn't going to be good.

"And...?"

"And he's dead. His clothes are gone, and the prison jumpsuit Drake was wearing was beside his body."

She couldn't control a shudder.

"This ups the ante considerably," Nick said. "Drake has nothing to lose anymore."

Amalie covered her face with her hands. She couldn't think—she couldn't breathe. It felt as if someone was sitting on her chest.

"Don't, baby. We'll get through this," he said.

She shook her head, crawled onto his lap and hid her face against his shoulder.

Nick silently cursed as he wrapped his arms around her. She was shaking so hard he could feel it. He couldn't quit thinking that this was all his fault. He was the one who'd found this house. He was the one who'd led three desperate men into her life and nearly gotten her killed for it. And just when he thought everything was finally over, this had to happen.

"I'm sorry, Amalie…so, so sorry."

She didn't move. She couldn't speak. She was holding on to the only bit of sanity she had left.

The house grew silent. Nick's phone didn't ring. There was nothing more to be said. They were all waiting—waiting for a killer. Would he come? Or would he disappear? Would she spend the rest of her life looking over her shoulder?

She was still in Nick's lap when the sun went down.

Seventeen

Lou charged through the underbrush, holding tight to his weapons. He was desperate to check out Amalie's visitors and see how their appearance impacted his plans. By the time he reached the tree line surrounding the house, the men were just getting out of the Jeep. As he'd thought, they were dressed like soldiers, and unless they were just stopping here to ask permission to go hunting on her property, it seemed an odd choice of clothes.

Suddenly the front door opened. He leaned forward, expecting to see Amalie Pope emerge. Instead a tall, dark-haired man wearing gray pants and a red knit shirt came out onto the veranda.

Lou grunted as if he'd just been punched in the gut. Unless his eyes were deceiving him, the man looked like Aroyo. He even moved like him. But how was that possible? He'd watched the Feds take Aroyo into custody. He wanted to get closer but didn't dare. Even the slightest movement could call attention to himself, and then it would all be over.

He kept watching, expecting to see the woman come out. But she never showed. The idea crossed his mind that maybe he should just discard this notion of revenge and get out while the getting was good.

But no one had ever accused Lou Drake of being an intelligent man. He'd operated on gut instinct and knee-jerk reactions his whole life, and he wasn't about to change. If he didn't get satisfaction for what Amalie Pope had done, he knew he would regret it the rest of his life.

When the men got back into the Jeep, he expected them to drive out the way they'd come in. Instead they circled behind the house, at which point he lost sight of them. Then he realized the dark-haired man was gone, too. The front door was closed again, and instead of answers, he was left with more questions.

Muttering beneath his breath, he quickly circled the house, taking care to stay deep within the trees. He wanted to see where these men were going and what they were up to. But by the time he reached a point where he could see the backside of the house, the Jeep was already out of sight. Frustrated, he started to retrace his steps when he saw the men emerge from behind the barn, only this time they were on foot and carrying rifles.

This did not look good.

As they paused, he tensed, then watched as the three men split up and headed into the woods at three different locations. When he realized one of them was coming his way, he panicked and ran deeper into the trees. When he was finally satisfied that he'd found a safe place of concealment, he settled down to wait until dark. Obviously they were set to guard the place. He assumed to protect her from him.

But instead of letting that throw a kink in his plans, Lou grinned. He liked a little competition. It should be an easy task to slip through the woods after dark. He knew the place and the house better than they did, and he had a few tricks up his sleeve. He would have preferred some firepower, but would gladly settle for the long wicked knife with the serrated edge and his nice sharp hatchet.

Right now his plan was to get inside the house, dispose of the guy who looked like Aroyo and then have a little fun with that bitch before he cut her in pieces.

A phone rang.

Amalie jerked, blinking in confusion as the deep rumble of Nick's voice sounded above her head. The last thing she remembered was crawling up onto his lap, where she'd obviously fallen asleep. What touched her was that she was still there. No telling how long he'd sat, quietly holding her safe within his embrace.

She listened long enough to know he was talking to Edwards again, then got up, waved goodbye and blew him a kiss before leaving the room. After a quick trip to the bathroom, she thought about making them some supper. Sunset had come and gone, and the moonless night promised to be a long and tense one.

She dug around in the pantry, then the refrigerator, before deciding on hamburgers. They would be hearty and quick, and she had some chips to go with them.

She washed her hands, then got to work, and was taking the last burger out of the pan when Nick came into the room.

"Smells good," he said.

"Thanks. You might have had better fare if you hadn't let me sleep so long."

He kissed the back of her neck as he passed.

"You needed the rest, and I wasn't going anywhere."

Amalie began putting the burgers together as Nick washed up at the sink.

"Mustard, right?" she asked.

"Right, and onions if you have them."

"Absolutely," she said. "If we both eat them, then it cancels out the smell."

He laughed, then made their drinks and got out the chips as she carried their plates to the table.

Nick dug into his food with relish, but Amalie only picked at hers. She kept glancing out the windows into the darkness and wondering if Lou Drake was out there somewhere, just waiting for his chance to get revenge.

"Eat, honey," Nick said. "The team is out there, and I'm in here. There's no way he can get on your property without us knowing it."

"Right," Amalie said, and made herself eat.

"Feel like talking?" he asked.

"Absolutely," she said. "About what?"

He shrugged. "Stuff."

She smiled. "So what stuff are we talking about?"

"Like…what's your favorite color…your favorite flower…your favorite holiday? You know…the kinds of things we would know if we'd done this the right way."

It touched her to realize he was serious, and so she treated her answers the same way.

"My favorite color is blue. My favorite flower is lilac. Christmas is for sure my favorite holiday. What about you?"

"I like red, I guess. I love Christmas, but I think Thanksgiving is my favorite. It comes with my mom's pecan pies."

Amalie's eyes widened. It was the first time he'd ever mentioned family.

"How much family do you have?" she asked.

"My dad's been dead since my senior year of college. Heart attack. He was a cop in St. Louis. Mom lives in Miami now, not far from my condo. I have a brother who's an electrical engineer. He has a wife and four kids, and lives in Denver. I have a younger sister who lives in Oregon. She and her husband are teachers. They don't have any kids. And there are the usual number of aunts, uncles and cousins scattered around the country."

"Wow! You do have family…. And you have a condo in Miami, as in Florida?"

"Yeah, that's where I live when I'm not on a case. As for my family, they'll be your family, too," he reminded her.

The thought of belonging to a clan like that was comforting. "I can't wait to meet them," Amalie said.

"As soon as we get this mess behind us and you feel like taking a trip, I'll take you back to Miami with me. I need to either put the condo up for sale or see about renting it out."

Amalie realized he was about to reorder his life to fit hers and was touched that he understood her bond to this place.

"What about your job?" she asked.

"I'll still be DEA, but I can do that from anywhere."

"And the undercover part?"

Nick frowned. "No. This one put a bad taste in my mouth that I'm not willing to ignore. Enough is enough."

"You're sure? Because I don't want you to have regrets later and blame me."

"That's not going to happen. Besides…what kind of a father would I be if I was gone all the time?"

Amalie grinned, her cheeks a little pink.

"Father?"

"You do want kids, don't you? I mean…you being a teacher and all, I just assumed—"

"Of course I want kids. It's been a long time since children lived here. It's time this house had some noise and laughter beneath its roof again."

"This whole place is amazing."

"It is, isn't it?" Amalie said.

Nick's phone rang again. This time it was Babcock.

"It's my boss," he said.

She waved to indicate she was giving him some privacy and left the kitchen. Making sure all the doors and windows were locked would give her a measure of confidence. For now, it was all she could do.

Lou was beginning to fidget. It was time to make his move. He'd already found the location of the guard closest to him and made sure to give the man a wide berth when he headed for the house.

And there was no moon—a fact that helped his plan along.

It was as if the world was accommodating his needs as he moved through the trees and then across the clearing to the house. He could only assume that the guard who was inside had already taken care of locking the windows and doors.

But there was one window in a very small room that he had found during his days of enforced inactivity that he would bet money no one had checked. He didn't know what the room's initial purpose had been, but it was now an empty closet, with nothing but an assortment of wire and wooden hangers and a few boxes of old clothes stacked up beneath the window. He knew it would be unlocked because the lock was broken. The fact that it was on the ground floor and at the back of the house made things even better.

Careful to stay away from the rooms that were lit, he made his way around the house. When he got to the window and pushed, it slid part of the way up, then stuck. He pushed a little harder and grinned when it rose the rest of the way without a hitch.

Bingo.

So far so good. Taking a chance that the boxes would still be under the window, he dropped his hatchet and fillet knife inside, heard them land with a soft plop on top of the clothes, then hefted himself up and through the opening.

The room was just as he remembered. He used his memory and sense of touch to maneuver around the boxes as he pulled down the window. Then he slipped the hatchet between his belt and the waistband of his pants before palming the knife as he moved to the doorway. Once he opened the door, he would be in the utility room just off the kitchen. After that, it was just a matter of finding the guard.

His hand was on the doorknob when he heard a deep voice and realized the guard was in the kitchen. He listened closer, his ear against the door, to see if he could hear what was being said. But it wasn't what was being said that shocked him. It was when he recognized the voice.

Son of a holy bitch!

It *was* Aroyo who he'd seen!

What could this possibly mean?

He needed to hear what was being said, and ever so slowly he turned the knob and cracked the door—

Nick was at the counter, writing as fast as he could, taking notes as Babcock talked.

"Yes, sir, that's right. The last shipment that French sent off went via a man named Armentrout. The last payment came in via a man named Curtis. No, I don't know if Curtis was his first name or his last. And I only saw him once. Most of the time a man named Prejean made the drops."

The floor creaked behind Nick. He turned, a smile on his lips, expecting to see Amalie. It was the creak that saved his life.

Lou Drake was coming at him with an upraised hatchet and a look of unadulterated hate on his face.

"You son of a bitch! You turncoat son of a bitch!" Lou screamed, and chopped downward, catching the edge of Nick's shirt and cutting into his shoulder.

The blow was deep and painful, knocking Nick backward off his feet. He fell, taking a chair down with him. The phone clattered onto the floor as he reached behind him for his weapon, only to remember that he'd taken it out of the back of his jeans when he sat down on the sofa. It was still in the living room, right on the end table where he'd put it.

Blood was pouring from his shoulder, and he was fighting not to pass out from the pain. He kept scrambling backward in an effort to get out of Lou's reach and

get back on his feet, but Lou kept coming, swinging t.
hatchet and cursing.

"How did you do it?" Lou screamed, as he kicked
over a chair and swung again, this time cutting a slash
through the sole of Nick's boot.

Nick felt a sharp sting and knew that the blade had cut
through enough leather to draw blood, but he didn't have
time to worry about how deep or how much. He rolled
over onto his hands and knees, and crawled beneath the
kitchen table, pulling it with him as a shelter.

Lou followed, chopping downward and splitting the
tabletop in half. The salt and pepper shakers fell onto
the floor and shattered, along with the plates and the
leftover food, scattering even more debris.

Lou kicked another chair out of the way. It hit the
wall with a bang.

"You and that bitch were in it together from the start!
You're the one who found the house for us to shelter in.
You knew she was here. You kept us pinned down until
Tug was so sick you knew he wouldn't make it. Then
you helped her get away and gave us up. I'm gonna take
you down, and I'm gonna make you watch while I fuck
her till she bleeds. Then I'm gonna kill you both."

Nick's blood ran cold. He had to get the upper hand.
He couldn't let Drake leave this room alive.

Edwards had his cell on vibrate, so when the call
came in, he almost missed it. He answered just as it
was about to go to voice mail.

"This is Edwards," he said softly.

It was Babcock, and he was yelling.

"Drake is inside the house! Nick and I were talking when I heard him break in. From what I could hear, he's armed and Aroyo isn't, or there would already be gunfire. Get inside as fast as you can and call me when it's over!"

"Yes, sir!" Edwards said, and then grabbed his hand-held and radioed the others. "Target is inside the house. I repeat. Target is inside the house. Move! *Move!*"

He couldn't believe it as he started running. How had the man gotten past them? But that was a question that would have to wait. He had unfamiliar territory and a lot of trees and ground to cover. All they could do was hope Nick would be able to hold his own until they could get there.

Amalie was on her way down the stairs when she heard a man shout. At first she thought it was Nick, and then she heard chairs crashing and things break-ing, along with more shouting and cursing, and that was when she knew.

The devil was back, and he'd come for her.

Her first instinct was to run—to hide in the secret room inside her closet until all the shouting was over. She was already turning for the stairs when it hit her. Not only had Nick not fired his weapon, she hadn't even heard his voice. Something had gone horribly wrong. And that was when she ran for her rifle.

Nick had managed to get to his feet and was trying to maneuver himself to the doorway. Even wounded, he knew he could outrun Drake. All he needed was time to get to the living room and get his gun, and this would be over.

But Drake wasn't stupid. The moment he'd realized that Nick wanted out of the room, he'd positioned himself between the door and the hall, the hatchet in one hand and the fillet knife in the other.

Nick could have run out the kitchen door, but that would have left Drake in the house with Amalie, and that wasn't going to happen.

"There are agents in the woods. They'll be here in seconds," Nick said.

Lou laughed. "No, they won't, because they don't know I'm even here. I moved right past the stupid bastards, and they never knew it."

Nick feared Lou was right, but he wasn't going to admit it.

"You're wrong," he said, trying to buy some time and hoping Amalie had heard enough of the ruckus to hide.

"No! You're wrong!" Lou screamed. "You're a backstabbing, two-faced bastard, and this time I'll make sure to finish you off before I move on to better things."

Nick's arm was beginning to go numb. He didn't know if it was from blood loss or if some nerves had been cut. But he was bleeding too damned much. He had to do something—and fast, before he passed out.

He made a run for the counter, intent on grabbing a butcher knife from the knife block and arming himself.

Lou roared and started running, the hatchet raised for a final blow.

The shot came out of nowhere.

It echoed within the walls of the Vatican as if some-one had just set off a cannon.

Nick froze, staring in disbelief as blood began to bubble and run from Lou's mouth and down the front of his shirt.

Lou didn't know what had happened.

His chest burned, and he could no longer feel his hands. The weapons he'd been carrying tumbled to the floor as he turned to look behind him.

"You are a stupid man," Amalie said, as she moved into the light. "You never did know when to stop. You should never have come back into my house."

Lou couldn't believe it. "You shot me," he mumbled.

"No. I killed you," she said, and didn't even flinch when he toppled forward, dead before he hit the floor.

Nick grunted, then leaned against the counter, holding his injured arm against his body.

Amalie tilted the rifle barrel toward the floor, then looked across Drake's body to Nick.

"Are you all right?"

"No, but I will be," he said. "You saved my life."

"I owed you…remember?"

Nick grinned, then winced. "So now we're even?"

"We're even," she said, eyeing the furniture lying about in pieces. Better it than Nick.

Then all of a sudden they heard footsteps coming up on the porch.

"Just like in the movies," she said, as she stepped over Lou to unlock the door.

"What's like in the movies?" Nick muttered.

"The law always arrives after the shooting is over."

He grinned, then winced. He would have liked to be sitting down, but all the chairs were in pieces, so he slid to the floor instead, too light-headed to focus on the agents who came racing into the house.

Amalie handed them her rifle.

"Nick needs an ambulance, and Drake needs a hearse."

Nick felt Amalie's hands on his face, and then pressure on his shoulder. She was staunching the flow of blood as he finally passed out.

Epilogue

The fireplace was ablaze.

Stockings were hanging from the mantel.

Garlands of greenery had been wound about the staircase and over doorways, and draped from chandeliers. Mistletoe hung over every doorway, tempting all who passed beneath to steal a kiss.

The house was alive with people and noise, and all manner of food and drink had been placed on every sideboard and table that would hold them.

Every member of Nick's family, from the youngest to the oldest—who happened to be his father's ninety-two-year-old aunt—had come to Louisiana for the Christmas holidays.

For the first time in almost a century, every bedroom in the house was in use, along with some cots beside the adults' beds for their respective children.

Amalie was carrying a tray of homemade pralines and hot mulled cider into the living room when she paused in the doorway, watching the tall, dark-haired man who was standing beside the fireplace, retelling the story of how she'd saved his life for what seemed like the hundredth time.

"I kid you not," Nick said. "Cool as a cucumber, she stepped over his body and let in the agents as if it was an everyday occurrence."

A murmur ran through the crowd, coupled with comments ranging from "What a gal" to "Are you man enough to handle a woman like that?"

Then Nick looked up and saw her and the tray she was carrying, and bolted through the crowd as if the room was suddenly empty.

"Honey! You shouldn't be carrying that heavy stuff in your condition." He took the tray out of her hands, then kissed her gently before setting it down on the only bare spot left in the room, which happened to be on the coffee table near the fire.

Amalie stood for a moment, thinking that she would never get tired of watching the way he moved, then followed him into the room.

Someone got up to make room for her in an overstuffed chair. As the mother of the latest impending Aroyo heir, she was definitely being pampered, but it was the fact that she'd saved Nick's life that had ensured her a permanent place of honor within the family.

"What gave you the courage to shoot?" someone asked.

Amalie leaned back in the chair, gazing around at all the faces of people who had yet to become familiar, then looked beyond them to the house itself.

"It wasn't the first time this old house had seen a woman fight to the death for a loved one," she said. "I'm the last of the Popes, but this is still the Vatican, and we don't allow justice to be swept aside."

"Have you picked out a name for the baby?" Nick's mother asked.

But this time Nick spoke before Amalie could answer.

"Yeah. We're naming him Jonathan Pope, and that was my call, not hers."

Nick sat down on the arm of her chair, then laid his hand on the top of her head, loving the silky feel of her curls against the palm of his hand.

"Jonathan Pope Aroyo. That has a nice ring to it," his brother said.

"No. Jonathan Nicholas Pope. There are plenty of Aroyos, and he'll always be my son. But Amalie more than earned the right to keep her family name alive when she saved my life. I consider it an honor to do my part to preserve the name. And a whole lot of fun to boot."

Amalie blushed.

The crowd roared with laughter.

She sat back in her chair, marveling at the family she'd inherited, and wondering how their lives would unwind in the coming years.

The secret room had been investigated and documented, and the names written on the walls were being researched. But it no longer mattered to Amalie if her theory was ever proved or not. She knew what she believed, and she was proud of the stance her family had once taken.

Then someone called out Nick's name, urging him to retell—one more time—the story of how his little wife had taken down the man who'd nearly killed him.

And so he did, relating her exploits until they were more amazing with each telling, making the story of Amalie Pope larger than life.

And for many Christmases after and through the ensuing years, the story was told and told again of a girl named Amalie, who was the last of the Popes, and how she refused to die, and how the name was reborn.

* * * * *

AWARD-WINNING AUTHOR

JOSEPH TELLER

Harrison J. Walker—Jaywalker, to the world—is a frayed-at-the-edges defense attorney with a ninety-percent acquittal rate, thanks to an obsessive streak a mile wide. But winning this case will take more than just dedication.

Seventeen-year-old Jeremy Estrada killed another boy after a fight over a girl. This kid is jammed up big-time, but almost unable to help himself. He's got the face of an angel but can hardly string together three words to explain what happened that day...yet he's determined to go to trial.

Jaywalker is accustomed to bending the rules—and this case will stretch the law to the breaking point and beyond.

OVERKILL

Available wherever books are sold.

MIRA®

www.MIRABooks.com

MJT2776

HARLEQUIN® A *Romance* FOR EVERY MOOD™

From passion, paranormal, suspense and
adventure, to home and family,
Harlequin has a romance for everyone!

Look for all the variety Harlequin has to offer
wherever books are sold, including
most bookstores, supermarkets,
discount stores and drugstores.

REQUEST YOUR FREE BOOKS!

2 FREE NOVELS
FROM THE SUSPENSE COLLECTION
PLUS 2 FREE GIFTS!

YES! Please send me 2 FREE novels from the Suspense Collection and my 2 FREE gifts (gifts are worth about $10). After receiving them, if I don't wish to receive any more books, I can return the shipping statement marked "cancel." If I don't cancel, I will receive 3 brand-new novels every month and be billed just $5.74 per book in the U.S. or $6.24 per book in Canada. That's a saving of at least 28% off the cover price. It's quite a bargain! Shipping and handling is just 50¢ per book.* I understand that accepting the 2 free books and gifts places me under no obligation to buy anything. I can always return a shipment and cancel at any time. Even if I never buy another book, the two free books and gifts are mine to keep forever.

192/392 MDN E7PD

Name	(PLEASE PRINT)

Address	Apt. #

City	State/Prov.	Zip/Postal Code

Signature (if under 18, a parent or guardian must sign)

Mail to **The Reader Service:**
IN U.S.A.: P.O. Box 1867, Buffalo, NY 14240-1867
IN CANADA: P.O. Box 609, Fort Erie, Ontario L2A 5X3

Not valid for current subscribers to the Suspense Collection
or the Romance/Suspense Collection.

Want to try two free books from another line?
Call 1-800-873-8635 or visit www.morefreebooks.com.

* Terms and prices subject to change without notice. Prices do not include applicable taxes. N.Y. residents add applicable sales tax. Canadian residents will be charged applicable provincial taxes and GST. Offer not valid in Quebec. This offer is limited to one order per household. All orders subject to approval. Credit or debit balances in a customer's account(s) may be offset by any other outstanding balance owed by or to the customer. Please allow 4 to 6 weeks for delivery. Offer available while quantities last.

Your Privacy: Harlequin Books is committed to protecting your privacy. Our Privacy Policy is available online at www.eHarlequin.com or upon request from the Reader Service. From time to time we make our lists of customers available to reputable third parties who may have a product or service of interest to you. If you would prefer we not share your name and address, please check here. ☐

Help us get it right—We strive for accurate, respectful and relevant communications. To clarify or modify your communication preferences, visit us at www.ReaderService.com/consumerschoice.

SHARON SALA

32633	THE WARRIOR	___ $7.99 U.S.	___ $7.99 CAN.
32596	BAD PENNY	___ $7.99 U.S.	___ $7.99 CAN.
32544	THE HEALER	___ $7.99 U.S.	___ $7.99 CAN.
32507	CUT THROAT	___ $7.99 U.S.	___ $9.50 CAN.
32352	NINE LIVES	___ $7.99 U.S.	___ $9.50 CAN.
66967	REMEMBER ME	___ $6.50 U.S.	___ $7.99 CAN.

(limited quantities available)

TOTAL AMOUNT	$ _____
POSTAGE & HANDLING	$ _____
($1.00 for 1 book, 50¢ for each additional)	
APPLICABLE TAXES*	$ _____
TOTAL PAYABLE	$ _____

(check or money order—please do not send cash)

To order, complete this form and send it, along with a check or money order for the total above, payable to MIRA Books, to: **In the U.S.:** 3010 Walden Avenue, P.O. Box 9077, Buffalo, NY 14269-9077; **In Canada:** P.O. Box 636, Fort Erie, Ontario, L2A 5X3.

Name: _____

Address: _____ City: _____

State/Prov.: _____ Zip/Postal Code: _____

Account Number (if applicable): _____

075 CSAS

*New York residents remit applicable sales taxes.
*Canadian residents remit applicable GST and provincial taxes.

MIRA®

www.MIRABooks.com

MSS1009BL